THE MONTEGIALLY SCHOOL OF SWEARING

Andrew HC McDonald

Andrew HC McDonald was born in the small town of Shackleton in the Wheatbelt of Western Australia, moving to the foothills of Perth at an early age. He has been a photographer, comedian, storyteller and a visual artist. He currently works at Curtin University.

For the angels & the Angels

Coq au Vin

The stench of rancid lime rose from the collar of his t-shirt, mixing with the bitterness of too-strong black coffee. His eyes bleared into the screen and ran ratlike across the unfamiliar words. '*Congratulazioni!*' he read. That was not good. That was not good at all.

* * *

Barely half a day earlier, Brian Chapman – Victorian Teacher of the Year runner-up – lifted the plastic bag left outside his apartment door. Toby took it from him and peered inside. 'Another pity food parcel from your nosy neighbour?' He stuck his own nose in. 'Tuna bake, I reckon.' He handed the bag back to Brian, who opened the door and carried it to the kitchen.

'I don't mind. She's OK. And now I won't have to scavenge for food.' The hum of the microwave echoed from the tiles of his bare apartment. 'You want?'

'Sure. But didn't she used to cook you a lot fancier food than tuna bake?' Toby sat himself down at the kitchen bench.

'Yeah. Got coq au vin once,' said Brian.

'What is that? Oh yeah. French. Cock with wine.' Toby scrutinised a grubby bottle of sweet chilli sauce, holding it up to the bare fluorescent strip like a doctor checking an iffy sample.

Brian waited for the bell, took the baking dish from the microwave and levered two solid cubes of pasta onto side plates. 'You must be the first person ever to make that joke. Cock with wine. Hilarious.'

'It has been a year,' continued Toby, twisting off the cap encrusted with dried sauce, then forcefully shaking way too much onto his food. 'Can't expect topnotch grub forever. Ahh! Ho-ho-hot!' Through a piece of scalding macaroni he added, 'Probably thought she was going to get some cock and wine in return. Surprised she didn't try it on, to be honest.'

To be honest, she had, but Brian didn't want to get into that.

Toby looked at him. 'You know, it could do you good.'

'Just ...'

Toby raised his hands in surrender. 'OK, OK, but "You Know Who" is getting on with *her* life for sure. And by getting on with it I mean ...'

'Yeah, I know what you mean.'

Toby stood and began to make several comical actions with tongue, hands and hips to suggest vigorous sexual activity.

'Thank you, Toby. This is just what I need right now.'

After a final thrust of his buttocks, Toby resumed his seat and blew on another forkful. 'Mate, you can't just sit around in a half-empty apartment living off humanitarian food parcels forever.'

'Well, I won't be sitting around here anyway,' said Brian. 'Settlement on this place is in two weeks.'

'Good, good, finally,' said Toby. 'Splash some cash, make a new start. Yes, yes, yes.'

'Well, I don't know how much splashing I'll be doing with thirty thousand dollars.'

'Your share is only thirty K? For this place? I know it's a crap hole but it still must be worth at least ...'

'Paying the mortgage off, the lawyers and everything else, yeah. That's it.'

'And everything else? Jeezus. Did your guy even go to law school?'

'I'm happy with it, Toby. Really. I'm sick of the fighting. Just glad it's over. And I've got money saved too.'

Toby released an extended and flamboyant pasta burp. 'If I'm going to have to continue this fucken conversation, I'm going to need a serious drink.'

'Beer in the fridge.'

'I said, a *serious* drink. You can give an advance on that payout and spend some of it on margaritas.'

Under a Neon Tongue

La Rana Loca spread across two former shopfronts, united by enough coats of black enamel that the texture of the brickwork barely showed through. There was a sign behind the bar claiming a selection of over fifty tequilas. The owner, Mrs Amarin, was an Aussie woman of Thai background and perpetually cheerful outlook. She was rumoured to have a Mexican boyfriend. It was Toby's belief that she spread the rumour herself, to explain why she hadn't opened a Thai place.

The restaurant area, taking up one of the former shops, held a few seated families, but the bar was all theirs for the moment. Toby claimed a corner under a neon frog perched high on the wall. As he ordered two mezcal Tommy's, the frog's tongue flashed in and out above them.

'Runner-up teacher of the century right here,' Toby tilted his head at Brian as the cocktail constructor – one of Mrs Amarin's minions – shook the last drops of margarita out of her shaker.

'Really?' she said drily. 'What does he teach?' She was wearing some kind of horror-metal t-shirt, King Parrot, over classic bar-worker black jeans and Docs. Her features were unmistakably Vietnamese, but her accent had its origins only an hour or so west of where they were sitting.

'One of Melbourne's finest *English* teachers,' replied Toby. 'One heartbeat away from legit teacher of the universe.'

'Does he talk too?'

Brian was attempting to ignore all this. Toby tapped him on the forehead. 'Mate, if you're not going to say anything, pay the woman.' Brian held his card on the machine.

'Ask him a question,' Toby urged her. 'He can teach any subject.'

'Don't take any notice,' said Brian.

'Nah, come on,' Toby raised his eyebrows, 'ahh ...?'

'Chelsea.' She looked back down the bar, hoping for another customer. Nope. She sighed. 'OK. Ahh, umm ... how would you teach, let's see, I don't know, statistical anomalies in quantum fluctuations in the cosmic microwave background?'

'She didn't put up her hand,' interjected Toby.

'Hush, Toby. Wow. Let me guess, that's what you're studying?'

'Masters.'

'Right. Isn't it the background buzz left over from the big bang or something? Like tinnitus of the universe? The cosmic microwaves, I mean.'

'Tinnitus of the universe. That's actually not bad. Maybe you *should* teach it.'

'Nice to meet you,' Brian said to her back as she moved away down the bar.

'Just a runner-up in Teacher of the Year,' he corrected Toby. 'As you know very well. Over twenty of us in the running. You're automatically a finalist if you don't punch a parent more than twice a term.'

'Well ya ain't going to win next year with that attitude, I can tell you,' said Toby, draining his Tommy. 'Ahh, good thing I've got a calming raft of tuna bake on board to soak up this piss. Do we need nachos too?'

'I absolutely *won't* be Teacher of the Year next year,' said Brian.

'You'll have a spring in your step when you finish your leave. Nothing to stop you. Stab the frontrunners in the back. Give out a few hand-jobs in the department car park! You've got to hustle. How do you think the last guy beat you?'

'By dedicating his life to teaching profoundly autistic children?'

'Oh Brian. You are too beautiful for this world. How could you be so naive? It's the value-adding that gets you there!'

'In any case. Not going back. Told you.'

'That's just the divorce talking. You love teaching those brats. I know you do. Anyone willing to hammer the joys of Shakespeare and Chaucer into the skulls of those nose-picking malcontents – and on a teacher's salary – must be doing it for love.'

'Nup. I used to. Not now. Leave was over a month ago. Department told me to make a decision, so I did.'

Toby was astonished. 'So this whole last month you weren't depressed on holiday, but depressed and unemployed? Brian, Brian, Brian. When you burn your bridges, you shouldn't be standing on one of them!'

Brian lifted his shoulders in a shrug.

'She won't be working at the same school, you know,' said Toby.

'Yes, I know that,' snapped Brian.

'Wow, I almost feel bad getting you to pay for drinks now,' said Toby. He waggled his fingers over their empty glasses to signal for another round. Chelsea raised a thumb in response. 'But consider this an intervention.'

'I'm paying for my own intervention?'

'Well, you've got to understand you're at rock bottom *somehow*.' The shaker rattled in front of them again. Toby rubbed his hands together 'Hoo, yesss. You're a lifesaver, Chelsea. And I think ...' He pointed at an option on the laminated menu.

'Perfect Tommy's. Thank you,' said Brian who began to return his card to his wallet. Toby whipped it out of his fingers and put it down on the bar. 'Not so fast. There's plenty more intervening to go yet. Haven't even begun, mate.' He savoured the sourness of his fresh drink. 'Haaaaaa.'

A small mountain of nachos arrived and, for twenty minutes, the impromptu intervention was put on hold.

While the pair crunched through an overdose of sodium under the relentless neon tongue, their section began to fill rapidly. Customers shed coats and umbrellas as they entered, then sat along the bar waiting for tables. Chelsea was joined by another staff member and two cocktail shakers clattered busily. The atmosphere began to buzz and Brian hoped Toby had forgotten any intervention intentions. He had not.

'So,' said Toby brushing yellow crumbs from his fingers, 'It's been a year. Traditional time for an intervention, I think. Anyway. High time to review the pluses and minuses of the sad fucken case of Brian Chapman, former golden boy of the Victorian Department of Education and Training.'

'Do we have to?'

'OK. Minusesezz.' Toby held up one finger. 'Whoa. That's tough to say after mezcal. Orright. The minuses and defe-shits of Brian Chapman. One: apparently, he's got no job now! Completely his own fault this one. Hundred percent. Two: he's got no woman. This one maybe he's not fully to blame for, so let's call it ninety-nine point nine percent his fault.'

'I'll accept twenty-five percent,' said Brian. 'And you're single too, don't forget.'

'And three,' continued Toby, ignoring him, 'in two weeks, he'll also have nowhere to live. Again, one hundred percent his own, sad fault. What does that add up to? A basket case is what.'

'It adds up to two hundred and twenty-five percent,' said Brian.

'Jeez, really?' said Toby. 'That's even worse than I thought.'

'Can we get to the pluses?'

'No, wait.' The alcohol had loosened Toby's tongue. 'You're thirty-nine years old and are looking about fifty, mate. You're starting to resemble my granddad's scrotum. This is getting serious. You used to be funny – not deliberately – but funny. It's. Been. A. Fucken. Year. Time for a comeback.'

Brian was silent.

'But if you want pluses, absolutely. Well firstly, you've got your friend of over ...' Toby started to tap his fingers.

'Please don't try counting,' said Brian. 'It's not your strong point.'

'... of over thirty years,' Toby continued loudly over the top of him, 'one Tobias Young, Esquire. And two ...' Toby started to consider carefully. 'Nope that's it.'

'You know, you're right. This really is rock bottom,' said Brian.

Another Brick in the Wall

The night was still reasonably young as they took a left out of the chilly and empty alfresco area behind the restaurant, passing a number of tightly wrapped Corona umbrellas. The cold wind curled around their alcohol-warmed heads. One more had turned into four more. After finishing those, Chelsea had made it clear that a fifth would be contraindicated.

The cold did nothing to sober them up. The wet streets shone like only Melbourne wet streets can. As they rounded the end of the car park, Toby began to make a sound which Brian finally realised was singing. But what song was not immediately clear.

'Nar, nar, nar, nar ...' warbled Toby. Then, something, something, was it 'Cruise Control'?

Toby kicked into an even higher gear. 'Whoa, TEACHER! Leave them kids at home! Na, Na, Nananana.'

If this is supposed to be Pink Floyd, it's not going to worry the copyright holders, Brian thought.

Toby turned back to face Brian, singing and dancing in reverse.

'Whoa, teacher,' he began again, then fell straight onto his backside.

'If you'll shut up, I'll help you,' said Brian. But he was in as bad a shape as Toby and the attempt had him down on the freezing and wet footpath beside his friend.

'I'll stop singing if you promise to take a sex and drugs holiday,' said Toby.

'Granddad's scrotum? Really?' said Brian. 'That bad?'

'Yes, yes, but I know what you should do!' Toby finally managed to lift his rear off the footpath. He looked around conspiratorially, still on his knees, and whispered loudly into Brian's ear, 'You should call the wine-and-cock woman!'

They made slow and careful progress around the block and managed to not get arrested or run over. When the issue of who was seeing who home was resolved, Brian made his way a little unsteadily into his own building. Toby's brutal intervention had revived an idea. An idea that had been nagging at him ever since the real estate settlement had been announced. An idea that had gone from ridiculous pipe dream to completely reasonable with just a few mils of Mexican cactus juice. He leaned on his bedroom doorframe and walked over to the computer on his small desk. Waving the mouse over the pad to wake up the machine, he found he needed to cover one eye to be able to focus on typing the password, but finally managed to open the article from *The Age*.

> Buy an Italian mansion for just one euro! An initiative by the Italian Government to revitalise rural towns has seen buyers from around the world purchase centuries-old historic houses for less than two Australian dollars.

Brian opened the website he had saved from the article, which had links to the various Italian regions involved. With one hand on the mouse and the other still covering one eye to stop the screen from spinning sideways, he stopped scrolling at random. And clicked.

Did I Do That?

Brian felt surprisingly fine waking up next morning. That was going to end within a minute, but before that time was up, his head barely pounded. Certainly less than it deserved to pound. His tongue felt nothing like dried bark, which was its usual reaction to multiple margaritas. Good old tuna bake had been like some kind of superhero liver shield.

He rolled on his side, rubbed his eyes and saw the subdued light filtering through the blinds. Another wet winter's day. As he rolled back, he took in the blank computer screen and noticed his office chair was lying on its side. 'Wait, I must have …' He whipped his head too quickly back to the computer and, now, it really did start pounding. He dimly remembered turning on the machine the night before and his tongue immediately took on the consistency of pine mulch.

'Arrk.' Something was wrong. Something was bad.

Avoiding looking at the computer again, he lurched out of bed and into the kitchen. 'Water, Panadol, coffee,' he whispered to himself. 'Water, Panadol, coffee.' His phone was on the counter. He eyed it warily as he filled the base of the stovetop espresso maker from the tap. He spooned in enough ground coffee for an entire dinner party and put it on the element, throwing back two painkillers with half a litre of water as it began to heat. Finally he was ready to pick up the phone.

There were notifications for a text and an email. The text was from Toby. The email was not. Its subject line was in Italian. He began to smell rotting limes and realised it was his own margarita sweat. Better open this on the big screen. Back in the bedroom he placed the mug of coffee and phone carefully on the desk, pulled the office chair upright and, very slowly, sat down in front of the computer. He took a gulp of the black brew and finally opened the email.

Alright. Stay calm.

He rubbed some focus into his eyes and pressed the bridge of his nose. The attached PDF was in Italian and English. The word *'Congratulazioni!'* made his stomach contract around a slurry of semi-digested nachos and tuna bake.

This is not good. Really not good.

It went on in English, 'Congratulations, from Montegiallo, Sicily.' Scrolling past some more Italian, he continued to read, 'Welcome to your dream home. Ready to move in and renovate.' A dozen photographs followed. A house, apparently *his* house – Jesus, don't call it that – looked like some kind of rustic mansion made of rectangular blocks of light stone, with a wrought-iron balcony rail in a simple pattern. It was on the corner of an ancient-looking street which was paved in blocks cut from the same type of volcanic rock as the house. An old-fashioned street lamp was fixed high on the second storey over the footpath, but Brian was not ready to appreciate the archaic charm.

A text box claimed the house had 'Bedrooms – 8, Bathrooms – 2', plus a cellar and balcony. There were ticks against 'services connected' and another against 'furniture' with an amendment noting 'limited'.

Brian scrolled, temples throbbing, through photographs of the property, desperately looking for anything more in English. Assorted views of the front of the house travelled up the screen. Interior images were few, with the most prominent, a fairly underexposed shot of a gigantic kitchen area. It had a greenish stone floor. In the gloom, just about visible, was some kind of huge wood stove with a smaller oven next to it, which looked like it was from the 1960s. A stained hot-water heater of similar vintage hung over a triple sink.

There was an immense sepulchral cellar stacked with scrap metal. All the other interior photographs were very dark, exposed for the windows, through which could be seen an unbroken blue sky and the terracotta tiles of neighbouring roofs. A shot taken from the balcony showed a shaded and pleasant *piazza* below. Beyond the buildings on the far side of the square, just visible through a few gaps in the heavy foliage, rows of smaller trees, maybe citrus, descended towards plains in the distance.

Underneath the photographs, the text continued in two blocks, one in Italian, the second in English.

> Your payment of €1 has been accepted and the property has been reserved in your name. A non-refundable bond of €5,000 will be required within 30 days to confirm the purchase. As per the agreement, this bond will be released if you begin renovations within a year. Failure to deposit the bond will result in the property being returned to the pool.

'OK. That's OK.'

Phew!

'Got thirty days.'

His chair creaked as he sat back and breathed out. Either the relief or the Panadols had cleared his head a little. Buying a house in the Sicilian countryside had been – he could now admit when sober – more of a fantasy than a real plan. An escape option he had kept open to avoid thinking about the rest of his problems. Facing it as a reality had been a hard shock. He scrolled back and looked at the photographs again. The house could be absolutely wonderful if renovated, and the town looked stunningly beautiful too. *And* a cellar would be awesome. But no, no, no, no. Don't be ridiculous. Toby was right. 'Get yourself together, Brian. Go crawling back to the department and do what you are good at.'

His phone vibrated. Another text from Toby. 'Errrrrrrrrrrrk,' was the extent of the message. Brian laughed to himself. He texted back an emoji of a cocktail glass.

Brian *now* felt better than he had in ages. The sudden shock of almost buying a rundown house in rural Sicily had been just the wake-up call he needed. *Worth every cent of one euro,* he thought. Along with Toby's forthright intervention, it was just the kick in the pants required to start re-engaging with life.

He picked up the phone again and sent Toby another text. 'Feeling great over here! Might go for a bacon sandwich.' While he had the phone in his hand, another email notification pinged. Another Italian email. Opening it, he read, 'Thank you Mr Chapman. Your non-refundable payment of €5,000 has been accepted and processed.'

Yes, You Did!

Brian turned off his computer at the wall and pulled out the power plug. He shut the blinds completely, turned off the light and sat in the semi-dark on the side of his bed. The damn phone buzzed again. Another joke text from Toby.

'Not now, Toby!' he yelled at the empty apartment.

He tucked the phone under his pillow and put his head in his hands. *Maybe I should give up drinking*, he thought. But that wasn't going to help if the pledge couldn't be backdated to the previous evening. And, if he was now a homeowner in rural Italy, where he had no friends or job, or family or contacts, surely *more* drinking, not less, was called for.

'Why did you pay the bond, you total plonker?' he moaned.

'Wait, maybe the bank.' He went back to the computer and waved the mouse, forgetting that he had unplugged it. 'Grrrr!' He got it back on and checked his balance online. It turned out that €5,000 was the best part of $8,000 Australian. Most of what he had until the apartment settled. He checked the bank contact number and pulled the phone back out. It took him nearly fifteen minutes to get through, and when he did, the bank rep all but laughed at him when he asked if the payment could be reversed. 'Is sir claiming the transaction was fraudulent?'

Sir was not, but sir was not going to divulge that drunken stupidity was the cause either.

'Ask for a refund from the payee,' was the only advice he could get out of them.

He turned his phone completely off and pulled a pillow over his head. When he finally awoke, it was late afternoon.

Brian spent a long hour sitting with a blanket over his shoulders, trying to compose a letter, begging Italy to refund a non-refundable deposit.

Maybe something in Italian would set the right tone?

Brian had been good at Italian at school. But that had been primary school.

'*Mi scusi ...*' he typed, then backspaced it out. '*Il mio amico nuovo, buongiorno.*' Hello, new friend? Too desperate?

Like all teachers, Brian had been required to take classes outside his speciality for absent (hungover) colleagues from time to time, and he had sat in on a few Italian classes in his day. But like all stand-in teachers, he hadn't bothered with much prep, beyond finding out what page to tell them to open. He half closed his eyes and tried to remember the grammar from some of those sessions. Past perfect, was it? After I had paid ... when I had been paying ... after I had been paying? This was not helping his own regrouping hangover. Perhaps safer to stick to the present tense.

After years of strictly forbidding students to use Wikipedia for assignments or to look up information on their phones in the classroom, Brian had a strong aversion to reliance on technology for the answers to questions he should be able to work out himself. Whenever it was still possible, he remained staunchly analogue. Not trusting Google Translate for anything longer than a single word, he went to his wardrobe and pulled down a box from the shelf space above. Shuffling through the stacks of old books, he found what he was looking for. His school copy of *Personal Italian Grammar*. The initials of the title had been ringed in heavy blue ballpoint. *PIG*. Brian didn't appreciate the joke as much as he had then. His name inside was printed as by a child – which of course he had been – right next to the book's details on the inside front page. 'First printing 1965'. Brian's was a much later version, but it didn't look like it had been updated much since the swinging 60s and *La Dolce Vita*. But at least it was a real book.

The present tense was covered in the third lesson. The example dialogue was a scene from a classroom where a very strict teacher was laying down the law to some rather dimwitted pupils.

Those were the days.

Even when Brian was at school, some of his classmates would have told this teacher to go fuck himself and then torched his car, if he had tried this on. There was an accompanying ink illustration of the moustachioed educator in a dark suit and tie. The text did have one particularly useful phrase, *uno sbaglio grande* – a big mistake. Yes, *uno sbaglio grande* was exactly what it was! He scanned the vocab list for anything else useful and saw the word *balbettare*, to stutter. One of the students, Giorgio, had been cowed into stammering by the teacher. How utterly useless, thought Brian. It'd be more use knowing 'My bike pump is in the arse of my uncle' than *balbettare*.

He began trying to compose a sentence again. 'I really like Italy – *Mi piace*, err, *proprio, Italia* – but, but, but …'

'But' in Italian was '*ma*', he was sure. '*Ma, ma, ma, ma, ma, ma, maaaaaaaa*,' he muttered desperately, trying to think, realising he was *balbettare*-ing already. '*Ma c'è uno sbaglio grande*. But there is a big mistake.' He closed the document, almost gagging on the smell of his tequila sweat.

Jeezus.

While he was waiting for inspiration, he began googling Montegiallo. It was almost in the centre of the island. They grew lemons. Lots of lemons. Montegiallo was spectacular in its own way. It seemed like every day the skies were blue and the sun shone. The town looked ancient and beautiful, although it gave a general impression of shabbiness. It peered over a stone wall onto narrow valleys crammed with citrus trees. There were some new apartments way down the hill, every bit as ugly as Brian's own in Melbourne, but the town itself was a beautifully proportioned piece of stone sculpture. It was founded in 1360, like other nearby Sicilian towns, by Manfredi III Chiaramonte, 'scourge of the Arab pirates'.

Wow. A scourge, eh? Cool.

Brian leaned back in his chair. 1360 was one thing, but what about today?

Under 'Facts about Montegiallo' he found the following: 'Only a 50-minute drive to the beach town of Agrigento.' Agrigento had sun, the Mediterranean, beaches, palm trees as well as Greek and Roman ruins. A semi-silhouette of a woman, deliberately shot to be unclear whether she was topless or not, lay on the sand next to a rough chunk of volcanic rock. A tanned man waved from an impossibly blue, flat-calm sea. Fifty minutes from where Brian was now would get him to Port Phillip Bay and the bleak beaches of Port Melbourne or St Kilda which, outside midsummer, required a wetsuit and a tetanus shot before having a swim.

'Let's just wait a second.' Brian opened the blinds and looked out at the rainy afternoon.

Then he ran the hottest shower he could stand. 'Let's just think about this ...'

Gumboots of Style

Toby had sent him eleven separate texts of the turd emoji and there were two missed calls. Not a conversation he was ready for yet.

Still feeling a little shell-shocked, Brian decided to trial the reaction to what he'd done with someone unlikely to call him a 'total fucken plonker'.

Elizabeth opened the door and her face lit up. She was wearing a brand new Matisse-print apron and was holding a tiny art paintbrush loaded with warm red, which she balanced on the edge of the small table next to the door.

'Brian!'

'Hello, Elizabeth. I think these are all yours. I should have got some of them back to you sooner.' He awkwardly transferred an armful of designer food containers to her.

'Not sure about this one, Brian. Not sure at all. Doesn't really look like me, does it?' She turned a beige microwave container over with a critical eye.

'Don't worry, it's yours now. I'm not taking it to Italy with me, ha-ha.'

Elizabeth frowned at the container again, and then realised what he had said. 'You're moving to Italy? Oh my God! How exciting! When?'

'Well just thinking about it, you know. Just tossing it around, weighing it up.'

'Running it up the flagpole, you mean?' asked Elizabeth.

'Yeah, yeah, yeah, exactly. Not one hundred percent yet. Might or might not be happening.'

If I can still get out of it. If I really want to get out of it.

'But if it does happen, then soon. You know my apartment's sold right? So if I have to go somewhere, it might as well be rural Italy.' He gave an exaggerated shrug and a goofy grin and wondered if he looked as stupid as that had sounded.

'Oh, that's incredible! I have a really good Facebook friend in Milano if you need a contact. Her photos are amazing. The fashion and the art and the style. Oh, so wonderful.'

'Other end, I think. Sicily. Countryside. I guess the style might be gumboots. Not sure to be honest.'

'Even the gumboots will be stylish in Italy.'

'Will they?'

'*Absolutely.*'

Brian thought it was unlikely that gumboots would be stylish in Italy, but didn't want to argue about it now.

'You've got a job there?' she asked.

'No, not really.'

'Oh. And you're going by your ah …'

'By myself yes. Why not, eh? Who else?'

'Not, with …?'

'That's a definite no.'

She gave him a smile with only a hint of pity.

He decided to spill the lot and went on hurriedly, 'Look, Elizabeth, honestly, tell me what you think. I've bought a house off the internet in Sicily for one euro. It sounds like a scam but it's not. In a town that grows lemons. In the middle of nowhere. I don't have a job and my Italian learning finished in grade seven primary school.' Brian leaned back to judge her reaction, breathing a little heavily.

Elizabeth looked like she was going to cry. 'That is by far the most romantic thing I've ever heard!' she said. 'Oh Brian. I'll miss you a lot.'

She dropped the food containers on the floor beside her and wrapped her arms around him. She smelt nice. She smelt of happiness and she smelt of Tupperware, which to some people was almost the same thing.

'And I'll always remember that time. That night… After I cooked you…'

'Yes,' said Brian with a smile. 'The coq—'

'The boeuf bourguignon,' she sighed, and hugged him harder. 'Yes, we will always have the boeuf bourguignon.'

Brian felt thoughtful as he walked back down the corridor. Had she got the dish wrong, or had she been catering to more of the building than he realised?

I'll miss you too, Elizabeth. You got me through a tough time.

The Total Plonker

Toby stared at him for a full thirty seconds. 'I'm waiting for the punchline.'

Brian eyed him over the rim of his coffee cup. 'That's understandable, but …'

'You never had the most sophisticated sense of humour. I want to make sure this is not some kind of sick joke.'

'Not.'

'Mate, you live near Carlton! You've only got to walk out the door and you'll be knee-deep in Italians. Look, there's one now. There's another one.' Toby pointed at two random dark-haired strangers passing the café who glared back at them. 'Didn't you watch *The Godfather* or *Underbelly*?'

'*Underbelly*? The organised-crime show? What's that got to do with anything?'

'Nothing at all. Sicily? Why, they've never even *heard* of the Mafia in Sicily, what was I thinking?'

'Toby, come on.'

'You've bought a house for one euro that's already cost you eight grand. Wake up and smell the inside of a shallow grave!'

'It's completely legit. The Italian government is trying to regenerate rural areas. Some of the towns are half deserted.'

'Of course they are. Because they're all over here! Isn't Melbourne the largest Italian city outside Rome?'

'I think it's Greeks outside Athens,' said Brian.

'It's Mediterranean in any case,' insisted Toby.

'The Greeks? They're Aegean, I think you'll find ... Ionian also rings a bell.'

'You're the teacher,' Toby said coldly. 'But in any case. My point is, Mediterraneans or Aegeans *or Ionians* would all rather live in Melbourne than their own towns.'

'Well, no, I don't think that's true. Rural people have just moved to the cities. Their own cities usually.'

'What about that you don't even speak Italian?'

'I learnt it at school.'

'I know. I was there. Mrs Calalesina. What were we? Nine years old?'

'I remember heaps,' said Brian. 'You never forget it when you learn young. How about this? *Sopra la panca la capra campa, sotto la panca la capra crepa.*'

'What the fuck does that mean?'

'On the ledge the goat lives, under the ledge the goat dies.'

Toby could barely articulate. 'You, you, you, you ...'

'*Balbettare,*' said Brian under his breath.

'What?'

'Nothing.'

'Wait,' said Toby, 'I suddenly remember some Italian as well. *Vaffanculo! Vaffanculo!*' he yelled.

'Shhh, Toby.' Brian looked around nervously for any of those Italians they were supposedly knee-deep in. 'Elizabeth thinks it's a great idea,' he said, trying to deflect Toby from any more multicultural profanities.

'Who's Elizabeth? Oh yeah, coq au vin.'

'Yeah. Coq au vin. Her.'

'Show me this place again.' Toby took Brian's phone from him and scrolled through the photos. 'Eight bedrooms? With your love life, you barely need one bedroom, mate. Right. Plenty of space for me to visit, I guess. Put me near the cellar, but get rid of this attractive scrap metal and replace it with wine racks.' Toby squinted at the pictures. 'Haven't they heard of a camera flash in Sicily? Dark as a bloody tomb.'

'I think that's a gold bidet,' said Brian. 'If you look closer.' He tried to zoom in using two fingers.

Toby slapped his hand away and gave him a look. 'Bidet as it may, Brian. Bidets are waaaay down the list of discussion points, don't you think? When a bloke's best friend tells him he's moving to Sicily in a couple of weeks, the fact that his arse will be clean enough to eat dinner off – while generally admirable – won't be the first consideration! The plumbing probably went in around Caligula's time too and will be just as nasty. Lead piping for sure. You want lead-contaminated water sprayed up your arse, be my guest. It will be Mad Hatter's disease from the other end. Mad Hatter's arsehole!'

'It's kind of a shock to me as well.'

'Why don't you revitalise the *Australian* countryside?' Toby arced up again. 'Plenty of dead towns here. Some of the locals even speak English of a kind. Crying out for bloody teachers too. Granted there wouldn't be a single gold fucken bidet between here and Shepparton, but Christ, can't you get yourself out of this?'

'I wanted to at first. But now I'm set to do it, especially after your well overdue intervention. Don't forget you were the one who wanted me to make a change. Being told that I looked like a fifty-year-old ...'

'And like my grandfather's scrotum,' reminded Toby.

'Many, *many* questions there. But yes, putting his scrotum aside, you were completely correct. Although it makes no sense, getting out of Australia is what I think I need right now. I'm done. As you say, it's time for a comeback. This is it. The start anyway. Just helping me feel good about it would be great. That's all I need from you right now.'

Toby puffed out his cheeks. 'Sure, mate. Nice to hear it's my fault by the way.'

'Actually, that's not all I need,' continued Brian. 'Not going to get everything done before I'm kicked out of the apartment. Might need a couch for a week. Maybe three. Maybe five. Got to get the visa sorted and all that.'

Toby furrowed his brow. 'Wait, I've got some more Italian. Umm. *Il mio casa*, ahhh … *sono*, no wait, *è la tuo casa*?' said Toby. And then, '*Io non* have *una bidet*.'

'I told you,' Brian tapped his head. 'Mrs Calalesina, Year Five. It stays with you forever.'

Say Goodbye to Harold Holt

Despite being on such short notice, Brian found time wasn't passing quickly enough. He thought he would worry about missing Melbourne, but surprisingly he felt little emotion for the place he had grown up in. What was left for him anyway?

Almost nothing and almost nobody.

He felt hollowed out, and the city felt the same for him. What could there be to miss? He liked the coffee culture, pubs and wine bars. But one thing he was sure of was that good coffee would be available in Italy. *And* good wine. Those volcanic soils. He looked up Sicilian wine on the internet. 'Mmm.' Looked good. Rich purple reds. What else would he miss? Melbourne's art, architecture and culture? Again, Montegiallo was apparently only fifty minutes away from actual Greek temples from back to 500 BC, at Agrigento. Although Montegiallo itself was small and remote, it looked like he could have culture up the wazoo in less than an hour from his new place. *My new palazzo.* A fifty-minute drive might be a long way in Italy, but from a country which took five days, driving full-time without sleep or toilet breaks, to get across, it was a joke. He found himself planning trips to Agrigento, and San Leone in his imagination. A hike through the hills seemed a pleasant idea, although he remembered he didn't like hiking. Or exertion. *Let's not run away with fantasy, Brian.*

Unsurprisingly for Brian, online visa sites gave wildly contradictory advice. The consulate on St Kilda Road was much more helpful and booked him in for an application appointment. The consulate official accepted with polite smiles Brian's documents, brief forays into primary school Italian, proof of address in Italy and a few of the half-truths in his statement. Paying the deposit had been very well received. Seemed to have tipped the balance. The visa he applied for wouldn't allow employment, but Brian didn't want to work in the near future anyway. The process was so civilised that Brian was shocked when it ended with being fingerprinted.

Things at the Italian end were going relatively smoothly. Moving in a month or whenever the visa came through was apparently no problem. He checked again to make sure. In English. Carefully. Although renovations would certainly be required, the house was habitable, and power and water were connected. Limited items could be purchased in Montegiallo, more substantial goods in Agrigento.

Emails arrived in mostly Italian, then more in mostly English. The mostly Italian ones came from Franco Messina, the local real estate agent handling the transfer. The mostly English from Viviana Messina, a wife or some other relative, Brian assumed.

An email from Franco included the words '*Possiamo uccidere ogni insetto con lo spray. Molto efficace contro ragni e scarafaggi.*'

'*Lo spray*' was, he assumed, 'the spray', but what were *scarafaggi* and *ragni*? *Scarafaggi* sounded like Scarface. If they had to spray the place for gangsters, maybe Toby was right.

The English version from Viviana came hot on its heels with a translation. It was an offer to spray for cockroaches and spiders.

Ah, scarafaggio is cockroach. Good to know. Yep, and ragno is spider. He didn't know what spiders there were in Sicily, but maybe best to start with a clean slate? Brian looked up 'Spiders in Sicily' on the internet. 'Jesus, yikes!' There were a *number* of venomous spiders in Sicily. The Sicilian tarantula, various black widows, and the yellow sac. The thought of a spider with a yellow sac boggled his mind. That would be more terrifying than a tarantula.

Yellow sac? Really? Wow.

'Normally,' wrote Viviana, 'this would not be considered renovations,' but if Brian wished, money from his deposit could be used for pest control. The house did not have linen either, so if he wanted, then they could arrange that too.

'Yeah, no. Get that crap right out of there. Especially any yellow sacs.' That's not what he wrote though. '*Sì, grazie.*' Brian hit send with a flourish, very pleased to be able to reply in Italian to an Italian. Then he suddenly worried whether this would encourage too much Italian in return that he wouldn't understand. Maybe he should have checked the price too? But what would he know about the cost of discouraging *scarafaggio*s – and killer *ragno*s – *or* the cost of sheets in rural Sicily? He vaguely remembered there was a dance, the tarantella, during which you spasmed uncontrollably, the result of being bitten by a tarantula. Maybe Mrs Calalesina had told him that too? It was a dance that he would prefer to avoid.

Brian was tempted to look up Sicilian venomous snakes as well, but he could hardly, as a self-respecting Australian, start asking nervously about spiders and snakes. He'd be a laughing stock. He thought there were no great white sharks in the Mediterranean, Aegean or Ionian. But maybe that was not right.

When Brian received the details of his full address from both Franco and Viviana, he had an idea. He took out his phone and thumbed a text to the ex. 'Please direct any future correspondence to *Piazza Spirito Santo numero 5, 93014, Montegiallo (Agrigento), Italia.*'

He set the phone down and looked at it, expecting a surprised and rapid response. None came. When there was no reply by that evening, he finally deleted her name from his contacts.

He moved out of the apartment two days before the settlement date and into Toby's rental. He gave Toby his computer, his microwave and the rest of whatever wasn't total crap. What was total crap, including most of his clothes, he either dropped in the communal bin, or left out on the footpath late on the last night in direct contravention of council by-laws.

Going through his stuff, Brian came across a Skeletor action figure toy, with battle-damage armour, still with his ram's-horn staff and sword. Not received when he was a child, but bought, embarrassingly, while stoned as an adult, well into his twenties. What was the cartoon? *Masters of the Universe*? Something like that. It was too good to throw away, and who could he give it to? His suitcase so far was barely clocking over eleven kilos balanced on Toby's bathroom scales, only half his entitlement, so he packed Skeletor as a good-luck companion.

Might need all the friends I can get over there.

Toby had done better than a couch. A spring folding bed that rang like a zither whenever he turned over. Brian's feet stuck over the edge, but he was grateful. When Toby was at work at the university, dispensing what was described as 'student wellbeing', Brian's doubts and fears were difficult to banish, but when he got home, both of them tried to keep his spirits up. Toby even promised to visit the following year when he had leave again.

The visa and the money came through within a day of each other, so Brian confirmed his one-way ticket to Palermo via Hong Kong, Heathrow and Milan. Twenty-eight hours in total. *Plus* a train trip.

Two days before he was due to fly out, and, telling Toby he needed to get some last-minute things done, he borrowed Toby's scratched silver Avalon. After dropping Toby off at Monash, Brian took a drive out to the Mornington Peninsula. He intended to visit Dromana, a little beach town on Port Phillip Bay where his family had used to holiday. But the weather was bad again and the closer he got, the more he realised it was a terrible idea. What was the use of reviving those memories?

Leave them where they lie.

Instead he drove on, almost to the tip of the peninsula, then turned left, away from the bay and towards the sea coast. Just a few minutes from the calm bay beaches, the wind drove in from Bass Strait, almost knocking him over as he made his way to the lookout. The surf boiled, the wind picked up further and he had to hold on tight to the insubstantial weather-blasted wooden railing. This was the spot where former prime minister Harold Holt had disappeared while swimming, never to be seen again. A savage, violent coast where the nation's leader could just disappear while having a dip was a scenario so Australian that Brian for the first time felt a little sadness at being about to leave.

* * *

Two days later, Brian turned his head back one last time to Toby, who, one hand raised in farewell, watched him drag his suitcase containing not much more than the treasured *Personal Italian Grammar* and a Skeletor, past the metal bollards of Melbourne's Tullamarine airport, and he was gone.

Flighting for Arrival

Nothing will put you in a better mood to start a new life than a twenty-eight-hour flight. If the will to live hasn't entirely departed before you reach your destination. Ten hours to Hong Kong, with the wait for the connecting flight to London not quite long enough for a quick trip into Kowloon. He would be trapped for three extra hours in the world of $38 burgers and $9,000 watches.

Brian was not much of an in-flight chatterer, but he had been excited about his adventure and confided it to his window-seat companion out of Melbourne. The man was absolutely convinced that the one-euro deal was some kind of scam. As were the occupants of seats A and C, Row 32, on the soul-crushing fourteen-and-a-half-hour leg to Heathrow. After his assurances about the bona fides of the Italian government began to sound unconvincing even to himself, he kept his mouth shut, making exceptions only for the linguine option and three tiny plastic bottles of Australian wine.

There was another wait at Heathrow, again not long enough to do anything with, but Brian was too disorientated to have done anything anyway. Large, square, beige tiles stretching off into infinity had become his whole world and he trudged in a daze past what could have been the same Burberry, WHSmith, Gucci and Seiko stores just to get some feeling back into his legs.

There was a complimentary snack on the two hours to Milan, but by this stage, everything he ate on a plane tasted like metal. He took it from the attendant anyway and, as with all airline food, wished he hadn't. Airline meals were more a rite of passage than sustenance, markers that divided off the journey. He wished even more this time that he hadn't eaten, because they began to fly over some extensive mountain ranges. The scenery was wonderful, but the peaks, maybe the Alps he guessed, were throwing up some spectacular turbulence and, if he wasn't going to throw up anything spectacular himself, he needed something else to think about. Despite the soothing British accent of the pilot, the jolting was bordering on terrifying. This time he told his neighbours, both of them tightly belted to their seats, that he was going to Sicily to be a writer. He wished he'd gone with this earlier, as they seemed to find it more believable than buying a house for one euro in a semi-abandoned town. He had the inspired idea to tell them he was writing a male version of *Eat Pray Love* and *The Joy Luck Club* combined, which was such a horrifying concept that it took all their minds off the plane falling apart in midair.

When booking the flights, Brian had of course concentrated on the destination. Twenty-eight hours in economy doesn't register as a reality until you are living through it. By some miracle of foresight, Brian had booked a night at the Sheraton near Milan airport to break up the journey, particularly so he wouldn't arrive at his final destination in Sicily as a drooling zombie. Even though Palermo was less than two hours from Milan, his body and his sanity could not have taken any more. The thought of lying straight out on clean sheets was the only thing he could think about as the British pilot gifted them the smoothest possible landing, touching down at Milan's Malpensa Airport.

Brian was tempted to try a little Italian at the hotel check-in, but the clerk's expert level English – switching to a smooth and rapid Italian with a colleague, then to French for the guest before him in line – was so intimidating that Brian could barely mumble in English when his turn came.

With his key, the desk clerk gave him a brochure for Volandia,

Milan's museum of flight, which was apparently just five minutes away from the airport, and offered to organise it if he wanted to visit. Who on earth would want to see another plane after the torture of travelling on one? He tried some Italian after all. '*No, grazie*,' were his first words of Italian in his new country.

He showered, and lay down on the bed. So, so wonderful. When he switched on the TV with the remote, an American appeared, talking gravely about the German economy. As soporific as that promised to be, Brian decided that since he was in Italy, he might as well go native at the first possible opportunity. Switching through the channels, he stopped at the first one in Italian and lowered the volume a little. To the sound of five talk-show participants, speaking over each other at the pace of machine guns, he slipped into one of the best night's sleep he had had for months.

* * *

With the clarity afforded by a good night's sleep, a certain trepidation returned as he took a window seat for the final leg of his journey. About an hour and a half in, he cupped his hands over his eyes, and pressed his face to the perspex, getting his first view of his new island home. He wasn't sure what he was expecting, but Palermo slid into view as the plane began to descend, as green as Ireland, way greener than his mental image of it. A small coastal plain, with ancient rocky hills backing it, slowly crossed his window. The houses *were* exactly what he was expecting though. Big white blocks with terracotta roofs on spacious green plots.

Palermo's Falcone Borsellino Airport was relatively small and had the slightly raggedy feel of many regional hubs. It had the same brightly lit ads for expensive products, but there was a much more relaxed feeling. It was like they were just going through the motions and would completely understand if Brian didn't buy a $2,000 pashmina. Brian took advantage of the airport wi-fi to confirm his arrival in Montegiallo that night, with an email to the Messinas.

An information booth stood right in the centre of the arrivals hall. Two brightly lipsticked women stood behind its narrow counter. Brian summoned up the courage to try some Italian again. '*Buongiorno*,' he began, even rolling his R's a little, wondering whether he could be mistaken for a local if he used only one word. 'Good afternoon,' they replied in synchronised English. He abandoned the Italian right there and asked how to get to the central train station, simply as a confused Australian. When they had given him directions, he replied, 'No wukkas.' He took some satisfaction that they didn't know how to respond.

Ha-ha, take that, Italy.

A Train to Nowhere

The streamlined Trenitalia electric train was brand new and bright blue. It followed the coast out of Palermo Centrale, a station that managed to be both grandiose and charming. Hotels and the occasional home on the waterfront separated car parks and small factories. The sun showed no intention of setting, although it was well after 7pm. As if shying away from a particularly large and ugly industrial centre, the tracks suddenly turned due south and began climbing into the heart of the island. The ground rose slowly and the green of the coastal strip ended abruptly. For much of the journey from this point, with the addition of a stand or two of gum trees, some roos and a few bullet-riddled road signs, it could have been rural Australia. Brown, yellow, grey. This was more the Sicily he had been picturing. There were long periods of almost no buildings, or any activity at all. Brian couldn't tell if the crushed dry grass, turning gold as the sunset finally began to bite, was natural, or the by-product from some kind of agricultural activity. Every now and then, huge highway bridges, like aqueducts for cars, crossed and recrossed the tracks. The train was mostly empty. The few, well-dressed passengers on board slumped listlessly in their seats, not engaged at all by the passing scenery. *Seen it all before.* Brian, in contrast, acted like a tourist, regularly swapping seats from one side of the train to the other to get every angle.

Sudden stands of citrus groves began to appear, almost right up to the tracks. And by the time the train began to slow as it arrived in Casteltermini at the end of the line, they dominated the area. Evening finally arrived and the glossy leaves were black against a barely lit sky.

Brian had a folded printout from Viviana Messina with the number for a taxi service that would take him the last thirty kilometres to Montegiallo. But two new-looking Volkswagen taxi vans were waiting outside the old brick terminus building and Brian tried them first. The drivers were chatting and smoking. Brian said, to either of them, 'Montegiallo?' One of the men threw down his cigarette, got into the driving seat and started the engine. Brian dragged open the side door, pushed his suitcase onto the rear seat, and sat next to it.

'*Nuovo?*' asked the driver.

'Ahh?' said Brian. '*Nuovo*' sounded like 'new', but new what? Was he asking if Brian was a newcomer?

Isn't it obvious?

Crouching down, he pushed his piece of paper forward over the console. 'Agenzia Immobiliare Ideale,' Franco's real estate office address. Brian pulled his *Personal Italian Grammar* – crammed with post-it notes marking useful phrases – from his backpack.

'*Sai dove?*' he said, which he hoped was 'Do you know where?'. The driver glanced at him in the rear-view mirror, then down at the paper, which he handed back to Brian, who hoped the driver had noticed Viviana's approximate cost for the trip.

'*Sì*.' Although the man had several low conversations on his phone during the journey, that was the only word he said to Brian.

The road twisted like a cut serpent during the dark drive. The headlights picked out white rough stone and thick walls of trees. Dirt tracks peeled off the main asphalt at regular intervals pointing to building-shaped chunks of darkness. Now that the sun was down, the night was quickly intensely black. A few streetlights were set, apparently at random, on the road's edge and the occasional yellow glow showed at an infrequent window. No traffic travelled with them. On some of the tight turns, Brian could see lights below and in the distance. They were climbing.

Unexpectedly, a double row of curved modern streetlights suddenly lined both sides of the road, then a normal apartment building of modest height appeared, then more streetlights, a service station and a small town centre. The sudden brilliance was like a slap in the face. Several smaller and newer-looking apartments went by, these also lit brightly. Cars were moving through car parks, and in and out of the service station, and the driver slowed a little. Brian had assumed they had reached Montegiallo, but the driver sped right through this lit piece of civilisation. As Brian watched the meter revolve, they began to climb again. On one of the few straight sections, they met a tiny black vehicle speeding down the hill at a dangerous pace. Sharp valleys full of dark trees, presumably also citrus, dropped from the road's edge. Finally, after one more hairpin, they slowed almost to a walking pace, edged through an opening in a heavy stone wall and crept into the old, old town of Montegiallo.

Montegiallo

The town was as still as old bones. Brian lowered his window and a lemon-scented warmth filled the vehicle. The tyres of the taxi echoed strangely off the stone walls and squeaked like birds on tight stone-paved corners. They hit some cobbles, which widened from a hemmed-in alley into a wedge-shaped, open market space with closed and dark roller-shuttered shops along one side. The taxi stopped behind a silver Mercedes saloon parked haphazardly across the only shopfront that was shutterless. The lights through the windows of the real estate office – whose window said: Agenzia Immobiliare Ideale – made the rest of the square look even darker. As Brian was settling the taxi fare, a man came out. He was barrel-chested, around sixty years of age, and wore a grey suit jacket, jeans and an open collar that was filled with a cravat.

'*Signor* Chapman? I am Franco Messina.' Franco shook Brian's hand with both of his large paws. As Brian looked around, Franco put his head into the cab and said a few words to the driver.

The glass office door opened again and a serious-looking woman holding two bundles of keys came out and locked the door using one set. Daughter, not wife maybe, thought Brian. But he remembered a former Italian prime minister who was always surrounded by bikini-clad nineteen-year-olds, so possibly things worked differently in Italy. She was slightly younger than Brian's thirty-nine in any case, or was his age but had looked after herself better. She was elegantly dressed in a brown silk blouse, with a matching skirt and boots.

For some reason the word for skirt, *gonna*, came to his mind. And the word for woman, *donna. Good old Mrs Calalesina! A donna in a gonna*, he thought, and laughed quietly. The woman stared at him and it was immediately clear he should stop doing that.

'Mr Chapman,' she said, giving him a brief, businesslike smile. 'I am Viviana Messina. Welcome to Montegiallo.'

'*Grazie,*' he said too loudly, and after the bubbling smoothness of the pair's Italian honed vowels, his Australian accent bounced off the walls like a dying raven.

Viviana opened the back door of the Mercedes and handed him a stack of packages.

'Ahh, my sheets and towels.'

'OK, we go.'

'We walk?'

'We walk. Very near.' Franco led the way.

The pair had a brief conversation which Brian couldn't follow. He wasn't sure if his poor Italian was to blame or if they were speaking in an impenetrable Sicilian dialect.

Boxed street lamps fixed on the walls were just one of the things that gave the town a medieval feel. Burning torches wouldn't have seemed out of place. They followed a curving street. They were all curving streets. Their shadows bent and flickered across the stone curves, arches and steps. The few lights showing were gold. Everywhere was the yellow scent of citrus. In less than a minute, Brian was completely disorientated. Each dark curve was the same as the last, rising with each step. In five minutes they reached a small *piazza*, which could have been the one photographed from his balcony. The same old-style lamps, but now on ornate metal poles, shed uneasy light on benches and the darkened stone buildings. Tree roots were pushing up the stone blocks, buckling across the ground. They looked like creatures from the underworld elbowing their way to the surface. Brian realised that this description, although accurate as far as it went, would have received some red pen from him on a Year Eleven's essay.

Nice writing, Hannah, but overdone descriptions can distract from narrative. Consider revising. BC.

That might be all very well on the page, but in person, it was impossible to shake off the ominous theatricality of the location. Montegiallo *was* overwritten.

They came to a chipped enamel sign. 'Piazza Spirito Santo'. Below that, some metal lettering bolted straight to the wall. 'Bar Limone'.

'Ahh, Bar Limone?' queried Brian, peering at the building.

'It is a, ahh,' Franco turned back to Viviana, '*incantevole?*'

'Delightful. Charming,' she said brusquely. The place looked anything but delightful and charming.

As they crossed the square, Brian looked up and around to find his balcony, but the contrast between this shadow world and the vivid blue of the daylight photographs was too difficult to piece together. Two out of three buildings in the *piazza* were in darkness and it was only the lightness of the stone that gave the park lanterns anything to reflect off. The air was like lukewarm water. Only patches of stars showed the gaps between black branches.

On the opposite corner to the bar, they stopped. Franco used his phone torch to illuminate the front door. A new lock looked incongruous next to the huge lion's head doorknocker. The lock was the only thing on the building – in fact in the whole town – that didn't look five hundred years old. Brian stepped back, and Franco obliged by shining the light across the rest of the exterior. The shadows of the iron railings moved across the upper level like the scales of a snake. The photographs had not conveyed the proportions. His house looked double the size of the neighbouring building, as far as he could see in the darkness.

'Tch,' clicked Viviana, annoyed, and Franco moved the spot of light back to the lock while the correct key was finally found.

Brian would have been disappointed if the door had *not* creaked spookily as it opened. Viviana pushed it wide and strode straight in. Franco gestured for him to follow her, and he stepped into his new home.

A Ruined Mansion

Beyond a stone hallway from which narrow stairs without railings rose, Viviana was switching on some dim lights. Were there any other kind in this town? He might need night-vision goggles to live here. Brian and Franco walked together through a small arch and into a wide, open room. On a rug so threadbare that it had almost no colour stood a solid wooden table and three dilapidated 1960s kitchen chairs in red, white and blue. There was nothing else in the room. Viviana put some paperwork and the keys on the table and looked around.

Am I supposed to say something?

'Would you like to see? Or you would prefer to do that by yourself?' She put one hand on her hip. Franco grinned at him.

Brian put the stack of linen on the table as well. 'Water and services connected, right?'

'I have transferred the accounts to you. There are three internet providers that are reliable for this area. All in your folder.'

'This is the best house in Montegiallo, for one euro,' said Franco. 'And the biggest.'

It felt like Franco had used that phrase before because this English was quite confident. If real estate agents were the same as in Australia, they would *all* be the best house in Montegiallo for one euro. It was certainly a 'renovator's dream'.

The room opened up further under another arch as Brian moved through. Also big. An open kitchen and living area which he recognised from the photographs. An oversized wood stove big enough to cater for a moderate-sized army barracks. A gas stove which looked tiny in comparison. Very old. An even more ancient curvaceous refrigerator with the door open, showing a chrome and icy-green pressed-metal interior. The type of thing that would be restored and sold for a fortune in a Melbourne antique shop. It had a huge crown logo above large silver letters saying INDES and a solid chrome handle as big as a car jack. It was much older than Brian. Any older and it would have been powered by kerosene.

One door off the kitchen hid a high cistern toilet with a black plastic seat that reminded him of childhood visits to his grandmother's house in Geelong. It had no water in the bowl, only dust. In the far corner of the kitchen area was an extensive wooden bar, built solidly into the fabric of the building.

A doorway and another set of dark steps led to the cellar.

Of course they are dark steps.

An earthy and cementy smell met his nose as he poked his head through the opening. He decided to leave investigating that space until later.

One thing he was pleased *not* to see were any *scarafaggio*s or more particularly *ragno*s and especially yellow sacs.

He walked back into the room as Viviana's long, slim fingers leafed through the laminated sleeves in a folder. There were two documents left on the table. 'All the information you need should be here. If you have any other questions, come and see me in the office. Just the final sign-off here. Or if you want to look around first?'

Brian was going to ask them to wait while he examined the rest of his house, but he suddenly wanted them gone.

And what difference would it make anyway? What could he say? 'No thanks'? And stumble back down the dark hill, all the way to Melbourne?

'Do you know if there are any other Australians here?' asked Brian.

'Yes. English. Some Americans.'

'But no Australians?'

She shook her head. 'Maybe now you are the first, there will be many.'

Brian was suddenly unsure of whether he wanted that. Australians not actually in Australia were often not particularly good ambassadors.

He signed the two copies with Franco's absurdly chubby fountain pen, then Viviana scooped one up and closed the plastic folder. She handed their copy of the signed papers to Franco and they made to leave.

At the door, Franco turned, grinning like a demon again, and said in confident English, 'Welcome to your dream.'

Home Alone

It was all a dream. But Brian had been in a dream since his plane had left Melbourne. Standing alone in the cool, quiet stone building should have felt like the end of the trip, but the unreality continued. Maybe only daylight could offer a real conclusion to the journey. The other rooms downstairs, devoid of furniture, could have been for anything, but he assumed they were some of the eight bedrooms.

Paying a lot of attention to where he placed his feet, he ascended the perilous stairs, hugging the stone wall. A stair rail might be a good idea for the first renovation project.

More bedrooms. One contained a cheap blondwood desk. Others were totally bare. A full bathroom. Disused and covered in dust. Opening the door was like discovering an ancient temple. He lost count of the toilets. Maybe seven including the one downstairs? Some of the cisterns were shaped like seashells, but none of them seemed in working order. Most were dry and full of grey powder; another, for some reason, was filled with tiny pieces of torn cardboard. A small bedroom had a dresser and mismatched stool under a multicoloured 'modern' light fitting. One square space contained only green metal shelving and a door four centimetres thick that was stuck at forty-five degrees; another room contained nothing at all, not even a window. Why was the place so large?

The master bedroom was the most completely furnished and, apart from a door at the top of the stairs, was the only access to the balcony.

The bed itself was a dark wooden monster which was not quite a four-poster, but the posts it did have rose high and in an unmistakably phallic manner at each corner. A matching wardrobe like a quadruple-width coffin with a curved Deco exterior stood ominously on the side wall. He opened it briefly, but decided to investigate its contents properly later. There was a dusty cover over the mattress. Brian lifted it and pressed down. The mattress was fortunately not as old as the bed.

New mattress first, then the stairs.

Brian grated open the door to the balcony and stood outside, realising how cool the interior was. Through the trees and across the square, the door to Bar Limone opened, releasing a wedge of uranium-coloured light. Sound, possibly from a jukebox or radio, escaped with a figure, then was cut off as the door closed. Two more dark shapes left a moment later.

Closing time.

Brian went carefully down the stairs, retrieved his linen packs and returned to the bed, hoping that the brand-new cotton would shield him from anything that might be lurking.

There was a large bathroom next door. There was indeed a gold bidet and a matching gold toilet! He turned the worn chrome of the basin tap, and water flowed. He wouldn't have said gushed, but it definitely flowed. *Good.* He pressed the lever of the toilet. After a little reluctance it flushed as vigorously and as noisily as a Cessna taking off. *Even better.* He pulled his phone out of his pocket and took a photo of the bidet and texted it, hoping that his roaming set-up would get it through to Toby. *Wait, what time would it be there? Oh. Probably early morning. Will do you good to wake up early, Toby.*

The thought of his friend and his former life sent a wave of loneliness through him.

He lay on his new sheets and put his head on his new pillow. He had barely closed his eyes when the frame gave way and the head of the mattress dropped to the floor. With a sigh, he took his pillow to the higher end, which followed suit by dropping out as well. He turned over until his thoughts stopped swirling with the cloud of dust he had raised and waited, exhausted, for sleep.

A New Dawn

And that's how it came to be, that on one Sicilian summer morning, in a year that has never been explicitly stated, a man pushing forty years old could be found lying asleep on his back. On a mattress on the floor. Under the frame of a bed that nobody alive would remember had been made – along with a matching wardrobe – by two brothers in 1923.

Dust turned slowly in the sharp blades of sunshine that cut through the curtainless windows. The ghosts and shadows of the night, along with various *scarafaggi* and *ragni*, had crept back to the cellars, cracks and holes in the venerable town's walls. The warmth of the night had retreated to the yellow plains below the town.

The man's possessions were contained in just one soft suitcase, a backpack, and some electronic ones and zeros in the computers of an international bank.

The suitcase contained little more than a few clothes, a second pair of sneakers and a blue fifteen-centimetre-tall muscled and hooded action figure with a skull face and a ram's-head staff.

The backpack contained a bottle of water, a toothbrush, a wallet and a baseball cap with the words 'Monash University' on the front. Also an old-fashioned Italian grammar book with dictionary.

His phone, lying next to him on the floor, had recently contained hundreds of photographs, many of himself and a brown-haired woman with a long face and a beautiful, lopsided smile, but no longer did so. One of the few images now in its memory was of a gold bidet.

Daylight

The night before, Brian hadn't registered that the bedroom windows did not have curtains. 'Errk.' There was no mistaking it now. Light from the window roasted the wallpaper behind the bedhead like a rectangle of polished aluminium. Brian had stayed with his head at the foot of the bed when the mattress had dropped to the floor the previous night. He now threw his pillow back to the head end, turned over, sat up and looked over the dark varnished foot board into a piece of infinitely clear, cloudless blue sky. Indeed, it would have been fairly infinite even with a few clouds in it. After the gloom of the previous night, which felt as unreal as a scene from a noir movie, the difference was dazzling.

I will definitely need curtains before ever getting a hangover.

He sort of remembered seeing, during his investigation the night before, some kind of black-velvet drapery somewhere, but that could have been a night-time fantasy.

He had slept well, despite the mattress being on the floor. Although the room looked like it should be mouldy, the scarifying blaze of the sun had kept any aspiring fungus at bay. It was hard to describe the colour of the peeling wallpaper, what it was now, and what it had been in the long-ago past when it had been applied. Now the barely visible oval pattern referenced nothing less than the dull grey shapes of Sicilian tarantulas.

That got him thinking about getting off the floor. Brian climbed out of the bed frame and went to the window. The sun was already drawing deep, indigo shadows between the rows of terracotta tiles of his lower neighbours, which stepped down the street on one side. He forced open the balcony door again and stepped outside in his underpants onto the elaborately patterned brown-and-white tiles. Eight o'clock. Despite the sun, the air on the hill was cool. The leaves of the trees in Piazza Spirito Santo below him were squeezed straight from a tube of emerald-green oil paint, shading the wood and iron benches below. Brian stood with his hands on the metal railings. A woman carrying a large cloth bag in each hand exited the square and glanced up at him. He gave her a small wave, and then realised that, with both hands full, she couldn't wave back. Even if she wanted to. She didn't really look like she wanted to, to be honest.

Well, I am in my underwear, I suppose.

Brian wondered if her bag held groceries and he suddenly felt hungry. Especially for coffee. But first, make use of the facilities.

He went to the bathroom and turned on the shower. The showerhead was old, with the chrome worn back to brass, but the knurled fitting attaching it gleamed new and bright. After what seemed forever, the low-pressure sprinkle that emerged reluctantly turned lukewarm, and then, at last, hot. As the water rinsed the floor of the shower and the dust drained away, the spectacular patterns of the bathroom tiles became apparent. Wet, they blazed with a vivid green-and-red geometric pattern that was a tribute to 1960s Italian style. Brian mentally added a mop to his 'to buy' list to properly reveal the garish beauty of the rest of the grime-covered bathroom floor. After towelling off, he went back through to the bedroom, speculatively pressing the flush lever on the bidet on the way past. Brown water barely bubbled out, the nozzle almost completely blocked. Brown, thought Brian, is not going to make the back door sparkle.

Time to look over his *palazzo* properly. He went downstairs, again wondering what had happened to the stair rail, and went back into the room where his copy of the contract and folder still lay on the table. Through the arch, he looked more closely at the wood stove. A real behemoth, but not as old as he had thought. It was so wide his arms could not stretch wide enough to touch either side. Dials and temperature gauges were set into the enamelled doors which were black, blended into brown, creating a half-burnt look. It seemed at the same time old but also trying very hard to be modern. 1970s? 1980s? In any case, you could roast a large proportion of most edible beasts in the main oven section. There were various doors and compartments for wood and cooking. Maybe he could learn artisanal (or artist-anal as Toby called it) baking. The brand was Becchi, and he would think of her as 'Becky' from now on.

The only spot he had not looked at properly was the cellar basement. The stone stairs were smooth and worn, and went down like the steps to a dungeon. Besides the earthy smell, he detected the remnants of the pest control work. He felt he should have been holding a candelabrum as he descended. At the bottom of the stairs, bare globes down one wall gave out a brownish light. *Natch.* The floor was sand-covered stone. The space was large but, apart from the mystery scrap metal, mostly empty. The far wall was arched and blocked with broken, rubble-like masonry held together by roughly applied concrete. It looked relatively recent, in a rustic sort of way. He clapped his hands, and the sound was flat and muted, as if he was clapping inside a grave.

Brian went back up to the main room thoughtfully. The place was a wreck. A magnificent wreck, but a wreck nonetheless. Suddenly his $30,000 felt like an extremely inadequate sum. His plan, vague as it was, had been to live comfortably off his savings in a cheap rural town for a couple of years and, at his leisure, decide what to do with the rest of his life. What did it even cost to fix a bidet in Sicily? He had the horrible feeling that the answer might do quite a bit of damage to $30,000 Australian.

He walked over and plugged in INDES the refrigerator, which jolted into life like kickstarting his old Honda, during his fortunately brief – and even more fortunately fatality-free – motorbike period. As the vibrations subsided, he pulled out the shelves and ice trays and put them into the largest of the three basins of the sink. The plug was as cracked as a piece of oak from a sunken galleon. The handle of a dish scrubber and a brown bottle were the only items in the cupboard beneath. The bottle had no label except the remains of what was obviously a skull and crossbones. He unscrewed the lid. Whatever the poison was, it had a sweet smell. He put it back.

Never know when I might need some unidentified poison.

He went through the whole place and opened anything that had a door. He placed every item he found on the big main table. Bathroom cupboards – empty. He moved to the bedroom wardrobe. A brass rail with half-a-dozen empty wooden hangers which clacked together at the opening of the doors.

Ahh, here they are. At the bottom, some solid black velvet, presumably curtains. He glanced at the windows. Substantial metal wrought-iron hooks, but no rail.

The top shelf of the wardrobe held a large tan suitcase made of indeterminate materials. As he pulled it down, he could see it bulged. Filled almost to bursting with something soft. *More sheets maybe? A body?* The clasps were locked or jammed, so he took it down the main room and added it to his modest pile.

Behind the solid bar were two big cardboard cartons lettered in faded blue. 'Detersivo in polvere'. Some kind of washing powder. But that was not what was in them. The first was filled with glassware, including several vintage Messina beer glasses with much of the paint still visible. Not trusting the ageing cardboard, he pulled the items out two by two and put them on the table. Solid-based wine glasses, several ashtrays, one with a novelty rubber-tyre border that advertised Pirelli.

Almost worth taking up smoking again to use this.

There was a water jug filled with tiny, cut-crystal shot glasses. The other box had crockery. A full set for a dozen diners in a simple cream-

and-blue pattern with scalloped edges. Looked old. Even a gravy boat and a butter dish, which could have taken the output of several cows. He put it aside. Various mismatched plates and cups with daring 1960s and 1970s colours and patterns. Some cutlery with bone handles, knives that had been sharpened so often that they were little more than narrow strips and a hand meat-grinder in green powdered enamel. He turned the handle thoughtfully. On the lower shelf of one of the rooms was a wooden fruit box filled with oak-handled tools. Chisels ground back to a few centimetres, hammers, nails and bits and pieces. A thin cupboard in the basement held a mop, the head of which turned to powder when he moved it. At the bottom were two and a half boxes of the same lurid tile that graced the bathroom. He left them there. There was also a reeded rail which looked to be from the windows of the bedroom. There was a gold decorated knob on one end, the other end missing. Still, it might be enough to get the curtain back up. Lastly there was a dangerous-looking ancient electric iron with a frayed cord and a dubious bakelite plug.

He'd now done a careful count. There were six toilets. On top of the cistern in one of them was a small stack of very old pornographic comics which, apart from dull glossy monochrome covers, were printed on paper of the lowest possible quality. No date. *Got to be 1950s?* The comic was called *Pussycat*. The dialogue, such as it was, was in Italian, but few of the nouns or verbs were likely to be covered in his grammar's dictionary. 'Spruuuut!' was a frequently used sound effect. Wait, there was one word he could translate easily from the image. '*Idraulico*', plumber. This *idraulico*, however, didn't even get a chance to get his plunger out before being distracted by the lady of the house. There was also an *Ultra Pussycat*, some sort of special edition with a poorly registered three-colour cover, on which a woman in a cat costume sported an enormous red strap-on.

'Err, right,' said Brian, flicking through, not sure whether the magazines could strictly be called assets. Not the kind of publication you could claim to be reading just for the articles. The paper threatened to disintegrate in his hands, so he placed the stack very carefully with the rest of his possessions.

And that was about it. The inventory barely covered the tabletop. He bent Skeletor's muscle-bound thighs and sat him on top of it all. 'King of the hill, mate.'

Actual rubbish he put into one pile. He kept the *Pussycats*. He put his hands on his hips and scrutinised the rest.

He grabbed a flat screwdriver with a broken blade from the toolbox. It looked a century old. He used it to lever open the suitcase. From under thick, old, crackly plastic, the very vaguest of mothball smells rose. It covered tightly packed clothes. The top few items were cotton dresses, the first with a textured elastic waist, which had long ago given up its stretch. Under the womenswear was some men's stuff. On top, half-a-dozen ties, some silk, some wool, all carefully rolled. No labels. One cravat of plainly patterned green. Half a dozen thick white shirts, folded. Folded so long they might be permanently set in that shape. They could have been carved from marble. Under those, wrapped in brittle brown paper, a dark, midnight-blue, wool pinstriped suit with wide lapels and a pearl-grey satin lining. Brian lifted the jacket and held it in front of him.

Might even fit me. If it didn't fall apart. He put the jacket on carefully. 'What you reckon?' he asked Skeletor. He held the trousers up. Too short by the looks, but the hems were turned up generously inside. Right there he dropped his jeans. Who was there to object? He pulled on the trousers, which ended several centimetres above his ankles and the waist was a little loose, but otherwise it fitted as well as any other suit he had worn. In the spotted mirror of the bathroom upstairs he took stock.

I look like the drawing of the teacher in the grammar book!

He unfolded the shirts, took the suit off, and hung all of it in the wardrobe.

Brian pictured himself sitting on the balcony in the dark suit, insouciantly glancing through a *Pussycat* and sipping a latte. Then the reality of the place hit him again. Then the reality of not having a latte.

OK. High time to look at Montegiallo in plain daylight.

Whoever the Hell He Was

Pulling his jeans and sneakers back on, dropping the keys in his pocket and leaving Skeletor in charge, Brian walked out the front door and looked left and right. He examined his neighbour. Closed up. Dark. It had a look of being abandoned. Dust covered the stone doorstep. The door itself was dressed in peeled black paint. Maybe he'd get some one-euro neighbours sometime.

But not today.

Retracing the route from the night before was going to be impossible, but he remembered they had gone steadily upwards and then through the *piazza* to get there. So through the *piazza* and steadily downwards was the plan. Piazza Spirito Santo was already in deep shade. Through the gaps in the branches, small blue patches of sky dropped the occasional bright pool of light.

As Brian began crossing the *piazza*, a man emerged from Bar Limone with a small cup of coffee with an even smaller saucer and sat at one of the benches. He was almost comically big, sturdy and solid like the buildings surrounding them. A stained apron inadequately covered black shirt and trousers. Dark hair sprouted on his brown arms and from the neck of his shirt.

Brian half thought of going into the bar, especially as it looked like you could get a coffee there, but the exterior, even in daylight, was a little forbidding. He stopped in front of the seated giant. No time like now for some Italian interaction.

Here goes nothing.

He cleared his throat, and began hesitantly.

'Ahh, *buongiorno* ...'

The man's eyebrows contracted towards the bridge of a nose that could have ruddered a small boat. He rumbled something in a low voice that Brian couldn't catch.

He wished he'd brought his Italian book with him. '*Io sono* ...'

'*Inglese?*' the man asked. 'English? *Americano?*'

'Australian. I mean *australiano*. I have just bought ...' He pointed back at his *palazzo*.

'So the foreigners have made it to the top of the hill now? Ha!' the colossus said in heavily accented English. 'Americans, English, *Faaarkaarza!* All-a *faaarkaarza*,' he elaborated.

Without saying another word the man got up and, taking his cup and saucer with him, stomped back into Bar Limone.

'Umm, Australian actually,' Brian called hopelessly after him.

Faaarkaarza? Did that mean what he thought it meant? Brian was not sure what to make of this outburst. Perhaps subconsciously and almost certainly arrogantly, he had assumed that he would be received as some kind of minor saviour, revitalising a struggling town and all that. He decided to keep his head down and his mouth shut for the moment. Just the first day after all.

Faaarkaarza? Whoa!

Through the square, and after a couple of wrong turns and more stone steps than he remembered from the night before, he found himself back in the cobbled triangle containing the real estate office.

Although the office was closed, the roller shutters around the rest of the area were up or being raised. There was a *supermercato* which looked more like a *minimercato* to Brian. There was a shop that looked like it was mostly for cigarettes and a laundromat in front of which some tiny tables had been set up. Brian realised they were for the coffee bar next door. Finally. This place looked much more inviting. There was a couple inside receiving their takeaways. A bluff-faced man with a round head on a rectangular frame said to the server, 'Have a nice day.' A distinctive American accent. His torso was draped in an olive t-shirt hanging like a curtain above shorts and Crocs. Brian pushed past him with a nod, turning sideways in the narrow shop. The thin woman inside received a tray of coffees. 'Thank you, lovely.' English accent this time, and Brian realised they were not a couple.

Brian turned to the very young woman behind the counter. He knew that Italian coffee ordering could be quite complicated. He knew that 'flat whites' popular in Australia were not a thing, and he wasn't sure about 'lattes'. So he tried to keep it as simple as possible and simply asked for a coffee with milk. '*Un caffè con latte, per favore.*' Despite Brian's accent, which here, sounded as broad as a Queensland farmer, she satisfyingly complied without comment.

The man stepped out of the door, turned back and addressed Brian from the threshold.

'New fellow, am I right?'

'Yes,' said Brian.

'One euro as well?'

'Yeah. You too?'

'Uh-huh. Another impoverished bastard just looking for a cheap spot in the sun. Murray Purdue.' He moved further back out of the doorway to allow Brian room to continue the conversation. He put out his hand.

'Brian Chapman. From Melbourne, Australia.'

'An Aussie, eh? And that was Martina,' Murray said, releasing a firm handshake. The woman turned to look back at them and raised her coffee tray in greeting, but she continued across the cobbles.

'English,' said Murray. 'You'll get to know everyone pretty soon. Us one-euro expats keep pretty tight.'

'I just arrived.'

'Which one you get, huh? The double level on Via Magellano or the three-bedroom on Via Pirandello?'

'Which house, you mean?' Brian looked back up the hill. 'Ahh. Piazza Spirito Santo. Three levels with the basement. Six toilets. Apparently. I only moved in last night. Trying to get my bearings.'

'That huge dump up on the hill? Were you drunk or something when you bought that? Ha-ha.'

Brian gave him a thin smile. 'Of course not,' he lied. He turned back into the shop to pick up his coffee and took a long swig. 'Ahh, *molto bene*,' he called back.

'All the expats basically live in one spot,' said Murray. 'We call it "The Ghetto". Best views in town. Come on. Let me show you.'

Following downhill in the direction Martina had disappeared, they went through an arch and under a covered stone walkway open on one side. At the far end, where steps began descending yet again, Murray stopped and they looked down at the rows of tiled roofs below them.

'This is Viale Virgilio Marone, whoever the hell he was. Past it, you got The Ghetto. Half the places are Brits and us Americans. The other half mostly empty. None of us live up the back on your part of the hill. No views because of all the trees. Also, the locals are not all that friendly up there, as you'll maybe find out for yourself.'

Brian looked past the roofs, and the lemon trees, out to the dusty plain below. The dark, low hills beyond were already in a slight haze of heat.

'Looks beautiful,' said Brian. 'I do have a nice little *piazza* under my balcony though,' he added, already a little defensive of his *palazzo*. 'And six toilets.'

'Yeah. Where that rundown bar is. The Lemon Pit.' Without waiting for Brian to respond, he went on, 'You don't have to go in there. *Ever.* We have a great Saturday drinks regime down in The Ghetto. Different place each week. As a one-euro expat you are automatically invited.

Martina and Eric are hosting the next one. Come down. It's kinda compulsory.'

Brian realised that with the travel, the time zones and the general bamboozlement, he had absolutely no idea what day it was.

'Tomorrow night, six pm,' said Murray, his Crocs already slapping down the stairs. 'Corner of Madonna della Vita and Via Salieri.' He turned his head back over his shoulder. 'Whoever the hell he was.'

Brian finished his coffee. While speaking to the American, he had not noticed it was beyond *molto bene*. It was *magnifico*! He went straight back for another.

No Yellow Sacs

At the *supermercato*, Brian bought a mop, a broom, a plug for the sink and two large bags which contained mostly cleaning products, apart from a couple of panini, wrapped in waxy paper and bulging with sliced meats and pickled vegetables. Remembering the old glasses he had found, he had also purchased four bottles of Messina beer. He hoped this would be enough to keep hunger at bay for the day. Coming out, he saw that the Ideale offices were open. Laying his shopping on the footpath outside, he went in. No sign of Franco, but Viviana came out from behind a beige room divider. Daylight confirmed what a striking woman she was. Hair to her shoulders, a necklace of rectangular amber blocks complemented an apricot floral knee-length dress, above the same heeled boots she had worn last night. She reminded Brian of one of the classic Italian movie actresses he couldn't remember the name of, whose eyes were always toggling between points of fire and dark, mocking pools. Usually while conversing with Marcello whatshisname. The effect, which might have been startling in the equivalent-sized rural backwater in Australia, seemed perfectly appropriate here, where, apparently, even gumboots would be stylish.

Out of my league, he thought. Or maybe leagues are different here?

'Yes?'

'Ahh, *buon* … Oh, sorry I forgot what time to stop saying *buongiorno*, and start saying *buonasera*. I think you're supposed to switch in the afternoon sometime?'

'That's what you came in here for?'

'No, no, sorry, I actually wanted to know what the process was for releasing funds from the bond for renovations. What do I have to do?'

'*Allora*,' Viviana said. 'Get a written quote, and bring it in here. We do the administration for the government. I've also got your receipts for the linen and the pest control.'

'Great,' said Brian. 'Haven't seen a single yellow sac so far. Please give my compliments to the sprayer.'

She stared at him like he was an idiot. There was a short silence.

'Get a written quote, bring it in here, and the deposit will be paid direct to the company,' she repeated deliberately, as if he was a little slow-witted. 'Once work begins, the rest of the funds will be transferred.'

'Good. I've got six toilets and a bidet. One of them works.'

'You got a large house in Italy for one euro, remember?' The eyes were trending towards points of fire.

'I know. Thank you for reminding me.' The claims 'ready to move in' and 'furnished' were, while not straight-out lies, at best misleading, was his opinion. He now understood why the photographs were all so dark.

Brian turned to go. As he reached the door, Viviana said, 'About lunch.'

Brian's brain scrambled to understand what she meant. She was asking him to lunch? First day in town, and a gorgeous Italian woman was asking him out? But the only thing his brain could come up with in reply was, 'I would love to, but I've got paninis.'

She looked at him like he was an idiot for the second time in a minute.

He *was* an idiot for the second time in a minute.

'Around lunch. That's when you start saying *buonasera*. Afternoon is *buon pomeriggio*, but you can leave that out. Really most people say *buonasera* anytime after lunch.'

'Oh, right. Great. Sorry. Goodbye, err, Viviana.' Brian scuttled towards the door red-faced. He was sure he heard her snort, 'Lunch? Hah!' He didn't turn back, but no doubt her eyes were already forming mocking pools.

Cinghiale

Throwing himself into repairing the bed, Brian tried to forget about the embarrassing encounter with Viviana. He had briefly wondered about his chances, speculating that he might now be a big fish in a small pond, but was now sceptical about the advantage any pond-shrinking might achieve when it came to romantic encounters.

It took all four beers to fix the bed. After that, Brian had to make two more trips back down the hill for *more* Messinas. His plump INDES fridge hummed and jiggled away happily downstairs as he worked, sounding pleased to be back doing good honest work chilling Brian's beer.

From the old toolbox, the rusty claw hammer was almost all he had needed to get the bed frame fixed and the mattress back off the floor. The frame had separated slightly, leaving the flat wooden slats that were the base with nothing to hold onto. Fortunately the wood was still sound, in fact it was like iron, and he just re-slotted the slats and hammered the frame back together with brute force and a few archaic, square-headed nails from the bottom of the toolbox.

Once the bed was back together, he hauled the lined, black velvet curtains out of the wardrobe and laid them on top of the sheets. The bottoms were a bit crusty, but they looked substantial enough to keep out a nuclear blast. The strip that held the heavy rings had half come away, so, one more trip down the hill for a needle-and-thread kit. This stair climbing was going to make him fit, or ruin his knees. He'd consumed all his food during the stair-climbing and physical activity. He didn't want to test the old gas stove just yet, certainly not without cleaning it, and the big wood burner looked like it needed a doctorate to operate. So for dinner later he also bought a loaf of bread, some olive oil, and a salami that turned out to be made of wild boar. 'Cinghiale, eh? Wild boar?'

Hmm. Good to know. A sample coincided exactly with what he would have thought a wild boar would taste like, had he been asked to think about it.

Very much so.

Into the INDES went the wild boar. On top of the fridge went the bread, and out of it came another beer, which he poured into one of the old, etched glasses.

Right. The curtains.

The light from the Sicilian sun busting through the windows was brighter than any artificial light in the place, so Brian knelt in front of the bed and slowly resewed the curtain strip with a lot of concentration and a very ugly stitch. He brought the rail back up from the basement and, in a job that would really have suited two or even three people, he hoisted the unbelievably weighty curtains up onto the hand-forged iron hooks. Even dragging them closed took some strength but, when he had done so, apart from a slight glow at the top, it could have been midnight.

He opened them again, and using his brand-new broom, swept every piece of dust out the door and over the balcony, including the three centimetres that had gathered on top of the wardrobe. While mopping the bathroom floor, he ran a bath into the light green enamel tub imprisoned in its rectangle of garishly tiled concrete.

Before getting in, he realised he had forgotten to buy soap, so he put in a drop of dishwashing detergent and had a relaxing bubble bath, sipping at a half glass of Messina.

Worries about a future without enough money notwithstanding, and it may have been the Sicilian beer talking, but he felt *good* about his first day. Apart from making an idiot of himself at the Ideale office, he had made some practical achievements. He'd fixed the bed and curtains. He'd made *some* attempts to speak Italian, with admittedly mixed results, but it was early days. The thing he was most glad about was that he was not living in The Ghetto with a lot of other expats. That was the best. That was the best of all.

Black Velvet Dawn

Brian woke late. The darkness imposed by his wall of velvet had kept the night going for far longer in his bedroom than out in the *piazza*.

Before tackling the stove and the rest of the cleaning, Brian decided to look around the town a little. He went and bought two large coffees and brought them home.

Yep, this is home now.

Drinking the first coffee, he wrote a long email to Toby, thumbing it awkwardly on the phone, telling him about The Ghetto and how much he dreaded meeting the other expats. He wasn't even sure why. Well actually he was sure – he hated social situations involving strangers. God, remember those excruciating parent–teacher meetings? But he might need their help sometime. Be nice to talk to some real English speakers from time to time too, wouldn't it?

Get over it.

He wondered if he should get a computer. In this house on Holy Spirit Square, modern technology might feel a bit alien or maybe, more accurately, '*fuori moda* – out of fashion', as expressed in the grammar book. He'd need an Italian phone or at least a SIM card. But he had a month of international roaming paid for so that could wait a bit.

One thing I do want to look up, though.

He thought that it was impolite not to know who the streets were named after. That was one of the reasons he had felt a little negative about Murray the American the day before. The man had not known who his street was named after. Brian didn't know either. The difference was, Brian would find out. *If I was living on Viale Virgilio Marone, I'd want to know who that was.*

Salieri was, he assumed, Salieri the composer – *Amadeus* the Mozart movie and all that – and Madonna della Vita seemed reasonably self-evident. But who was *Signor* Virgilio Marone? Oh. It was just Virgil. Great! An old friend. Brian knew Virgil very well as the ghost tour guide of Hell in Dante's *Inferno*, which was compulsory reading for Year Twelve literature. Virgil had been sentenced to Limbo for the poor judgement of being born before Jesus arrived. Brian had always made a joke 'Whaad I do?' to the class, which, he recalled, never really went over well. Hadn't the church abolished Limbo? Poor old Virgil was probably out on the streets these days.

Before going out with the other coffee, he started to fill the sink with hot soapy water and took anything removable off the gas stove and the big wood stove as well – knobs, trays, and even the burners. He still had not done the fridge trays and plastic fittings either.

Wait. Too much.

He stopped filling the sink and took the whole lot up to the bath, dripping water up the stairs in front of him. Adding more dishwashing liquid, he ran the water until it covered everything in a giant mound of warm bubbles. Leaving it all to soak, he grabbed his other coffee and a map of Montegiallo from his welcome folder, popped the *Personal Italian Grammar* in his backpack – or *zaino* as they called them in Italy – and took to the streets.

Turning away from the *piazza* and orienting his map, he turned left at the corner of his *palazzo* and up what was left of the hill behind. He nodded and *buongiorno*-ed at the few people he saw, to which he didn't get specific replies, but no actual hostility either. Nobody called him a *faaarkaara*, in any case, which was definitely a good sign.

Music and voices, from televisions, radios and other devices, emerged from the obviously residential street. Buildings not made of stone were painted bright red and green, with the pockmarked render giving a generally pleasing effect.

Dodging around parked scooters and motorbikes, he took several photos of these places, and then stopped.

You're a resident now, not a tourist. These are your neighbours. Stay cool.

As he met more people on the street he continued with his cheery *buongiorno*s. Most reactions were either non-existent or neutral, but a couple of times he got suspicious looks and bare grunts in reply.

Maybe a little disappointing.

A middle-aged man in a snazzy green-striped shirt and rumpled cap was attempting to secure a cardboard box to the rear of a scooter propped on the footpath. Although it would have made a charming tourist photo, instead, Brian decided to make another attempt for the day at testing his limited Italian vocabulary. He addressed the man. 'Ahh, *buongiorno*, ahh, *mi piace il tuo …*' he was intending to say he liked the man's shirt, but at the last second the word for shirt fled his memory. He hastily ended the sentence with the only appropriate word he could remember, *cappello*, hat. The man stared at him. He slowly took off his cap and turned the sweat stained piece of cloth in his hands as if seeing it for the first time in his life. 'You like my … hat?' he asked in puzzled English.

'*Sì*,' said Brian.

A pause threatened to extend indefinitely.

'… *Grazie*.'

That seemed to be it. They faced each other. Brian ended this intense encounter with a wave, and a jaunty '*Arrivederci!*' but he could feel the man's eyes burning on his back as he continued up the street. Brian decided to chalk that one up in the positive column.

Stopping at the Stations

Just five minutes from his home and the *piazza* was the church. Also named after The Holy Spirit. La Chiesa dello Spirito Santo. Despite being on nearly the highest spot in town, some undoubtedly magnificent views were blocked by the thick, gnarled trees crowning the top of the hill.

Brian hadn't been to church since he was a boy. He remembered midnight mass fondly, but wasn't sure why. The idea of going to church at midnight on Christmas Eve was mildly insane.

Pushing open the door brought back the smells and atmosphere of his childhood both vividly and unexpectedly. It hadn't occurred to him that a Catholic church would smell the same in Italy as in Melbourne. He guessed the incense would be identical, but what was the rest of it? The polish on the wood pews? Or was it just the feeling of the place? There was a clam shell set into the brick door arch with a sponge in it, and he almost reflexively crossed himself with holy water. And then, for a laugh, did so, although the sponge was as parched as the Sicilian countryside. That muscle memory had not left him. Up, down and across. He put his coffee a little irreverently on the back pew and stepped further in. He had forgotten about the Stations of the Cross set on the walls. *These* were certainly different from the memories from his childhood. In Melbourne they had been some kind of stylised wood carvings, reducing that last journey to a series of angles and abstractions. Not here. These were highly detailed and saturated with colour, the blood dripping liberally down the anguished face, with some vicious and realistic scourging, nailing and wailing during the trip. Each image was as graphic and unsubtle as a page from one of the *Pussycat*s sitting on Brian's kitchen table.

The lightly robed Jesus that hung behind the plain altar was much more familiar, and Brian realised that those sculptured pieces around the world would probably all have come from Italy. He remembered a Melbourne news story. Hilariously, one Italian community there had raised money to have a statue of a saint imported, but when it had arrived, the arm raised in blessing had – in an Australian context – appeared to be making an obscene gesture. The whole thing had been shipped back to Italy to have its hand remodelled.

No saint here. Way more top tier. Almost next to the altar, and totally stealing the stage from Jesus up on the cross, a starry-eyed Madonna sat on a gilded throne. Her ecstatic face was as brown as if she'd been picking lemons for a month, which, if he thought about it, was probably closer to the complexion of the original Mary than many representations of her. The face was turned slightly upwards and over the heads of the absent congregation, the wide eyes with their painted lashes seeing something wonderful through the back wall of the church. Tiny lights, currently not switched on, lined the back and arms of the throne around her. Brian walked down the aisle quietly. She looked like she was made of wood, brightly painted and way more colourful than the simple sky-blue that he thought was usual. Around her shoulders was a kind of cloak in sheer grey silk, extravagantly beaded and embroidered.

Wow. If I was Jesus, I would be complaining.

There was no statue of the Holy Spirit in the Church of the Holy Spirit. Brian couldn't even remember what she, he or it was supposed to look like, if anything. A flame? A dove? A puff of smoke?

There was nobody around, so he took a final deep breath of the faintly fragranced atmosphere and went back out the door. He crossed himself again without realising it – coffee in the other hand – and left. When he was halfway down the street, he turned and a priest, who looked younger than Brian from this distance, was standing outside looking at him, one hand on the open door. The man smiled and waved. Brian returned both smile and wave but didn't go back. It was his first really friendly gesture since arriving but, he thought uncharitably, the priest probably needs every customer he can get. Also, Brian needed to recharge the vocab before another possibly embarrassing bout with the Italian language.

Past the church, some glimpses of a view could be seen through the gaps in the branches. Peering through and downwards where he could, Brian could see just how small Montegiallo was. Outside the wall that circled the town was, it appeared, mainly lemon groves with the occasional clearer space devoted to some other agricultural activity. Brian couldn't tell what that activity might be. A small, red tractor toiled below, between the town and the beginnings of the rippling heat haze, so far away that no sound carried up the valley.

Checking the map one more time, he continued around the road behind the church, Via Piave. When Brian looked it up later, it turned out to be a river important in the First World War. Or another composer. Or even a cheese. Brian guessed it was the composer, but hoped it was the cheese. The town was small enough that he could probably learn the meaning of every single street name.

With just a few more twists and turns, Brian arrived back at his *piazza* from a totally unexpected direction. Wonderful. He felt like he'd had a minor adventure.

Insulting the Intelligence

Brian sat on one of the benches in the *piazza* and read a couple more grammar exercises. There was still plenty left in his cup and he sipped at it, not caring that the coffee was now stone cold. A handful of mostly elderly Sicilians drifted by, paying him scant attention. He felt he'd done his duty with *buongiorno*s for the day, so ignored them right back. Sick of study after half a page, he put the book down on the bench and turned his attention to the buildings surrounding him. Six homes on the longer side, the bar and two more at the far end. Four behind him, then his *palazzo* and the abandoned neighbour. Fourteen which were likely residences. How many showed signs of habitation? Half? Not even that. The Sicilians walking by, or, like him, taking advantage of the shade, didn't appear to be obviously connected with any of the buildings.

He remembered Elizabeth talking about Italian style. The men, particularly the older men, dressed like they had thought about it. Even in this country backwater. Ties. And hats. Polished shoes. His t-shirt and jeans felt shabby in comparison. He couldn't think of a single man that he knew in Australia that took the slightest effort when dressing. Toby's sole salute to sartorialism was making sure his fly was done up, and that effect was not always achieved, to be honest. A younger couple sat on one of the benches on the far side of the *piazza*. Even though they were wearing t-shirts and jeans, like he was, they did so with a kind of style that Brian just didn't seem to have.

Almost all the other women, though sometimes not as eye-catching as Viviana, wore what Brian would have considered 'going out' clothes back home.

Former home, mate, former home.

He thought about the suitcase of clothes he had found, and a memory flashed from childhood. The dressing-up box at his grandparents' house when he was four or five, full of moth-eaten fur wraps, broken hats and costume jewellery. He remembered how easy it was to become a totally different person – a different creature even – with just a tweed trilby and a towel for a cape. Was that kind of metamorphosis still possible as an adult? He hadn't really considered clothes making a difference since then.

Maybe time to rethink that.

He heard a door close behind him, then the buzz of a small motor. Turning around, a young boy, maybe four years of age, was piloting a remote-control car. Just as cats always make straight for the most allergic person in the room, the small red vehicle came directly for him. At the last second Brian raised his feet and it failed to make contact with his ankles, to the obvious disappointment of the child. The car went into reverse, and again Brian's feet avoided it like a matador.

'*Molto veloce*,' said Brian. 'Very fast.'

'Ferrari,' boasted the child.

The vehicle did indeed sport prancing horse stickers, but unless the company had started constructing off-road vehicles, they seemed misplaced.

Maybe this four-year-old would be at the appropriate level for Brian's Italian.

'*Come ti chiami?*' asked Brian. 'What is your name?' was one of the very first phrases Mrs Calalesina had taught them. Should have no problem comprehending him.

'Carlo,' responded the child.

'*Mi chiamo* Brian.'

Carlo received news of Brian's vowel-less name-ending like he was smelling a particularly pungent fart.

'Oh, Carlo, is it?' asked Brian. 'Wait, wait. *Aspetta*.' He had just seen an exercise in the grammar concerning a Carlo. He picked up the book from the bench beside him and flipped through it. Where was it? More of the present tense he thought. 'Ah,' he said. 'Here.' He spoke directly to the boy. '*Giulia è meno intelligente di Carlo.*' 'Giulia is less intelligent than Carlo' was another sentence that would probably not have survived a twenty-first-century editor.

The child gaped at him in astonishment. '*Dove?!*' he demanded.

Brian turned the book around to face him. Could he even read at his age? He moved his index finger slowly above each word. Carlo squinted intensely at the text, mouthing each word as Brian called it out. '*Giulia – è – meno – intelligente – di – Carlo.*' The boy roared with laughter, and sat down abruptly on the dirt in front of the bench, facing Brian. '*Ancora! Ancora!*'

Brian assumed he wanted to hear the phrase again. '*Giulia è meno intelligente di Carlo.*' Carlo beat the ground with his fists, crying with laughter like it was the funniest thing he had ever heard.

'*Ancora! Ancora!*'

Jeez, it's not that funny, thought Brian, but stood up and delivered the line once more. Carlo screamed with laughter again, and Brian was worried they were attracting too much attention. A couple of heads turned. A woman in a sun hat scowled at them both.

'*Ancora! Ancora!*'

Brian wanted to wrap this up. '*Troppo stanco*, too tired,' he lied.

'*Ancora! Ancora!*' demanded Carlo.

Brian was becoming concerned that this interaction was getting out of control and declined another recitation. The boy picked up his off-road Ferrari and shouted back across the square to the door he had emerged from. 'Giulia! Giulia!'

'Wait, what?' said Brian.

'Giulia! Giulia!' Carlo ran back across the *piazza* shouting and laughing. 'Giulia! Giulia!' The door opened and a young woman took a step out. '*Giulia è meno intelligente di Carlo,*' yelled the delinquent. The female, an older sister by the looks, barked something back at the boy. Carlo shouted the phrase again and yammered something else, pointing back at a horrified Brian. '*Giulia è meno intelligente di Carloooooooooooooooooo!*'

Brian shook his head and shrugged, hoping by these gestures to imply that the child was obviously insane, and he had no idea what he was talking about.

Giulia ordered Carlo inside. '*Il libro, il libro,*' he insisted. Brian took a step sideways to obscure the grammar book on the bench. Giulia shoved the boy inside, gave Brian a suspicious look, and then slammed the door on the scene. Brian felt it was a good time to retreat.

Wash and Wear

Returning to his *palazzo*, Brian went back inside, and rinsed the foam off the kitchen pieces in the shower. He took out the remaining beers and wild boar salami sitting in the bottom of INDES, and refitted the now sparkling metal shelves and transparent green plastic fittings. Putting back the items in the fridge except for one beer, he turned his attention to scrubbing and then rebuilding both the stoves. The work destroyed half-a-dozen metal scourers, but by the end, the vintage cookers were as close to spotless as they were ever likely to be.

Awesome!

The afternoon found him sitting on a bench watching his clothes, including the old white shirts, revolving in two of the laundromat dryers. The shirts came out of the machines with the fold lines gone, looking a brilliant white. A little bit of fraying of the long, pointed collars, but generally great-looking shirts, made of a dense cotton. *Hmm, need cufflinks for them though.* He didn't remember seeing any in his found treasures.

He had been planning to wash the suit jacket and trousers in the washing machine but had an instinct wool might not survive the process. There was a door with a hatch at one end of the *lavanderia* with the word '*Servizi*' written in black marker. He knocked on it and the hatch flipped open. A young woman with extremely dark hair and blacker eyes regarded him.

'*Si?*'

Brian pointed at the trousers and then at the washers. 'Ahh, *possibile?*'

'*No, no, no.*' She shook her head to make sure he understood. '*No, no, no!*'

'Ah. OK. *Grazie.* Hang on.' He went and got the grammar book and held up the trousers again in one hand while he riffled through the dictionary with the other. '*Loro sono troppo corto.* Too short, right?'

'*Corti.*'

Bloody plurals.

She opened the full door with two sharp snaps of the latches, and regarded both Brian's legs, and the trousers with a professional eye.

'*E troppo grande*? Too bigggg?' Her Italian accent held on tight to the last 'g' before finally releasing it into the steamy atmosphere of the *lavanderia.*

'Well, they're pretty close, I think.'

She produced a tape measure from nowhere, whipped it around Brian's waist in a flash, then down the outside of his leg, hip to ankle.

The tape measure disappeared, and she took the trousers, flipping over the hem. 'It's OK. *Mezz'ora.* Half hour. And iron shirts?' Brian thought about the dangerous-looking electric iron back home.

'Yes. Brilliant. I mean, *eccellente.*'

While he was waiting, he bought a couple more sporty pairs of undies in the *supermercato*, and a small trolley on two wheels, fit for a grandmother to go shopping with. He'd had enough of carrying bags back up the hill. He wondered what he was supposed to take to the expat drinks. Drinks, he supposed. He chose two bottles of Sicilian red wines at random from the shelves. Picking up the parcel of clothing from the laundromat maiden, he dragged the trolley – which really needed heavier suspension for this type of terrain – across the cobbles and up the stairs back to his house on Holy Spirit Square.

Dressed for Success

There was only one decent mirror in the place. The one in the bathroom was losing its silvering and had the diseased and spotted look of an old man's arm. Also, the green-and-red tiling threw up an odd light that would not flatter anybody's complexion. On the inside of the wardrobe Brian found an almost full-length mirror. He regarded himself in it. The suit now looked like it had been made for him. A him that lived in the 1960s. But looking at the lapels, he now wasn't sure of the era. Could it even be from the 1950s? He thought that both of those decades might have favoured thinner lapels. It was solidly made, that's for sure, and the suitcase had kept the moths at bay. Even earlier than the 50s? If he couldn't be sure exactly what decade it was from, he could surmise that the well-dressed but slightly short-legged man must be long dead at least. The cuffs of the shirt hung out, so in the absence of cufflinks, he simply stuffed them back inside the sleeves.

He draped the soft silk of three of the ties and cravat over the back of his hand. He didn't know how to tie a cravat, so chose the red, black and silver conventional tie and put it on with a simple school knot. He knew no other way to fix one. When was the last time he'd worn a tie? Wedding? First day teaching? Nah, not even then. Teacher of the Year award, maybe. He had definitely worn a suit that night. What had happened to it? The cheap ties he did have had been chucked out with the rubbish back in Melbourne. Maybe he had thrown out the suit as well? It wouldn't have been a good one. Nothing like the quality of this.

OK, if he was going to be a different person here, a New Brian in a new country, then why not look like a different person too? The suitcase really had been like an adult dressing-up box.

And I do actually feel different.

Who he was before hadn't been all that crash hot, to be honest. A suit-and-tie-wearing Brian might be just right for this new life. He did up the middle button of the jacket and turned sideways in the mirror.

You know, that looks pretty good!

Although he was looking in the mirror, the reflected Brian looked somehow taller than he was. He adjusted the tie knot, and New Brian gazed at him coolly, almost confidently from behind the glass.

Huh.

The trousers were the perfect length now, breaking gently over his shoes. They needed old-fashioned button braces, but they fitted so well that he didn't need to worry about them falling down at the moment, unless he lost a lot of weight climbing those damn steps all day. The Converse sneakers were a bit of a problem though? *Or are they?* He knew there was some kind of Italian word for style where you wore one item that was wrong deliberately. Or something. Started with 'Spr' he thought, but could only come up with 'Spruuuuut' from the *Ultra Pussycat* vocab.

The Ghetto was an area of Montegiallo that he hadn't yet explored, so he checked the map again for Viale Virgilio Marone and mentally worked out the way to Via Madonna della Vita. OK, cross Virgil at this unnamed alleyway, and take Salieri all the way down about one hundred metres to Madonna of Life Street. Seemed simple enough. Was there a Madonna of Death Street? La Madonna della Morte? That would be cool. He wouldn't put it past a Catholic Church that was so keen on death images.

The prospect of meeting new people and, even worse, trying to remember their names filled him with dread. He had been meaning to take both bottles of wine as a gift to the hosts, but at the thought of a social gathering, he opened one of them and poured a generous tot into one of the beer glasses.

Just a little bit of Sicilian courage.

'But don't overdo it,' he warned himself. The wine tasted wonderful, rich and dry. Well, they had been at it for two thousand years. Probably a lot longer. He washed the wine down with the remains of a bottle of mineral water and, after a deep breath, brushed an imaginary spot of lint from the half acre of his right lapel, and left the house. Destination: a ghetto full of expats. 'Don't worry, Skeletor,' he called out as he left. 'I'll be friendly. I'll be …' He thought about an appropriate Italian word. 'I'll be *cordiale*.'

In the Ghetto

Bar Limone was going to have to be dealt with at some stage, but this evening he walked past it again without stopping.

The mouthfuls of wine had worn off by the time he reached the steps down to Viale Virgilio Marone. Locating the right alleyway hadn't been as easy as he had expected from the map, but he eventually saw with relief the enamelled rectangle that let him know he had found Salieri. He was only going to be fashionably late.

The first thing that Brian noticed was the number of houses that were under renovation. Many were only half finished. There were some touches, including an American flag in a window, that gave the area an immediately different feel from his dark sleepy square. The streets were a little wider than up the hill. Fewer trees too, so the late afternoon light poured into the road and a warm breeze was rolling up from the plain. There were more cars but fewer scooters crowding the footpaths. Salieri bottomed out. The view over the wall showed black hills capped with small touches of green, backing up the yellow plains and the citrus groves below the town. Even the lemon trees had a slightly more organised look on this side.

Via Madonna della Vita dropped into Salieri in an abrupt T-junction that you'd need to hit the brakes pretty hard for. The house he was looking for was obvious. Lights were on. Bright lights. Brian wondered if it was the fittings or if they just got a better class of electricity down here. Singing 'In the Ghettoooo' to himself in an Elvis accent, he knocked on a newly varnished front door

***

About twenty people were holding glasses on half a living room floor. Tiling had been started, but ended like the foam from a small wave exhausting itself on a flat beach. Cardboard boxes and low stacks of unlaid tiles formed an inadequate barrier. The ground beyond was dusty. The kitchen, on the renovated section, was modern looking in a conventional and slightly boring way. A small, white, generic refrigerator was fitted into a light pine frame that also housed a mid-brand oven and stovetop. Brian thought with fondness of his 1960s INDES, humming and buzzing away back up in Spirito Santo.

'Brian, is it?' The woman, Martina, that Brian had seen at the café the day before, came over and pressed his hand lightly. 'Sorry I couldn't stop yesterday. Eric paces if he doesn't get his coffee in time. We try making it here,' she turned to the kitchen. 'But it's just not the same.'

Eric had a face that was both smooth and lined, as if he used moisturiser but also did a lot of grimacing. His remaining hair was trending comb-over. He shook Brian's right hand. Brian held up the wine in his left. Eric frowned. 'Some of the local swill, eh?' He had a featureless English accent. 'We generally drink Australian. The reds anyway.' He patted Brian on the back as if he had been personally responsible for the quality of Australian winemaking. 'Let me get you something from the Barossa or at least the Yarra Valley.' He circled his hand urgently at Martina.

'Yes, I'm doing the introductions, Eric.' She smiled to take the annoyance out of her voice. 'Brian, you already know Murray.' Murray was wearing the same outfit as the day before. Maybe it was a different olive t-shirt.

'Brian. Good to see you. This is my wife, Salina. It sounds Italian, but isn't.'

Salina was a cheerful-looking and diminutive woman wearing a summer dress and white sandals.

'Pleased to meet you, Brian. I hear you're up the hill. And by yourself? I'm sure it will be lovely,' she said unconvincingly. 'When you get it all fixed up.'

'In about ten years,' said Murray. 'Hah-hah. As you can see,' he indicated the untiled patch of floor, 'the locals are not exactly eager for our business. Our place is even worse. We've had a dumpster out the front for six months.'

'I've got some plumbing to get done, and the —' Brian began, before Murray cut him off.

'Get in line, pal!' and it really felt like the man was not joking. 'We've been waiting nine months to get our water feature hooked up. Gaetano and Gianni have that and about a million rain showers to fit before you'll get to the front of the line. You got six toilets, you told me? You might have to hold it a while, buddy, hah-hah.'

Where the hell is that wine?

Martina was hovering, but Murray grabbed one of Brian's lapels in two fingers. 'What, you get this off a corpse, Brian? Hah-hah.'

Brian had heard the man laugh only three times, and it was already grating.

This is good coming from a guy wearing Crocs, Brian thought, but he hadn't had enough to drink to say that out loud, thank God. Now he was absolutely determined to dress up every time he met the man. He'd buy a gold dinner suit if necessary.

'We're a casual crowd here.'

The casual crowd was about half Americans and half Brits. As he usually did after meeting people, Brian gave up any attempt to remember names or even faces. One Brit began to look like another American. There was an English Chris, and an American Christopher. A Jenny, a Michael, plus a Lars. Most were couples of around middle age, with a few divorced or bereaved singles. One of these, Samantha from Seattle, finally grabbed them each a wine from Eric. While half listening to Samantha's dramatic life story, he noticed, as Eric's bottle swung by them, that the wine had been produced only a few hours from his former home in Melbourne. He vaguely remembered visiting the estate for some music event. The wine was delicious, but was just another connection to his former life that he would be fine to break with. He'd swap to the Sicilian the first chance he got.

He left Samantha just before she could detail the unusual death of her third husband, and circulated a little awkwardly, listening here and there. The main topics of conversation were complaints about the quality or amount of work being done on their one-euro bargains.

'Is there anything worse than a broke expat?' A London accent aimed at Brian, came from a man dressed casually, but stylishly, in a coffee-coloured knit polo shirt, a short-brimmed straw hat, chocolate chinos and leather sandals. His outfit complemented his complexion, or maybe it was the other way round. His skin was the colour of mild butter chicken.

'Although you'll be one yourself if you could only afford a one-euro house.'

'Yeah, I guess I am.'

'We were crypto victims. Mere babes in the woods.' He sighed. 'Robinson.' Another handshake. 'Like the castaway!' he exclaimed. 'Montegiallo is like a desert island sometimes. We had dreams of The Argarve. You? Let me guess. Financial crash? Gambling problem? Running from the law?'

'Ahh, what? No! Divorce.'

'Painful. Love the *sprezzatura* by the way.'

'Huh?'

The man indicated Brian's footwear.

'Oh yeah. Thanks.' *That's what it's called.*

'Is this suit original nineteen forties? Very tasty.' A man joined them and laid his arm on Robinson's shoulder. 'Ahh, and this is Peter, my Man Friday.'

'Hi there.'

Peter shook Brian's hand. He was the opposite of Robinson in every way apart from the London twang when he spoke. He was pasty, almost deathly white, which was quite an achievement in this climate. He had mouse-coloured hair and a wide smile. He wore a Daffy Duck t-shirt and faded shorts.

'Don't expect Peter to appreciate your outfit,' Robinson said. 'Just look at this get-up.' He shook his head sadly. 'The crypto crash isn't the only reason we are here,' Robinson confided. 'We had to flee London because Peter insisted on wearing camouflaged trousers to dinner. We couldn't face the community. The shame, Brian! You couldn't imagine.'

Peter laughed so warmly that Brian joined in. 'I still have those. I should have worn them tonight.'

'He's got a lovely smile though. And huge cock, of course,' said Robinson.

'Greatly exaggerated, I'm afraid,' said Peter, shaking his head mock sadly.

'You couldn't leave me with that, Peter? Really?'

'So we're doing the snarky gay man performance for the new resident? OK then. Good to know.' Peter laughed again. He did have a lovely smile.

One of Brian's cuffs had flopped out of his sleeve. He stuffed it back in. 'No cufflinks.'

'Oh!' exclaimed Robinson. 'Stay right there.' He hurried out the front door.

'We're almost next door, round the corner on Salieri,' Peter told him.

'Is it really as hard as everyone says to get work done?' Brian asked.

'Most people are here because they can't afford to actually buy a place in Spain or somewhere on the beach in Italy or Portugal. As we had planned. And it's a tiny town. It's not like you have a choice of tradespeople. Just the plumber and electrician up here, and the builder and tiler down the hill in the new town. And most expats can't afford to pay enough for the locals to ignore the rudeness. That's it. You kind of get tarred with the same brush as the worst examples.' Brian was sure he had met one of those examples. 'Just to warn you though, if you poach somebody's tradesperson, they'll claw your eyes out. Us included. That's a promise. Everyone knows who paid deposits and when. To the minute.'

'Wow. I didn't know that. What about Franco or Viviana? Can't they help?'

Robinson bustled straight back in. 'Oh my God, he's already eyeing off the Devil Woman, Peter,' he joked. 'Jacket off. Arms out.'

'What?' said Brian, confused.

'Off, off, off.'

With Brian's jacket off, Robinson folded back the shirt cuffs and pushed a gold cufflink through on each side. 'Peter got these in a Christmas cracker last festive season. Just plastic, but *gold* plastic. Until you can get down to Agrigento.' He glanced at the Daffy Duck on Peter's chest. '*He's* not going to need them, believe me.'

'You're welcome.' Peter gave him a thumbs-up. And the smile.

'So you've set your sights on the lovely Viviana? Hmm, fast worker.'

'No, no, no, I have no idea how it works. I just thought she might be able to help get some of the work done a bit quicker. Put in a good word for you, err, us?'

'Ha! If only,' said Robinson. 'We are going to demand action. Viviana and her father get paid very well by the regional government to do the one-euro admin and promotion.'

Ahh, so definitely daughter.

'Before you've signed on the dotted line, they are very helpful. Once you're hooked, they can take their time. But more importantly, they also allocate out all the renovation jobs. Very strictly and by the book. You can understand it in one way. It would be chaos if everyone was fighting over one plumber, one electrician, a tiler and a builder. And they are all scared of her too. But the downside is, if you get on the wrong side of them, particularly Viviana, everything becomes ten times more difficult. And it seems the expats are always on the wrong side.'

'And you can try to get someone up from Agrigento or Palermo,' Peter chimed in, 'but who on earth wants to drive three, or even one hour, to do a job way out here and then back again? And if they do, it's triple the price.'

'And there was a team of illegal Albanians who were never seen ag—' Robinson began to confide, but out of the corner of his eye Brian detected a tiny but urgent shake of the head from Peter. When he looked though, the smile was back in place.

There was a pause. 'And that's why the expats call her the Devil Woman,' said Robinson.

'But she is *single*, if that's what you were *really* asking,' said Peter. 'Former husband. Long gone apparently. No surprise there. Dumped his name too.'

'Well, I wasn't asking that, no. Last time I spoke to her, I made a total arse of myself.'

'Ahh, well then, that's definitely true love, by the sound of it,' said Peter widening his eyes. 'Don't you think so, Rob?'

'Well as long he's not thinking of romancing his way to a priority plumbing job,' scolded Robinson.

Jeezus, alright, you guys! For fuck's sake.

He would never have thought that plumbing would be the number one topic of conversation here. Anywhere.

About 11pm, Brian drifted away. According to the boys, Agrigento was where you had to go to get anything above 'brutal rural ugliness'. So a taxi to Agrigento on Monday was the plan then. He needed to check his documents in at the *questura* – what they called the cop shops in Italy – within eight days anyway.

Is it really going to be months before I can get that bidet pressure-spraying?

Apart from a school trip to Japan when a teenager, he hadn't really tried a bidet before. And over there it had been all beeps and multiple button options that had made him too scared to use the thing. But now that a *gold* bidet was so close he could almost taste it, he bloody well wanted it working. And he'd need more tiling, the stairs, the electrics ...

As he got back home, he reckoned that the evening hadn't been as terrible as he had thought it would be, but it had still been a *little* dispiriting. The expats believed they were starting new lives, but were just continuing their old ones in a slightly less convenient location, it seemed to him. Were not any of them learning Italian? That astounded him. From now on he wouldn't think of it as The Ghetto, but as one of Dante's levels of Hell. What was it, Eighth or Ninth, sowers of discord? Stomachs ripped out? He tried to remember the Year Twelve text. Possibly they had their livers pecked by ravens? No, that was some Greek dude wasn't it?

And what about himself? Was he any different? Alone here in Sicily? Wasn't it just a more destitute version of being alone in Melbourne? Well at least he couldn't be accused of putting his work before his marriage this time, since he didn't have either. He clenched his jaw and straightened his tie.

No. New Brian is going to be different.

With a short prayer to Virgil, the former but now evicted resident of Limbo, to guide him home, he took the steps slowly upwards, his quads aching from the hundreds, maybe thousands he'd already climbed in the last days.

Genuine Genuflection

Brian listened to church bells ringing the next morning, and found it an unexpectedly pleasant experience. Surprising himself, and in the spirit of becoming New Brian, he got up and had a brief shower while they pealed. He liberated one of the new pairs of underwear from its plastic prison, put on another ironed shirt, his new 'links', a different tie, and the suit. And went to church for the first time since he was twelve years old. He was by no means abandoning his rusted-on atheism. *Absolutely not.* There were limits to what a personality panel-beating could achieve. But after the night before, he wanted to be part of *this* world at the top of the hill rather than with the other foreigners lower down. If attending a church service or two was a necessary part of that, then he could live with it.

The mass had already begun and he slipped into the empty back row. He had expected an older demographic, and he wasn't entirely wrong. But there were some younger faces. Fortunately, Carlo and Giulia were not among them. There were a couple of very young children and a few that might have been wearing school uniforms. *On a Sunday?* At one stage, these children sang. The rest of the age ranges, maybe apart from teenagers, were reasonably represented. Better turnout than a small church would get in Melbourne. Even a bigger one. Montegiallo was obviously not *completely* deserted.

He sat at the back and listened to the familiar rhythms of the service. Despite it being in another language, the tone of voice of the priest – who was dressed in enormous robes – reawakened all the standing, kneeling and sitting cues from more than a quarter of a century before. Brian didn't miss a beat. Up, down, sit, kneel, sign of the cross. He tried to concentrate hard on the sermon, but could only pick out a few words. It would perhaps have been bad form to bring in the grammar book.

He got a little worried as the priest came down the aisle giving out the communion. Was that new? You used to have to line up at the front for it, didn't you? But as the embroidered robes approached the rear of the church, he pretended to pray with his eyes half closed and he wasn't offered the wafer.

Thank Christ.

He recognised a couple of faces from the *piazza*. Some who had returned his greetings and some who had not. He worried a little about being thought of as an intruder, which he obviously was, both here and at the *piazza*. But the priest gave him a slight smile and nod after finishing the communion rigmarole, so he suppressed the urge to slip out the door.

He had kind of remembered the begging box on a stick that circulated during a mass, but he panicked a little as it travelled towards him, forgetting exactly what you had to do. A civilian member of the congregation on each side of the aisle was managing the process. When he got to the back row, still empty except for Brian, he and Brian both hesitated. Brian finally pulled out a one-euro coin, which felt extra symbolic in the room packed with symbols. And it dropped with a soft knock into the felt-lined collection box.

As he stood up for the final dismissal which was all about going in peace, he noticed the back of a stylishly coiffed head near the front. No. It couldn't be? He was beyond surprised. Viviana? And Franco! Viviana seemed too modern … too … he was not sure exactly what, for a churchgoer. *I guess it is as unlikely as me being here.*

But in any case. Look who was rejecting Satan and all his works. None other than the Devil Woman herself! He was *very* glad he had made the effort.

Protestants & Atheists

The priest was older than Brian had thought, after seeing him from a distance down the street, but still much younger than the eighty-year-old he would have expected here. An energetic mid-fifties perhaps. In the morning sun outside the church, Brian could see the lines around his eyes.

The parishioners were greeted one by one as they left. Some got a few words. Others a wave or a hand on the shoulder. He waited around as the church emptied. Viviana and Franco came out and had a conversation with the priest. It was the first time Brian had seen Viviana really smile. Her hair was up and she wore a tunic-like blue cotton dress, a shade or two lighter than Brian's dark wool. Franco was dressed soberly in grey slacks, white shirt and dark grey tie. As they came past him, Brian smiled himself. Viviana looked like she wanted to keep walking, and she viewed his suit with an odd look, but Franco stopped and she had to as well.

'*Buongiorno, Signor* Chapman. I hope you are …' he struggled for the English words.

'Settling in? Yes. Very good.' Brian racked his brain for something else he could say. *Think, man!*

'Oh! Your name is Messina? That's the same as my beers!'

Christ on a bike, where was Toby to tell him he was a fucken plonker? What was wrong with him?

Viviana was apparently genuinely amused by this inanity. Or by his discomfort. 'My father's English needs a little help sometimes,' she said, then translated it for Franco who replied in some confusion.

'Eh? *Grazie, grazie.*' Franco turned to Viviana with a look that suggested 'What the fuck was that?' and they left, heading down towards his *piazza*. Walking away, Viviana, without looking back at him, raised her arm vertically and flicked her fingers in what Brian interpreted as an ironic wave. Brian waited until they were out of sight before starting to step towards his own home, but the priest put his hand up for him to wait.

The last parishioner, the woman Brian remembered with the two bags he had seen on his first morning, was inclined to be curious and lingered as the priest came up to him. But he gave her a few gentle sentences and she left slightly reluctantly, disappearing around the side of the church. '*Grazie,* Rosa.'

'*Buongiorno, Padre,*' said Brian. '*Piacere.*' He suddenly thought it would boggle Toby's mind to get a photo of himself with a priest. 'Wait, could I …?' He held his phone up. Barely waiting for the man to agree, he took a selfie, one thumb up, standing next to him.

'Hmmm, bless you. Good to see a new face in church.' His English was excellent. 'Have you a moment?' After the photo, Brian could hardly refuse. 'Wait for me on the bench under the trees over there. I need to give Rosa some instructions and change my robes.'

The priest returned in five minutes, in his basic black suit and collar. 'Thank you for staying. I always like to meet a new parishioner.'

He sat next to Brian.

'Of course, I know exactly why you are here,' he said.

Really? 'You do, Father?' Had he seen into Brian's soul? He was fairly sure he had lost it somewhere in the Victorian education system.

'Dominic. Or Father Dom, if you prefer. Of course. Every tourist coming to rural Italy needs to have a spiritual encounter with a local priest. It is almost compulsory, I'm led to believe. Every story requires one apparently.'

Brian thought on that for a moment. It was true. Every Italian story he could think of. *Oh, and I've just taken a selfie, confirming it.*

'For our Instagrams too, I guess,' Brian said.

'Yes, and for some homely but strangely insightful spiritual advice,' said the priest.

'Speaking of local colour. That is a spectacular Madonna in the church. Do you do that thing where they carry her around town once a year?'

'With all these steps?' The priest looked at him in horror. 'No, but on the festival of La Madonna della Vita, we bring her out of the church and there is a celebration right here.'

Brian was tempted to ask the expert if there was a Madonna of Death too, but restrained himself. 'You know, I could just be a fervent believer on a pilgrimage,' he said.

'Are you?'

'Well, not really. But I'm not a tourist either. I have just bought a house around the corner.'

'Yes, that ruin on Spirito Santo. Lord have mercy on you.'

'You know it?'

In reply, astonishingly, the man crossed himself. 'An empty house, particularly an empty family home, will often have a sad story.'

'What do you know about it?' asked Brian. The priest shook his head. 'It has been falling apart from long before my time, and before Father Joseph as well, I think. Empty for decades. The Messinas did some work on it, so there must be some family member somewhere trying to get rid of it. For tax reasons possibly. You need to pay more on a second home, particularly if it's empty. And with so many people having left town, it's easier to be part of this arrangement.'

'So no other history that you know of?'

'You could ask Franco. If you really want to find out?'

Brian thought about that. *Maybe it doesn't matter. Maybe it would be better not to know.*

He changed the subject. 'No other foreigners at mass, Father?'

'The Americans and English? Not a Catholic among them. Protestants. Probably atheists as well.'

'Ahh. Of course,' said Brian. 'I should have thought. Yes. Bound for Hell, I assume?'

'Well, we have a more tolerant view of our brothers and sisters in Christ these days.' He patted Brian's arm. 'But between you and me,' he leaned a little closer, 'yes. Very much so.'

Brian had already decided that the expats were living on a level of Hell, so this wasn't news to him.

'You came alone? Will you have a family coming?'

So I have been noticed already. 'Divorced, sorry, Father. Back in Australia. And no children.'

'Well, you're not a Protestant ... so ... there's that at least. The way you were standing and kneeling at the right times tells me that. Oh, I have some relatives in Australia. Perth. They moved from Sicily in the seventies. Cremasco is the name.'

'I'm from Melbourne. Perth's about as far away as Moscow is from here.'

'Ahh, Moscow. They had a lot of atheists there too at one time, I believe.'

Brian was finding the conversation quite surreal until he looked carefully into the man's eyes and realised he was actually taking the piss.

Brian gave a short laugh. 'I actually came up here to pray for a plumber, Father. Can anyone in your flock fix a bidet or a toilet?'

'Ahh that is a sensitive topic. In more ways than one. I don't know if the Church should become involved in those matters. Wouldn't want to start another war with the Protestants. There have been mixed results in the past. I can come and bless it though, if that helps,' he said. 'Your house, not the bidet.'

'Wonderful.' Old Brian would have given a derisive rejection of anything like a house blessing, but here was New Brian, inviting a priest to Amen his drains.

Brian and the man chatted about Montegiallo and its people. Father Dominic apparently gave a later mass down in Montegiallo Nuovo, or 'Nuovo' as the locals called the new town built halfway down the hill. There was much less of the 'Monte' down there, fewer stairs, gentler slopes and modern apartments. Brian asked him whether all the former inhabitants had gone there.

'Some there, some to Palermo, some to …' he spread his hands to indicate the rest of the world.

'Like Perth, Western Australia. How do the locals who stayed really feel about the one-euro scheme?'

'I'm for it myself,' said the priest. 'Once the people become a bit more established maybe it will be good. Unfortunately, the foreigners keep to themselves and are generally seen as rude. Maybe that will change when everyone gets used to everyone else. I hope so. Small towns like this are in trouble across rural Italy, so it's not just the houses. What work is there for people? You can only get mostly retired foreigners here. All trying to live off very small pensions or savings. No young people. What's anyone younger going to do? Pick lemons? What are you going to do, by the way?'

'I don't know,' said Brian. 'I was hoping my money would last until I could decide. My visa doesn't allow me to work. Officially anyway. Maybe I can study for the priesthood? Does that pay?'

'Maybe it would be easier to pick lemons. Unofficially.'

Agrigento

Brian stepped out of the tobacconist with a handful of documents made on the shop's small copier, ready for his booked appointment at the Agrigento *questura*. Before booking it, he checked the reviews under the website. An American was outraged that he had been turned away because he was wearing beach shorts. One star. That wouldn't be happening with Brian. He touched his tie. He waited on the cobbles outside the *supermercato* for his taxi, wearing his suit and backpack. He might need a better bag than his battered *zaino* if he was going to level up his look. Through the window of the Ideale real estate office, he could see Viviana frowning at her laptop. He'd made such an arse of himself in their last conversations. Your name is like my beers? Yellow sac spiders? I already bought a sandwich? He needed to pull himself together. He wanted to make a better impression the next time they met. Maybe he could casually go in and thank her for all her help. Although she hadn't really been all *that* helpful, had she?

Brian knew he should really be round at the plumber or the electrician getting quotes, but wanted to buy a few things while he had that money in the bank, and before he saw how horrifying those quotes were going to be.

He had spent that Monday morning buying basic food in Montegiallo to stock the shelves with. He dragged some of the green metal racks from one of the upstairs bedrooms, pushing them down the stairs with the sound of a six-vehicle car crash. More metal screeching as he dragged them into the square, dark pantry. If that's what the room was. He had bought some higher wattage LED light globes, but the walls swallowed up the light much the same. He really wanted to buy some kind of wireless speakers. Place needed some music. Also some other pieces of furniture and a new mattress. Shoes to suit the suit as well. He hoped that Agrigento could supply everything.

Still no taxi. He was going to go and tap on the Ideale window and at least wave at Viviana, but as he looked through the glass, she was putting her phone to her ear. After listening for a moment, she stood and delivered a furious monologue into the device, using vehement hand actions with her right hand. Yikes! Brian wondered who was on the receiving end of the Devil Woman's invective. He couldn't hear if it was Sicilian to a local, or an in-English denouncement of a hapless expat. Tyres hit the cobbles around the corner and Brian guessed it was his taxi. He carefully moved away from the real estate office window.

He thumbed another short text to Toby as the taxi pulled up, sending him the selfie of himself and the priest. 'LOL.' *That should get him going!*

The vehicle rumbled across the cobbles.

'*Agrigento, per favore.* OK?'

'*Templi?*'

'No. Not temples. *Agrigento.* No *templi. La città. Negozi e questura.* The city.'

The man couldn't believe Brian wasn't going to the temples, and asked him three more times, in slower and slower Italian. Finally Brian gave in. He pulled out the grammar to compose a sentence and then realised he didn't need it. 'OK. *Uno, Agrigento. Due, templi. Tre, ritorno Montegiallo.*'

'*Sì, Sì, Sì. Bene, bene.*'

Brian had to wrestle his requirements a word at a time out of the grammar book. Against his strong preference for analogue, he had to resort to Google Translate on the phone for 'mattress', as the word was not covered in the book's limited dictionary.

It has 'stutter', but not 'mattress'? Really?

Brian hadn't been on the road during the day. 'Nuovo' Montegiallo was less interesting in daylight. None of the falling-down charm of the streets up the hill, but there were certainly fewer steps on these lower, gentler slopes. He saw what must have been Father Dom's new church as they went through, although it didn't look all that new. Ugly grey render and a circular stained-glass window. There was a gravel car park lined with mature frangipanis.

The flatter plains alternated between citrus and unworked land, similar to what Brian had seen from the train. Hills of granite stood bare of trees, with the occasional island of green amidst the golden grass.

Agrigento felt like a metropolis after Montegiallo, and there was even a traffic jam of sorts as they drove slowly into the centre, with horns blaring and cars jostling for a spot on the narrow entry. However, many of the modern apartments stood between older buildings with sightless windows and crumbling brick and stone. Which was a look that Brian was now used to. It was still a little early for his *questura* appointment so he'd hit the shops first.

Not surprisingly to Brian, a web search had failed in its translation duties. He had wanted a good bag to replace his backpack, but the driver had taken him to a handbag shop. *Una buona borsa* was not what he wanted, apparently.

He made an agreement with the driver to pick him up from Via Atenea, the main shopping strip, in two hours. '*Due ore, sì?* Yes, *sì, sì.* Then temples.' Goddamnit, they better be bloody good temples. The man had marked a glossy tourist map in pen with the *negozi* he needed. '*Scarpe, materassi, elettrodomestici, questura.*'

He got out of the car. The driver gestured at him, urging him into the shop. Brian began to compose a multi-claused Italian sentence explaining why he didn't want a handbag, but decided it would be easier to just go in and wait for the man to leave. '*Sì, sì, grazie.* Thank you, I'm going in, OK?'

He entered the handbag shop, which was next to a lingerie boutique, and peeked out between two sequin-covered purses on window stands waiting for the taxi to drive off. The shop assistant appeared behind him, greeting him in English. How could she tell he spoke English just from the back of his head? He hadn't said anything! Like a criminal can always tell a plainclothes cop.

Maybe it's my posture?

He pretended to be interested in a handbag for €800. '*Buona borsa, signorina*,' he said, before making his escape.

The bed and furniture shop was quite a few streets back. He sat on the corner of a few mattresses, then, as tradition demanded, took off his shoes and lay down on a few more.

He attempted to ask if they would deliver one, in his pidgin Italian. '*Consegnare possibile? A Montegiallo?*' He was delighted when the salesman replied in Italian, and he even understood!

'*Sì. Montegiallo Nuovo?*'

'No, *Montegiallo Vecchio*. Old. Very *vecchio*.'

He bought some colourful folding chairs for the balcony. A few more to fit round the main table. A round coffee table for the balcony too, plus some kitchen equipment, frying pans and saucepans. Almost against his better judgement, he bought the cheapest laptop and wi-fi router he could get. There was enough now to fill the back of the taxi while the mattress and furniture went by truck.

Pleased with his Italian progress that day, and not wanting to overdo it, he bought a set of wi-fi speakers, then a pair of beautiful black Italian calfskin boots at the first shoe shop he came to, doing the shopping all in English. He probably shouldn't have bought them, but he deserved them, didn't he? And New Brian couldn't wear two old pairs of sneakers.

Not with all the *sprezzatura* in the world. No way, pal. Brian waited for the assistants to package the boots and walked around the store. Whoa. Elizabeth had been right! On their own display plinth, under a spotlight was a pair of the most stylish gumboots Brian had ever seen, in a black-and-white houndstooth pattern.

'Huh. Wow.'

At the first menswear shop he came to, called Salvatore F., he got a nice pair of moderately priced cufflinks and a pair of red button braces for his trousers. They even had some great leather man bags! Brian chose a messenger bag with embossed spirals around the edge and a lime-green cloth lining. Too expensive, but too good to refuse. He emptied the contents of his backpack into it, and then folded the *zaino* in as well.

The *questura* looked more like a seaside villa than a police station. There was an ancient-looking shield crest on the front stone wall with a lion holding what from a distance looked like a foil-covered kebab, but closer inspection revealed to be a sword. Despite widespread reports of chaotic Italian bureaucracy, Brian was in and out in record time. *Looks like the paperwork is done for a year!* Disappointingly, they hadn't appreciated that he wasn't wearing beach shorts.

OK. Now let's have a look at these damn temples.

The Damn Temples

The damn temples were frankly stunning. Brian had only seen some small images on the Agrigento website back in Melbourne and was completely unprepared for how well preserved and impressive they were. The driver wanted to take him by car past the main sights (he thought), but Brian insisted on walking it. A bronze statue of Icarus lay out the front of one of them, as if it had just dropped from the sky after buzzing the sun. Amazing! He couldn't tell if the sculpture was thousands of years old, or had been installed last year by the Agrigento municipal arts committee.

And it wasn't just a *couple* of temples or a few piles of anonymous stones. There was a shitload of the things. Almost complete buildings! Stunning site after stunning site.

Most of the temples were so well preserved you could just about have whacked on a Colorbond roof, and the Vestal Virgins (or whoever) could have moved straight back in. It was unbelievable that he had never heard of Agrigento's attractions before. Maybe Italy just had too many antiques.

The temple site was framed by the town on one side and an ocean of clichéd blue on the other. It was a superb tourist location. And that was the main problem. *I'm not a tourist. I'm not sharing this with anyone. I'm not leaving and flying home with a phone full of memories.* For the first time Brian had a slight touch of homesickness and an almost physical feeling of loneliness. He suddenly wanted to do nothing more than take his new items back to Montegiallo to his new but permanent home.

'*Ritorno Montegiallo. Grazie.*'

They were damn beautiful temples though.

The driver stopped at a shop on the edge of the city centre, which had a large selection of fresh-made ravioli and other pasta dishes, for the driver to pick up an order for his family. Brian followed him in and left with a two-kilo bag of assorted stuffed pasta for himself for just ten euros. They were fat and juicy as Chinese dumplings and looked almost good enough to eat raw.

The Magic Mountain

The taxi sped away from the Greek temples and sparkling seas of Agrigento and back towards the yellow heart of the island. Cloud began to obscure the top of Montegiallo.

On the ninth level of Hell (or was it the eighth?), the expats cooked in their kitchens, completed or otherwise. Ice buzzed in blenders for afternoon daiquiris like any other day. *Like every other day.*

The Montegiallo locals went about their lives on top of the hill, trying to ignore the foreigners as usual.

Cats lay on the last warm pieces of ancient stone – before that late afternoon cloud cooled them – as they had done for centuries.

Birds hopped from one branch to another. And then back to the first branch again, like *they* had always done. Long before Manfredi III Chiaramonte had stopped there for a leak and decided it was a good spot for a fortified town.

Only the *scarafaggi* and *ragni* felt that, somehow, things were changing in Montegiallo. *Something* was different. They drew back a little further into the cracks and the holes of the town wall, and waited to see which way things would go.

Quotable Quotes

At the end of a sandy road outside the gates of Montegiallo, *Servizi Termoidraulici Gaetano* was roughly daubed in lime paint above a half-closed metal roller shutter. It looked more like graffiti celebrating the victory of some lesser-known Roman general than the premises of a plumber. *And Electrics* was painted below, for some reason in English.

Brian bent down and looked under the door. Now it looked more like a plumber's. Copper, plastic and metal pipes sat on racks above a tiny three-wheeled van. Cardboard boxes with illustrations of vanity units and toilets lined one wall. A box of old taps and bits of chrome sat just inside, next to rolls of thick, red, white and blue electrical cable.

A solid man with ferociously thick eyebrows sat at a wooden desk at the back, scribbling on a pad, trying to get a pen to work. Behind the desk an open door showed weeds and more stacked pipework. The outside of the town wall rose at the rear of the yard. Still bending, Brian rapped on the metal door, went inside, and straightened up.

'Ah, *buongiorno*.'

The man gave up on the pen and tossed it at a drum on the other side of the workshop, missing it by a wide margin. He looked at Brian.

'Gianni!' he shouted. 'Gianni! *Inglese!*'

'Actually *australiano*,' Brian tried to explain, but the man got up and went out the door, yelling even louder. The words 'Gianni! *In-gle-seeeeeeee!*' faded into the far corner of the big yard.

A young man was almost pushed through the door by his elder.

He had curly hair and was wiping his hands on a white rag. He wore boots and narrow overalls which he struggled to fill, and spoke as quietly as the man had been loud.

'English?' He spoke so softly that Brian struggled to hear him.

'Australian. *Australiano*.'

'No. You speak English?'

'Oh, yes. Sorry.'

The man was obviously uncomfortable in the role of translator. He spoke in Italian to the other man, presumably Gaetano, and maybe his father. Whatever it was, he didn't want to do it. Gaetano, if it was he, replied with something which Brian couldn't understand, apart from the words '*Spirito Santo*'. It was probably, 'That idiot who bought the house on Spirito Santo.'

Brian was already on the back foot here. 'Ahh, ahh, ahh ...' *Balbettare* had surprisingly turned out to be one of the most useful verbs in the Italian language.

The man swallowed nervously. 'I am Gianni. You have the house on Spirito Santo?'

'Yes. Brian Chapman.'

'*Sì?* So, yes?'

'I've got six toilets and a bidet. Only one of the toilets work. So I want the others to work and the bidet as well.'

The young man shook his head sadly and apologetically, his eyes on the floor, not meeting Brian's. 'No.'

'No? You can't do?'

'No, means you need more.' He looked behind him as though seeking an escape route.

'You know my place?'

'Yes. Franco ask us to fix. Few months ago. So it could be lived in. Why one toilet and the shower are good. Nothing working before.

Is empty for many years. My fixing is why hot-water heater doesn't explode for short term.'

Gianni's hesitant delivery was at odds with the brutal bad news he was giving, and an icy chill settled around Brian's wallet.

'Right. And what if I wanted the hot-water heater to not explode in the *long* term?'

'That would be a good idea.'

'Right. What if I'm happy with only one toilet and I just get the bidet fixed.'

'I'm sorry. The toilets are no problem. Easy to install. All pipes to them need to be replaced. Very old.'

From Caligula's day, no doubt.

'They might last a few months. Maybe.' Gianni gave a Mediterranean shrug. 'And you need to do them before new water heater. Won't take pressure of new system. And electrics too,' he said apologetically, looking at the other man, who said something in Italian.

'My father says you don't plug in that iron if there's anything else on.'

Brian's phone buzzed. His deliveries were arriving. 'I've got to go.'

Gianni promised to give him an official quote as soon as possible.

'And, how long to do the job?' That was a question apparently too difficult to answer.

'We have many jobs to do first. But as soon as we get to you.'

'Perhaps before the hot-water heater explodes?' said Brian.

Both Italians shrugged in reply, even though Brian was sure that the older man spoke no English.

Brooding

Back at Spirito Santo, a van blocked the entrance to the *piazza*. How it had got there, up the tiny curving streets, Brian had no idea. His new mattress, plastic wrapped, was leaning against the front wall. Two men were unloading the rest. Brian unlocked the front door, and the men grabbed the mattress and took it in after him. They seemed like they intended to leave it in the hallway, so Brian pointed upstairs with a hopeful question on his face. They eyed the rail-less stairs, and for a second Brian thought they were going to refuse. He put his hands together in a praying action. 'Please, please, please? *Per favore?*' They looked doubtful. Brian went to INDES, pulled out a sixpack of Messina and held it up as an offering. It was the traditional Australian way of informal payment. At home, most jobs could be divided or multiplied into sixpacks or cartons of beer, but he didn't know if it applied in Italy. Apparently it did. They looked at each other one more time and then complied.

The remaining items they left in the hallway. Once they'd gone, he unwrapped and unboxed the rest, which now looked like a hideous extravagance after the interview with the reluctant young plumber. But he couldn't live with two broken chairs and a table.

Buyer's regret merged with his anger. For an absurd moment, Brian considered legal action. But what would be the outcome he would want anyway? To get one euro refunded? He'd need a Sicilian lawyer. Most likely he'd just be laughed at.

He then wanted to storm down to Viviana and Franco and tell them what he thought of them. But again. To what purpose? And had they actually lied? No. The house was liveable. They had told him it would need renovations. Yes, they had. He had seen the photos. He had paid the deposit. He had signed the contract. It was all his own fault. They were not to blame.

In reality, I have a huge house for one euro. It is positive. So be positive.

'And don't catastrophise, Brian,' he said out loud to himself. 'First get the quote.' Maybe it won't be as bad as you think.

But he wondered if anyone, right back to Roman times, had ever got a plumbing quote that was lower than expected? Could be a first. *Be positive.* With the boots, the mattress, the furniture, the laptop and router, the frying pans and saucepans, he had spent what, in Australian dollars, in Agrigento? He made the calculation roughly in his head. About three grand. Actually, closer to four. He didn't have enough of such grands left. With the plumbing and electrics he'd be lucky to get away with less than another fifteen or twenty surely? He did still have most of the eight thousand left in the bond. Could it be done? Could it last, with careful spending, until he could find a way to get some cash?

He couldn't go crawling back to Australia after a week. Minus eight grand? Could he? Absolutely not. He'd rather watch the water heater explode while ironing in the bath. If he left, he'd lose the deposit and any kind of self-respect. If he stayed, he'd be up for most of the rest of his savings as well. Probably. He realised he was as trapped as any of the other expats.

If you had enough money to do it properly, you wouldn't be here in the first place.

God forbid having to teach English again. He thought he'd rather pick lemons. Teaching English was very Old Brian. He seriously wondered if lemon picking was actually an option in a slumping citrus industry.

Sure, Brian.

His Italian wasn't good, but how much Italian did you need to pick a lemon? But could he drive a tractor? No, he could not.

He took the folding chairs up to the balcony, then went back down for the round table and the last of the Messinas remaining after bribing the delivery men. Maybe he would have to change beers. The name 'Messina' was not his favourite at the moment. He sat on one of the stylish and beautifully designed chairs and put the heels of his new boots up on the balcony rail. He looked between them through the wrought-iron railings, and calmed down a little as he took in the peaceful *piazza*. The thing is, he really loved the place. When it came down to it, he wouldn't want a refund or to get out of it. He loved the town, and he loved the house, despite the plumbing nightmare that threatened, like the slow-moving molten lava under Mount Etna, to erupt at any moment. And the people? Well, the people were always the hardest, weren't they? With the expats, he would make an effort. Or avoid them entirely where possible. And the locals? Well, he would keep *buongiorno*-ing until they came round. He was going to have to make an even bigger effort with them. He stared across at the shuttered windows of Bar Limone on the far corner. He made a sudden decision.

'Cover me, Skeletor, I'm going in!'

Bar Limone

Conversation didn't stop as he entered the bar, because none had been going on in the first place. Dark oak tables and benches soaked up the gloom, facing a wooden bar, equally dark.

Centuries of bloody grime.

The only window that wasn't completely shuttered was behind the bar. A crabbed and unhealthy-looking lemon tree clawed at the glass outside with thorny fingers, like a sailor tearing at a porthole as his ship went down.

This place will be crawling with scarafaggios and yellow sacs. Brian watched his feet as his eyes adjusted. The man behind the bar did not stop polishing it because he had not been polishing it to begin with. It was the same man that Brian had encountered on his first morning, and the word *'faaarkaarza'* still rang in his ears. Brian had to resist the urge to go straight out again, but no. No, no, no. He was going to be accepted by the locals if it killed him. How could he face Toby ever again if he found out Brian was too scared to go into his own local bar? Two young men of possibly North African appearance, and a weary-looking older man eating some kind of stew, were the only customers.

There was quite obviously not going to be a selection of fifty tequilas here. *Probably a good thing, to be honest.* Brian approached the bar. Two black eyes, over that rudder of a nose, looked down on him.

He took out the old grammar from his new bag, but then put it back. It was only going to be *vino* or *birra*, wasn't it? He squinted at the row of dirty bottles of various shapes behind the bar, but didn't recognise a single one of them. As he finally opened his mouth, the door also opened behind him.

'Ah, *Signor* Chapman. I wondered if I might find you here. I was coming to bless your home.' The priest raised his hand to the sparse crowd. 'Giuseppe, Taysir, Akil.' One of the African men raised a hand. The tired man took another slow mouthful of stew.

Brian sat at one of the empty tables, while Father Dom did the ordering at the bar. After a brief conversation, he brought Brian back a greasy shot glass half filled with a yellow liquid, which looked like dishwashing detergent.

'It's the local speciality. A lemon liqueur. Called "L'Agrume".' Brian took a sip. It was at the same time overly sweet and very, very sour. It tasted like... concentrated lemon cordial mixed with vinegar. He made a face and wondered if he could accidentally knock it over rather than drink the rest. It smelled, he thought, remarkably like the bottle of mystery poison below his sink.

'You drink this?' he asked, making another face.

'Of course not! You have to be born here to be able to tolerate it. But civility requires that you at least try it once. What they don't drink, they export to Germany and Austria, I think. Best place for it, perhaps.'

The barman came over with a wooden carafe and two wine glasses. 'Ahh, you will probably like this better. *Grazie*, Pola. *Signor* Chapman, one of my parishioners.'

'*Buonasera*,' the giant rumbled reluctantly.

'*Buonasera*,' Brian replied brightly, feeling a little bolder with the priest by his side. He sipped his wine and looked around. Taking advantage of a local translator, he asked, 'What's the dish he's eating? What's in it?'

The priest looked over at the man in the corner. 'Giuseppe. *La caponata è buona oggi?*' The man turned around and gave a bare nod.

'It's fried vegetables. Eggplant it always has but every village will have their own version.' Brian took out the grammar, which had a few blank pages at the back, and wrote in *caponata*, which he then sounded out. 'Ca-po-na-ta.'

Pola the barman came over with a chipped bowl, a spoon and some bread, which he plonked down in front of Brian.

'Oh, no, I ...'

Father Dom put his palm up. 'You just ordered the *caponata*.'

Civility, OK.

'*Grazie*, Pola. Nice to meet you,' Brian called out to the retreating wall which was the back of the barman.

Melbourne Brian, that is to say Old Brian, actively disliked eggplant in almost all its forms. There was no recipe he could think of that wasn't tasteless slime, from Greek to Italian to Indian. But maybe New Brian would love it?

The dish was excellent, and although Old Brian would still have preferred leaving out the eggplant, New Brian was prepared to tolerate it. As for the lemon liqueur, drinking *that* might be taking assimilation too far. He very much wanted to take a picture of the bar for Toby, but decided to leave that for the moment as well.

Although the place looked like it might only accept lira, or even a purse of gold coins, Pola pulled out an iPad with a tap payment attached. The bill was surprisingly cheap. '*Grazie. Io ... ritorno?*' That seemed easy enough.

Pola did not reply, but he didn't call him a *faaarkaara* either, so Brian was satisfied. Despite everything, he had made some progress here, with the help of his religious representative.

'Right, Father,' Brian said, wiping *caponata* gravy from his mouth with the back of his hand, 'this house isn't going to bless itself.'

Blessing It Both Ways

'English or Italian? My English blessings may be a little rusty, but I'm sure it would be received in the right spirit ...' The priest waited, one hand raised and ready.

Brian only had to think for a moment. 'This old place would probably appreciate Italian more, don't you think?'

'Well apart from the television or radio, these walls would only ever have heard dialect. People here don't speak standard Italian at home. I can barely understand dialect myself, although I have been here for ten years. But you may be right. How about I do a little of both?'

Despite his frequently humorous pronouncements, Father Dom took the house blessing very seriously, and Brian felt a little ashamed about treating it flippantly. All the major rooms got the benefit of his soft but firmly spoken prayers, gestures and Amens in English and Italian. He also diplomatically pretended not to see the stack of *Pussycat*s on the kitchen table, which Brian hastily covered up with one of his new frying pans. He also paused at, but made no comment on, the demonic-looking Skeletor doll, currently ruling over the top of INDES the fridge.

'It's a childhood toy,' Brian lied.

Jeezus, I'm lying to a priest while he's blessing my house? The real explanation might have been too difficult, so he forgave himself the deceitfulness.

'Hmmm,' said Father Dominic.

'If you could use Italian for the bathrooms, maybe, Father. I want to make sure the plumbing really understands.'

A long pause. '*Bene.*'

While the bidet didn't get a specific blessing, Brian hoped the bathroom and the plumbing in general would feel the positive vibes.

When Father Dominic arose from the cellar, which had received an extensive set of prayers, Brian asked him, 'Ahh, do I need to …' Brian rubbed thumb and fingers together. He had not even considered whether you paid for a blessing. Or if so, how much.

'Consider it the next time the collection plate comes past,' said the priest, patting him on the arm.

'As you can see, it does need some work.'

'Eight bedrooms? Two bathrooms? Six toilets? What you need most is someone to share it, perhaps?'

'Well, Father, if you know any single females who can rewire a house, send them my way.'

'Hmmmm.'

As the priest made to leave, Brian suddenly asked, 'Wait, are you hungry?' Despite consuming the *caponata*, Brian still had the best part of two kilos of assorted stuffed pasta to get through.

After putting the *Pussycat*s out of sight and wiping down the table, Brian and Father Dom sat across from each other and ate. The ravioli was very, very good. If Brian didn't already have to start counting his pennies, he'd take the taxi back down to Agrigento and bring back enough to fill INDES to the top.

'No, no, you can get this at Nuovo,' the priest told him, and promised to take him down there when he did the second mass one Sunday. 'Up here though, you'll need to find someone to make it for you. Keep practising your pronunciation.' Brian thought of Viviana, but he didn't think she looked like she cooked a lot of pasta. Didn't look like she ate a lot of it anyway. He envisioned a jollier woman of

Italian tradition and wide bosom. If he saw such a one, he would give her his absolute best *buongiorno*. And if she could rewire a house, all the better.

Purosangue

Brian realised that the house as a whole was going to be too difficult to deal with given his lack of funds and lack of person power. He decided to consolidate just the main rooms, and shut the doors of the rest, particularly the other five toilets.

Just for now.

He unboxed the wireless speaker and plugged it into the charger. Every time he plugged something in, or turned on a switch, he half expected the lights to dim, if it was possible for them to dim any further, or, even though it wasn't connected to the electrics, the hot-water heater to explode. Nothing. Good. He piggybacked the power point again with another plug for the router, which he set up on top of INDES and set Skeletor on top of all that, his ram's-horn staff raised proudly between the antennas.

Brian wondered if the phone roaming was going to be enough to stream music. Probably not. Anyway. Bleh. Time to set up the laptop and wi-fi. Between pressing 'continue' more than twenty times, he flicked through his folder and chose a provider at random. SIC-NET. The price was about the same for all of them. He checked their cheapest package. The laptop asked him for language preferences. He hovered over the Italian option for a moment, and then chose English.

Better make sure you understand every word of the fine print you are not going to read.

He spent some time walking between the laptop, the router and his phone, each of them giving unhelpful and contradictory instructions. Many times, ninety-nine percent promised a resolution, but it always led to another sluggish five percent. He left them to fight it out between themselves for a while. He had bought a small stovetop coffee maker, and a tightly vacuumed brick of espresso, but he left both untouched and opened the front door. Light streamed in. The cool evening of the night before had departed. He decided to try the coffee at Bar Limone instead of making his own. Before stepping out, he checked the laptop one last time.

'Yes, yes, yes! Continue! What do you think?'

* * *

He ordered an espresso without incident. Pola was tending the bar again, and he also attended to the hissing of an impressive-looking Rancilio coffee machine. He grunted '*Prego*' not too severely at Brian's '*Grazie*'.

Brian took his coffee in its tiny cup and saucer out into the shade. The same woman (Rosa, was it?) with the same two bags crossed the same square in a re-run of previous days. Brian trotted out one of his stock *buongiorno*s, and then added a touch adventurously, '*Mi chiamo Signor* Brian.' But wait, he wasn't Mr Brian, was he?

Should have said 'My name is Signor Chapman'.

As he was thinking about correcting it, the woman replied with a smile. He didn't catch what she said, but it was a smile, right? Should he offer to help with the bags? But, not being sure of the etiquette, he returned the cup to the bar instead.

* * *

Still buzzing from the thick coffee, he wasn't going to take any more nonsense from his technology.

'OK,' he announced to his empty home and Skeletor, 'time to get your crap together.'

There ended up being only three more continues to press on the laptop and two more resets of the wi-fi. Seemed to be done. Try some music? What was contemporary Sicilian music like? He had no idea. He got YouTube up and had a look. First piece he brought up was Sicilian hip-hop. From the video, he could not work out if it was a parody, serious, or something in between. Men in gold chains drove Ferraris, smoked cigarettes and grabbed each other's hands in aggressive greetings. It was muted, but as soon as he clicked on the icon, his wi-fi speaker jumped into life, and despite its size, managed to fill the big room with a booming sound.

He could barely make out a word of the song. Probably in dialect. Would he have understood what was going on had it been American or even Australian hip-hop? Probably not. He scanned the comments. *'Purosangue siciliano.' Sangue* was 'blood', and *puro* was not hard to work out.

Yikes.

That didn't sound good. Or did it?

Pure Sicilian Blood? What the hell does that mean? That was the problem. He didn't know. Could be a bunch of comedians or neo-fascists or, slightly less likely, both. He decided to postpone any investigation into contemporary Sicilian music for the moment and, despite it being a kind of backwards step for New Brian, found a playlist of Hunters & Collectors and put that on shuffle. To this soundtrack he busied himself arranging his too few household items, into his too large and numerous spaces, to some semblance of homeliness.

For the kitchen, he chose a corner near the stove to concentrate his assets and then, remembering the conversation with the plumber, swapped to another spot that would hopefully be beyond any blast zone from the hot-water heater. His phone shot cropped out the reality of the general emptiness and disuse and, with a filter or two, looked pretty good. He discovered that his *palazzo* best suited the 'cross-process' filter. He did the same on the balcony, where he balanced the phone on a piece of polystyrene from the router packaging and in his finery took what he regarded as an excellent selfie, managing to include both the elaborately decorated tiles and the lush shadows of the *piazza*. He took another selective shot that included the bed (which he superficially made and tucked in), the black velvet curtains, the sky and the terracotta roof tiles. So, on the surface at least, and with a couple more judicious crops and filters, he could certainly give the impression of living *somebody's* Italian fantasy.

He sent the pictures to Toby. There was nobody much else to see them. The rest of his friends – those that had been able to tolerate a year of acrimony – turned out to be her friends in the end. The rest were other teachers like she was. So the world of staffroom gossip was the last place he had wanted to revisit, even before leaving Melbourne. Toby could spread the images around a little if he felt like it. He hoped his rigidly curated shots didn't give the impression of a *'vita'* so *'la dolce'* that someone would try to visit and see the slightly desperate reality. But who would that be anyway? Apart from Toby?

Nobody.

He had deleted his few social media accounts nine months before, and he had no overwhelming reason to resurrect them. If he did, New Brian would be posting. A New Brian with a 1960s fridge, a 1980s stove, wearing an ancient deceased Sicilian's woolen suit and living in a house, some of which at least, had been built when the plague last went through. But a New Brian nonetheless.

A Visitor from the Lower Levels

About this time, Brian began to feel he was *living* in Montegiallo, and not just a tourist. He got his coffee regularly at Bar Limone every morning instead of at the cobbled market café, and so had only encountered an expat once, one Friday, when he needed some olive oil at the *supermercato*. That was more than enough contact as far as he was concerned. As he came out with his bottle of oil, English Chris had come past carrying a white cardboard box of pastries.

'Oh, Brian. I'm glad I caught you. Haven't seen you for a while.'
Errrk.
'Just wanted to let you know, drinks are at ours on Saturday. Number seven Via Risorgimento. If you go up Madonna from Eric and Martina's, it's the next street.'

'*Risorgimento*, as in the Italian reunification? Garibaldi and all that, right?' Brian was fairly hazy about the reunification of Italy. Even on what century it had happened. He wanted to think Napoleon – or *a* Napoleon – had been involved. Could there have been several Napoleons? Didn't feel too guilty though. Couldn't think that a single Italian in Melbourne would know the first thing about Captain Cook, let alone Bennelong or Bungaree.

'Yes, everything's a composer, writer, or Garibaldi here, I suppose,' said Chris. 'If it was supposed to mean reorganisation, then they need to do it again, if you've ever tried to get anything done around here.' If it was a joke, neither of them laughed. Chris looked sourly at the offices of Ideale Real Estate, where Viviana moved gracefully behind the glass, again with her phone to one ear. Her eyes briefly took them both in before turning and disappearing behind the office dividers. Brian kept looking, hoping she'd reappear.

'Anyway, just making sure we'd see you again tomorrow night.'

'Hmm? Oh, I'll do my best,' said Brian, determined not to do his best if he could at all help it. 'Still clearing up and organising. You know…'

'Good, we'll see you then.'

'Looking forward to it!' said Brian, not looking forward to it. He probably should go, but knew himself well enough to know that he had already decided not to. 'See you Saturday,' he lied.

* * *

Gianni's quote had still not arrived and Brian found himself right in the middle of trepidation and blissful ignorance. It meant that his bank balance could still give the illusion that it was full of money. Until that bomb dropped, he could just continue to settle into a life in Spirito Santo square. Nobody even looked twice at his new dress habits. *People get used to anything in a few days.* He had even learned to tie a cravat.

Now that it was more convenient to type on the laptop than the phone, he was able to write at more length to Toby, but he had started to review and send in the mornings rather than at night after he'd had a couple of glasses of Sicilian, when he still sounded a bit sorry for himself.

Enough of that.

Toby kept him informed, in several casual breaches of confidentiality, about the funniest tragic stories from the world of student wellbeing, which cheered him up considerably. As Toby put it, some people had fucked up, or had fuck-up thrust upon them, overwhelmingly, and often hilariously. It brought Brian's own problems into perspective. 'Maybe I am doing OK?' Compared to some. Some who may have reversed over both of their cats on the way to an exam for instance.

* * *

On Saturday morning after he completed his coffee ritual in the *piazza* he was on his way upstairs when he heard the lion doorknocker toll. The thickness of the old door and the big stone-clad open areas magnified it to the sound of someone using a battering ram.

He had the hideous feeling that it was Gianni or Gaetano banging on it with an oversized plumbing and electrics quote. Since he was nearly at the top of the stairs, he continued up, went out onto the balcony and looked down, not onto the curly head of the young plumber as he expected, but a comb-over mostly successfully covering a bald head.

'Oh, Eric?'

The comb-over tipped back and was replaced by Eric's smiling face. 'I was in the neighbourhood…' He looked a little uncertainly behind him at the *piazza*.

'I'll be right down.'

Brian ushered the man in and through to the kitchen–living area.

'I'm sorry to barge in on you…'

'No problem. What can I do for you?'

'Only saw this place in the photographs. It's very…' Eric struggled for something positive, 'spacious!'

'Six toilets. I think. The number comes out different every time I count.'

Eric laughed. 'Must have been a big family. Or planning one. Italians used to like that sort of thing. Now they just have one or none like everyone else.' There was a touch of regret in Eric's voice and Brian felt some pity for him. He wondered what family the man had. He hadn't seen any expat offspring in Montegiallo. Most would be adults by now anyway. Maybe the priest was right. Despite the filling of a few empty houses, the one-euro scheme was still just another dead end.

'Would you like a coffee?'

'Oh, no, I won't trouble you, I just—oh my God!' he stared back over Brian's shoulder.

'What? What?' Brian spun around, half expecting a biblical swarm of yellow sacs to be emerging from the cracks in the walls.

'Those things are deathtraps! Don't tell me you are using it?' He pointed at the hot-water heater over the sinks with a craggy, bony finger like Death selecting a new victim.

'Oh. No. It's all been checked out. All safe.'

For now.

'Well, that's ... good,' said Eric hesitantly, still staring at the unit. INDES chose that moment to rumble into life, and the flagstones beneath their feet trembled.

'You know you could get a brand-new Miele sent up from Agrigento, or even Palermo?'

'Was there something you needed, Eric?'

'Ahh, really, no, I'm just here to make sure you were coming tonight. I saw Chris yesterday and he said he *believed* you were coming but ...?'

Brian thought he had escaped the whole thing, but now he felt trapped again. 'Well, I was thinking of it.'

'Going to be a special event. Can't say more. But want to see you down there. Everyone would. Don't bother to bring anything. They'll be well stocked.'

Brian thought they'd all be well stocked as maggots by the end of the night.

'Yes. I'll be there. Of course. Always intended to.'

'Wonderful.' Eric took one more fearful look at the water heater. 'Marvellous.'

OK, Virgil, Brian thought resignedly. Saddle up. We're heading down to Hell again.

The Delegate

Brian knew he had made a mistake. When he arrived at number seven Via Risorgimento, the chairs were all facing a single direction. A classroom or parent–teacher gathering came to mind. Which was always bad for all concerned. The room was pretty well full, and people did seem happy to see him. Drinks were already in hand, and Brian didn't resist as one was placed in his.

Chris and Ilse's place on Risorgimento looked relatively complete downstairs, but in conversation with Ilse, there were hints of dark times in the ensuite.

'Do you have a bidet?' Brian asked as he drained the first wine.

Easy, big fella.

She smiled. 'Plumbing and tiling are always on everyone's mind here, Brian. That's why we thought you might be able to —'

She broke off as Murray and Salina came in.

Able to what? Brian's mind whirled. He looked at the chairs again. He hoped he wasn't supposed to give some sort of speech? He felt like he was being lined up for a timeshare.

'Brian Chapman, man of the moment!' Murray and Salina came over smiling. 'Best-dressed of the broke-assed foreigners, hah-hah.'

Brian suddenly felt a tightness around his neck, and tugged at his cravat. *What man? What moment?*

'I think you look just gorgeous, Brian. You're putting Murray to shame.' Salina put her hand on her husband's arm with a smile.

'I like to be comfortable,' he replied irritably. Murray's stomach pushed out the front of an over-large polo shirt. Sneakers instead of the Crocs were below the shorts tonight. Maybe that constituted formal dress for Murray?

Brian was decidedly not comfortable. 'What's happening tonight? Is it some kind of meeting?'

'Oh, I ...' Salina was embarrassed. 'I didn't realise ...'

Someone else he had met, another Brit who he had forgotten the name of, came over. 'Oh, Brian. So good to see you.'

He tried to look like he remembered.

'It's Lars. My wife is Susan.'

'Of course.'

'Great to see you here tonight, Brian.' English Chris and American Christopher (or was it the other way round?) joined in. The group blocked any escape route to the front door, even if Brian could have moved.

'Once a month we start with a little bit of an informal meeting of the expats association,' said Chris. 'The One Euro Club. You're automatically a member.'

Grrrr, thought Brian but tried not to let that show on his face.

'It's very informal,' Salina agreed.

'Absolutely,' said American Christopher.

Brian surrendered without further protest to the well-stocked alcoholic resources of Chris and Ilse.

Eric, with Martina in tow, finally bustled in with a manila folder and smiles for everyone.

'Evening all, please take a pew.'

Brian tried to get a spot right at the end of the back row. If there was any prospect of getting out, he didn't want to have to trample on anyone.

'Thank you, everyone,' Eric stood at the front, and waved his folder. 'Welcome to the monthly meeting of the Montegiallo expat association. Only a couple of items. Firstly, for those who haven't met him, let me formally welcome the newest member of The One Euro Club – although he has decided to spurn The Ghetto to live up the hill with the natives – Brian Chapman, our first Australian.' That was followed by a mock whisper. 'Don't hold that against him.' Eric clapped his folder with one hand and the rest of the crowd followed. 'There's no paperwork to do, Brian, just the monthly subscription of a bottle of Beefeater, which you can leave on my doorstep anytime.' Eric put up his hand to quell laughter that had already stopped.

Is that it? thought Brian. If so, he'd got off pretty lightly. *But if Eric thinks I'm going to give him a bottle of gin every month, then he…*

Eric went on with some items that were of no interest to Brian. Barry and Jen had some excess cactuses available for free. The English-speaking vet in Agrigento was offering a discount on cat spaying for this month. A reminder that the Sicilian power company was raising tariffs again, blah, blah. But Brian's ears pricked up as Eric went on, 'And that leads me to the last item on the agenda, that Brian may even be able to help us with.' Heads turned from the forward rows.

Oh God, what now?

'Last month it was discussed making a formal complaint, and even sending a petition, to the Messinas as the representatives, managers and promoters of the one-euro scheme in Montegiallo, demanding that they take some action regarding the slowness and quality of the services offered. Just because we've only paid a single euro, that doesn't mean we are second-class citizens.'

Brian could hear general muttering. 'Disgraceful. Time for some action…' A ripple of applause went around the room. Even a 'Hear, hear!' from Murray.

'Now, after circulating the document, I have here…' and again the folder waved, 'signatures from almost every member of the Montegiallo expat community demanding they do something!'

Applause, more enthusiastic than Brian's welcome.

'Now, as you know, I was quite prepared to present this on your behalf, but a little bird tells me that our newest member, formerly of the convict colonies, now living in Piazza Spirito Santo ...' Heads turned again. Brian saw Robinson leaning forward in his seat and grinning at him from the end of his row. '... has quite an affinity with one of the Messinas – the female of the species, *the DW herself*, Viviana. So the committee – that is myself and Murray, Martina and Salina – has decided to give Brian the opportunity to make his first contribution to the cause, and beard the Devil Woman in her lair.'

The biggest applause of the night. And that was the only other item of business before the general drinking.

This was beyond horrific. Brian endured handshakes and words of thanks and encouragement as they stood.

'Good show.'

'Well done.'

'... our water feature.'

'Tell her what's what.'

'I haven't had a bath for a month and I can't abide showers.'

'Better you than me. I'm terrified of the woman.'

'Sorry to drop you in it, Brian. Oh, you got some new cufflinks?'

'Those two should be in gaol.'

'Welcome to Montegiallo, old man.'

Eric took Brian aside. 'I know it was frightfully rude of me, but when Robinson told me how well you had hit it off with Viviana ...'

Brian had simply told Robinson he had made a total arse of himself in front of her. 'Really, I've barely spoken to her!'

'And being an Australian, you can represent both groups more easily,' said Eric ignoring his reply. 'Plus, you're the only one that speaks Italian.'

'Well that's not strictly true.'

'Really? You were heard ordering your coffee in Italian.'

'Well, *un caffè con latte* is hardly fluency. I try and speak a few words, that's all. Seems like common courtesy. And Viviana speaks perfect English anyway.'

'Anyone who matters speaks English. Or wants to. Or should want to, don't you think? But in any case, if you can demand some action, it will help you too. At this rate it will be many months before you get your turn.'

Eric held out the petition folder. Brian felt he had no other choice but to take it from him.

No, You're Pixellated

'I've no idea what you're talking about,' said a heavily pixellated Toby.

'Wait, you've gone a bit blurry.' Brian reduced the size of the video frame, which then froze. When it moved again, Toby was mid-sentence.

'... course I'm blurry. It's nine am on Sunday morning!' Toby's voice echoed around the room.

'I thought it was ten am. Sorry. It's one in the morning here.'

'A friend doesn't call a friend at nine. Or ten in the morning. Or in the middle of the night. Are you wearing cravats now?'

'Yes. You like?' Brian fluffed up the silk a little. Toby ignored this.

'So you've been there just a few weeks and now you're heading a mob of villagers with torches and pitchforks up to storm the castle.'

'Well. Kind of. By myself though. I'm the whole mob.'

'To present a petition to a demon real-estate agent?'

'Yes.'

'Why?'

'Well, I kind of got trapped into it.'

'Trapped, eh?'

'It was a nightmare. They're all scared of her.'

'But you agreed?'

'Apparently.'

'What does she look like?'

'What?'

'What does this Devil Woman look like?

'Why?'

'I just want to see.'

'What for?'

'Because.'

'I don't see what difference it makes.'

'Whether it does or not, just show me the fucking picture.'

Brian sighed. 'Hang on.' He clicked off the video messenger and searched for the Ideale real estate website. A shot of a ridiculously beaming Franco and Viviana together was the only one he could find. He cropped out Franco, who looked like a wolf who had unexpectedly come across a flock of lost lambs. When the rectangle only contained Viviana, he saved it and sent it off to Toby.

Toby took a moment. 'OK, now I get it.'

'Get what? She doesn't usually look so friendly. She's usually more like ...' Brian leaned into the tiny camera lens until his face completely filled the screen and made the face of someone looking at someone else like they were an idiot.

'Now I get why you've agreed. Very nice. Although you just finalised getting away from another devil woman, don't forget ...'

'Well ...'

'Good icebreaker, by the way,' said Toby. 'Issuing a list of demands. Very smooth. And they wonder why you're single.'

'What am I going to do?'

'Ask her for a drink!'

Brian tried to visualise a meeting amidst the filth of Bar Limone, but couldn't. 'What about the petition?'

'Throw it in the bin. Fuck those idiots. Better still, throw them under the bus. Be the concerned citizen warning her against the peasant rebellion brewing.'

That sounded better. 'Yeah, that could be something. I'll try and see her after ...' he was going to say church, but caught himself. 'Yes, I'll see her first thing tomorrow morning.'

'It's already first thing tomorrow morning here. We're eight hours ahead of you, for future reference. I'm going back to bed. Good morning.'

'Thanks, Tobe. Great help.'

Nuovo Mondo

Father Dom's small black Fiat rocketed out of the Montegiallo gates with the noise of a nitro-powered lawnmower.

'Jeeeeezus, whoops, sorry, Father.' Brian braced one hand on the inside of the flimsy roof.

That morning, slipping late into mass again, Brian was still not a hundred percent sure of what he'd say about the petition. With a mixture of relief and disappointment, Brian noted that Franco alone took any sacraments on offer to the Messina family. No show, Viviana. Brian wondered about her soul, then about the rest of her.

Brian hoped that Father Dom would realise that the ten-euro note in the collection box – surely plenty for a house blessing – came from him. Should be plenty change left over from the blessing for some sage advice on his situation, but the noise of the car, the priest's rapid and frequent gear changing and the heavy braking, deep and late into every dangerous hairpin, made conversation a little difficult for the first half of the journey.

As the road began to flatten out a little, Brian was able to tell him about the petition.

'Hmmm,' the priest said, accelerating around a tractor. 'Seems like a bad idea.'

'I'm a bit stuck, you know, between the expats and the locals.'

Nuovo approached in the middle distance. 'Why did they ask you? You've been here only a few weeks?'

Brian braced for another bend in the road, which the priest took in third gear. 'Because I'm not American or English, I'm apparently seen as more neutral.'

'Hmmm. Let me think about it a little.' Father Dom's brows furrowed as they were mercifully forced to slow for the church's car-park entrance.

Brian wasn't going to take in another mass. One per Sunday was plenty for an unbeliever.

Very little besides the service seemed to be going on in Montegiallo Nuovo that morning. Brian wandered. Strolling around the town took much the same time as it would have up the hill. Just a lot less interesting. There was a much larger *supermercato* with a lot more on offer, but he didn't really need much more than he could get at his own shop. Three different varieties of wild boar salami. Did anyone need more than one? The pasta selection didn't seem as good as in Agrigento. There was a bright new café with tables covered in alternating red and blue tablecloths. Brian sat with a coffee and a small cake watching the cars enter and leave the service station opposite. Everything else was just about closed on this Sunday morning. He drained his coffee and squashed the last few crumbs of his cake together with his thumb as Father Dominic waved at him through the plastic net curtains. A man came up to the priest carrying a large, yellow plastic sack. They had a brief conversation, and the man left without it.

Brian emerged from the café. He looked at the sack.

'A present from a parishioner, which I'm giving to you.'

'What is it?'

'Cut wood for the stove. I didn't have the heart to tell him that I only use the electric now. Too much work. But I saw that you had a wood stove, so I thought ...'

'Sure, great, thanks.' Brian hadn't really considered using the huge wood stove. *But why not?* Especially since he'd spent so much time cleaning the bloody thing.

'Are we ready to go back up the hill? I was thinking of your situation during mass. Just during the hymns of course.' Father Dom raised his eyebrows in a smile.

'Sure. I had a look at the pasta in the *supermercato*. Didn't look as good.'

'Oh, wait, of course. I totally forgot. This way.'

Brian couldn't find a comfortable way to carry the lumpy sack. He ended by holding it in front of him like a pregnancy, as they walked past the square of shops and down another street.

'Maybe we should have left that at the car,' Father Dom said, eyeing Brian's burden. 'But it's not far.' He knocked on a bright-green roller shutter.

The door was raised to reveal three women working on a huge row of pasta products that stretched to the back of the building.

'Ahhh, Maria.' The priest spoke in rapid Italian, once indicating Brian.

'Fifteen minutes after mass, and they're already doing more of God's work,' he said to Brian with a smile.

A few minutes later they left with a couple of plastic bags full of fresh ravioli, which swung from the priest's fingers as Brian humped the firewood along.

He was relieved when they reached the car parked behind the church, and Brian managed to stuff the firewood into the tiny back seat.

'One of these is for you.' Father Dom gave Brian one of the blue bags of goodness.

'Do I need to pay? You've been so good to a former Catholic, Father.'

'Hmm. Not this time.'

Like drugs, the first time is always free.

'I will give you Maria's number. Next time you are down the hill, you can negotiate a price.'

The priest started the Fiat with an introductory revving of the motor. 'Now, to your problem.' Gravel flew up from the reversing tyres and strafed the trunks of a row of frangipanis like a machine gun. Then into first, and the stones scoured the chassis.

'Matthew six: twenty-four might be of help here,' said Father Dom, looking across at Brian and taking one hand off the wheel, both of which Brian wished he wouldn't. 'A man cannot serve two masters. You are aware of it?'

'I didn't know it was from the Bible, but yes.'

'Of course, originally it was about choosing between God and money, but this wisdom can equally apply to this situation. You need to decide where your loyalties lie. I hear that you have been speaking to locals in some sort of Italian and trying to be part of the community.'

'Yes. I don't think there is the same sentiment from some of the other foreigners.'

'Exactly. Everyone is surprised. Incredibly suspicious, but pleasantly surprised. If you keep that up, after ten generations and two hundred years, your family might be considered local.'

'Ha, really?'

'No, but it would be a start. Take Pola, the barman.'

'Yes?'

'One ancestor on one side of the family *might* have come from France, *maybe* in the sixteenth century. Some people still call him "The Frenchman".'

'Right.'

'But I think you will endanger your good start if you are bringing up lists of complaints and demands from the other foreigners.'

Brian sighed, which was drowned out by the shriek of a downshift as the car struggled on a steep section. 'Yes.'

'Don't give her any demands, just meet her. She's a reasonable person...' He paused. '...in many ways. Franco too. But Franco's English is *così così*...' He took one very needed hand off the wheel again to tilt it in the 'so-so' gesture.

Toby, Father Dom and possibly even St Matthew had recommended not giving the petition. Probably a good idea to take the advice of this substantially holy Trinity.

'What about the expats?'

'Hmmm. That relationship you will need to work out for yourself. But don't do their dirty work for them.' He thought a little more. 'I could perhaps speak to Viviana for you...' The Fiat shifted down for two seconds as they rounded another hairpin, then quickly back up to third and fourth on one of the rare straight sections. Brian briefly considered this offer. Despite how difficult the subject of the peasant rebellion would be to raise, he still looked forward to another encounter with the beautiful Sicilian.

'Thanks Father, but I'd better do that on my own.' *If I survive this drive.* He kept that thought to himself.

Plumbing the Depths

Twelve thousand, two hundred and eighty-six euros gets you:

- Enough pipework to reach halfway to Palermo;
- Six toilets and a full drainage overhaul;
- One bidet;
- One total electrical replacement, including enough wiring to reach halfway to Catania, and;
- One hot-water system.

Or to put it another way, which Brian did, eighteen thousand, nine hundred and ninety-five Australian dollars plus eight cents.

- Ten percent deposit to even get onto the list.

Estimated start date: about eleven months, or to put it another way, which Brian did not, roughly three hundred and thirty days.

Gianni and Gaetano had come in person to deliver the quote. And both took a brief further look round, to make sure that they hadn't missed another half-dozen toilets or electrical deathtraps to add to the bill. Gianni didn't need to do any translating. There was nothing left to say.

Artist-anal

Well at least he had a proper excuse to see Viviana, now he had the quote.

I'll take it down to the office today.

He took a deep breath. Before committing to the payment, he made himself consider one last time attempting to get the deposit back and pulling out. He looked around at his stone room, now looking almost lived-in. Hammond organ jazz bubbled out of the speaker from some random playlist. INDES sat in its corner, broodingly silent for a change. Becky the stove was ticking away as Father Dom's gift of wood provided heat. *Nope.*

'This is it,' he called out to Skeletor. 'Suck it up. We're staying!'

He would raise the other demands more softly. With a gift. And that gift was going to be artisanal bread. Taking his inspiration from Elizabeth, free food was a solid approach. Coq au vin was way too ambitious, and possibly inappropriate under the circumstances. Bread was just right and handmade was the perfect touch.

The ingredients had been suspiciously simple, all of them well within the *supermercato*'s limited stock. He didn't really know what artisanal bread was before starting. Was it anything more than bread made by arseholes? Looking online, apparently it was not. It really was just bread. Made by arseholes. He had scrolled through a huge list of bread recipes. Yep, arseholes all the way down. The recipes were also all reassuringly simple. 'Can't fail' was a frequent endorsement.

OK. Can't complain about that.

If the arsehole in question had an AGA, or ancient wood stove, which *this* arsehole did, then apparently it was all the better. He flicked his screen back to life. Leave three hours to rise. Perfect. Done. He looked under the tea towel and the dough was almost to the top of his biggest blue pattern bowl. He reviewed the recipe again. *All pretty simple.* He didn't have a rolling board so he sprinkled the old tabletop with flour, dragged the sticky dough out of the bowl, and scraped the rest out with his fingers. Using the one knuckle not covered in dough, he scrolled the recipe on the laptop. Form into two loaves.

OK. No need to knead!

Becky had been full of various metal moulds and tins, but this recipe called for just a simple flat tray.

Plenty of those.

Getting Becky up to speed had been the hardest part of the whole venture so far. There had been no instruction manual for a mammoth 1980s Becchi stove, either in the house or online, so he had to wing it. At first he wasn't even sure in which spaces you put the fuel, and which the food. But after going through about half Father Dom's bag of wood, he was kind of getting the hang of it. Maybe. There were various levers and vents, some of which appeared to have no effect. Others sent the temperature soaring and the flames roaring up through the stovetop. Move them the other way, and it was like throwing a bucket of water on the fire. Getting it cooled back down *just a little* was the hardest part. He felt like a scientist at the controls of a nuclear reactor. He wanted 230 degrees stable. He gave the flame-dousing lever the barest tap. Putting his hands on his knees he watched the temperature gauge intently. Like watching the hands on a clock, he couldn't tell if it was moving at all. He tapped the glass dial and the needle suddenly shot up to 265!

He couldn't be bothered playing around with the controls anymore, so he opened the door, wafted out some heat, put in the tray and slammed the door behind it, hoping for the best.

OK. Now to the angry expats. He wasn't going to give Viviana the page of signatures. That was for sure. *In fact …* He pulled the pages out of the folder and fed them into Becky's firebox. The paper turned from flame to ash instantly. 'Whoa there, Becky.' He hoped the sudden boost of combustion didn't affect his artist-anal loaves.

So, no petition. But he couldn't just ignore the whole thing.

He washed his hands, put the phone timer on for thirty minutes, poured half a glass of red Sicilian and sat down to wait. He canned the Hammond jazz and found a Frank Sinatra channel on YouTube instead. Frank began drawling about witchcraaaaaft. Baking. It was totally witchcraft.

The money, though.

One positive thing was that he had several months to find a way to earn some cash before paying out most of the rest of his savings. But he didn't dare spend any of it, in case he couldn't. Or if the job happened to start sooner. He would burn through the rest of the balance in a few months, unless he was very careful. He hoped Father Dom wasn't expecting a ten-euro note every Sunday. He must remember to get some fives and some coins from the *supermercato*, like he was planning a visit to a strip club. It must be expensive to go to a strip club in Europe, he thought. There were no one-euro notes and you could hardly tuck a euro coin into a garter. Or maybe they had special European Union garters?

Something to ponder.

The loaves that came out of Becky half an hour later, as Frank belted out 'My Way', although smelling divine, were difficult to describe visually. Brian thought they looked like a cross between giant croissants and dinosaur turds. How oval loaves going in could come out as these three-cornered obscenities, he didn't know. He took a photo anyway, but it was going to need a suite of filters to get them looking anything like the loaves the arsehole in the online recipe had achieved. He also took a photo of Becky's control settings for future reference, then shut every lever to what he hoped was its off position.

He cut off one of the corners. The crust was about as thick as car tyre tread. He took a bite. 'Delicious!' But it took almost all his strength to bite off a chunk. *That reminds me. Need to check where the nearest dentist is. Jeezus.*

He put the other loaf back in Becky with the door just ajar to keep it warm while he had a shower and put on his suit and best tie.

Coming down the stairs after his shower, he pulled the warm loaf out of the oven, wrapped it in a tea towel, put the quote from Gianni in his top pocket like a silk handkerchief, and strode determinedly down the hill towards the lair of the Devil Woman.

Viviana

The Devil Woman would be just '*due minuti*' according to Franco. They both turned their eyes to the ceiling and tried to frame some small talk in each other's language. Brian wanted to give the quote to Viviana not Franco, so was relieved when they both agreed it was better he wait. Franco put an office chair in front of Viviana's desk. '*Prego.*'

Viviana, when she came in, removing an enormous pair of bottle-green sunglasses, looked half pleased to see him. She was still rocking the Italian movie-star look, wearing a green linen dress with a square neckline that matched the colour of her sunnies. Brian stood up. He put the loaf on the floor to keep it out of sight for now, then checked the time on his phone. '*Buongiorno!*' he said confidently.

'Yes, still *buongiorno* time now. Well done.'

They sat and he pulled the quote out of his top pocket.

'Okaaaay …' She smoothed her dress as she read down the list. If she was shocked at the cost, she didn't show it. He had been hoping for just a little sympathy perhaps. She got up and made a duplicate on a small copier and handed him back the original. 'OK.'

Franco came up from the back of the office, his phone to his ear. '*Sì, sì, sì … Bene. No. Bene. No. Bene.*' He put the phone in one of his jacket pockets, and spoke to Viviana; the only word Brian understood was '*Nuovo*'.

Franco left, presumably to lever the Mercedes out of the square and down the hill to Nuovo. He'd certainly get a smoother trip than in Father Dom's demented lawnmower.

'OK. I will transfer the deposit to Gaetano today. Your jobs will be on the list.' She pulled out an actual paper list and added his name with some hieroglyphics Brian couldn't make out. He did notice that he was halfway down the back of the fourth page. She put the copy of his quote in the folder and closed it. And with that, it seems business was over. 'OK.'

'Thank you, ahh, I wanted to ask you ...'

'Yes?' She raised two pleasantly curved eyebrows in query.

'Oh, before I ask. Umm, I made you this.' He lifted the loaf from the floor, unwrapped it and started to hand it over, but as he did so, it slipped from his hand. Now cooled, the loaf hit the desk like a granite boulder. Viviana flinched.

She picked it up. 'Is it ... bread?' She knocked on the crust. It made a hard dull sound like knuckles on a wine barrel.

'Yes, I just baked it.'

'OK.' She turned it over in her hands and snorted a tiny laugh through her nose.

'And I also wanted to ask you, ummm ... look, I'm not sure how ...'

'Wait,' she said, holding up the loaf. 'Shall we take it to lunch?'

* * *

Directly behind the café, on a street that Brian couldn't remember if he had gone down or not, was a tiny restaurant barely more than the width of the four small tables. There wasn't even a name on the front.

They entered, Viviana still carrying Brian's loaf of bread.

'Simone!' she called out. And to Brian, 'Maybe a little early.'

'Ahh, would that be *troppo presto*?' asked Brian, racking his brains, and again noticing how harsh his Australian accent sounded.

She looked at him approvingly. 'Yes. You seem very determined to speak the language. That's unusual for foreigners.'

'Err,' Brian tried to think. What was it? '*Tutti tranne me.*'

'Yes, all except you. Again, very good.'

'Maybe I should learn the local dialect?' said Brian, getting more enthusiastic. 'Talk like a Sicilian!'

Viviana opened her mouth, but struggled to find words to address this startling proposal. Finally, she laughed. 'As amusing as it would be to hear you try, nobody would speak to you in dialect. Not even a child. Ever.'

Brian felt a little crestfallen as Simone came out from behind the tiny bar stacked with onion boxes. '*Buongiorno, signora.*'

Without translating a word, Viviana launched into rapid Italian which Brian lost track of after half-a-dozen syllables. Conversation turned at the end to the misshapen bread, which Simone viewed with wide-eyed astonishment.

'*Per favore,*' said Viviana.

Simone took the loaf away with him. Moments later, laughter erupted from the kitchen.

They sat at the table closest to the window. The overhead sun just managed to slant in, laying a bright strip along the edge of their table and across the glossy carmine of Viviana's right fingernails. Brian felt ridiculously nervous. *You're not in high school!* Unwanted, the memory of meeting his ex came up. He'd needed the help of a couple of wingmen on that occasion, as well as the assistance of several draught lagers. He suppressed the memory.

'So?' asked Viviana.

Simone brought over two glasses and a bottle of sparkling water.

'Well. Now that I've got my work booked. I was down with some of the other expats on Saturday …'

'OK. And I assume now you want to have your job done before theirs?'

Brian wondered if this was an actual possibility, seeing as they were apparently getting on so well. Viviana's next utterance made it clear that it was not.

'Because that won't be happening. It would be chaos. If someone jumps the queue, everyone will be at each other's throats. Our job is to make sure that the one-euro scheme runs smoothly for the regional government. And while I'm running it, it will be done properly ...'

Well, that good mood vanished quickly!

'Understood, understood,' said Brian, palms down, placating.

'But if you can get someone to drive all the way from Agrigento or even Palermo every day, then good luck ...' she said finally.

'I heard there might be some Albanians who are willing to work?' Brian asked casually. He remembered the half comment by Robinson.

'Who did you hear that from? Albanians, in Montegiallo? Not often seen.'

'I forget. Obviously a mistake.'

Brian would have been absolutely fine jumping the queue, but he said, 'I'm not asking to jump the queue. That's really not what I meant. I was wondering, well, *they* were wondering, whether you could help speed up some of the work. Some of them have been waiting for a long time. Maybe there is something you could help with.'

'And they sent you?'

'Sort of.'

'OK.'

Simone came out with two bowls of *caponata*, and a plate which had slices of Brian's bread, olives, and olive oil. Simone said something to Viviana, which Brian couldn't translate, but the sawing motion he made with his hand was an obvious reference to the difficulty of cutting Brian's bread. He all but made the sound of a chainsaw.

Thinly sliced though, it was quite edible, even delicious. They both ate a piece without too much difficulty chewing. Brian tugged at a crust between his teeth like a bulldog with a rubber bone.

'Maybe it would be better to soak it,' he said, laying a piece in the vegetable stew.

'I don't know what they expect,' said Viviana, ignoring this. 'They just bark at people in English. Barely one of them tries a word of Italian.'

'Except me. *Tutti tranne me.*'

'Yes. All except you.' She was still annoyed.

'Two months ago, one of the Americans called up shouting at Gianni. He's just a quiet boy. The American asked if they wanted him to take his business elsewhere. Gianni said *sì*. The American then went to Agrigento and shouted at another plumber. Who told him to ... well, he told him a similar thing. They want budget work done as fast as possible, and don't want to be a real part of the community. The foreigners barely talk to an Italian from one week to the next.'

'Except for ...'

'Alright, except for you.' She regarded him closely. Brian wondered what she thought of it all: his dead man's suit, his blundering Italian, the New Brian persona. He tried to push back a little.

'You know, sometimes the Italians can be hard to talk to as well. Even *in* Italian,' said Brian.

'It's their town,' she said. 'We have seen foreigners come and go for centuries. Thousands of years. The English and Americans will be the same, so ...'

'I know, but, but, I barely get a response even in Italian,' Brian interrupted, and she frowned. 'For every ten *buongiornos* I say, I get maybe one grunt in reply. Maybe the foreigners are just intimidated?'

'What specifically did they actually want you to ask? We only coordinate the jobs for the town and the one-euro scheme. We can't force the builders or the plumbers or tilers. How long they take is up to their business.'

I wonder if a few cartons of Messinas would help, Brian thought, but said instead, 'Well it's pretty hilarious actually, *i contadini si ribellano* ...' Brian was attempting levity – in Italian – and then, seeing her face, wishing he hadn't.

'Did you say ..."the farmers are rebelling"?' she asked.

'Well, I was meaning to say "the peasants are revolting"—you know, in English, "revolting" has a double ...' he petered out, sighed. 'They had a petition ...'

'What?'

'And a list of demands, but ...'

'Where are they?'

'The list of demands?'

'Of course the demands, yes.'

'Oh, I set fire to them when I was baking the bread.'

For a moment he thought she was going to *balbettare*. But instead – after looking at him like he was an idiot – she just shook her head, stood up and left. Brian paid. Simone handed him back the rest of his loaf with a sad shake of his head.

As he left, there was laughter again from the kitchen.

Laying Low

The door – and velvet curtains – remained firmly closed at *Piazza Spirito Santo numero 5, 93014, Montegiallo (Agrigento), Italia*, for the rest of the week, as Brian kept well out of sight. He stayed completely away from the market area in case he saw any of the expats. He didn't want to be quizzed about progress on their list of demands. Nor did he particularly want to see Viviana. Things had been going so well until he had raised the subject of that stupid petition. Toby had called him a total plonker *again* after he told him the bread and Viviana story. Which was fair enough. It was true. He was a total plonker.

To really feel safe out of sight and out of mind, he even went down and started cleaning out the cellar, a job that he spread out over several days. It had the added advantage that he couldn't hear anyone knocking on the door. He finally realised that the stack of ornately curved metal piled down there was the remains of what had been his stair balustrade. The bases seemed to have broken off somehow. Brian scrabbled around and found the pieces that bolted to the stairs. They looked like they had broken from pure age. He would need someone who could weld. *These are not going to be my top priority.* He'd just have to try hard not to fall to his death. He filled several buckets almost to the top with sand after sweeping the floor, which he then mopped. The stone gleamed. He had hauled the buckets of sand upstairs and taken them around the corner to spread under the trees near the church like the ashes of dead relatives. When he got back the last time there was a note from Eric stuck to the door. 'Sorry I missed you.'

I'm not.

That was annoying. He would have liked to have sat on his balcony drinking a Messina and chewing on a crust of artist-anal, softened with olive oil and wild boar, but he'd be exposed to all and sundry out there.

He made sure the black velvet was still shut, and went slinking down to Bar Limone. Nobody he knew would see him there. Nobody he didn't know would see him there either. The place was basically empty for most of that Friday afternoon. Brian spent a couple of hours slowly sipping alternately beer and coffee, wondering about what he was going to do for money. He leafed through the *Personal Italian Grammar* and completed many of the exercises out of straight boredom, including a difficult one on the future conditional. A conditional future is exactly what he was experiencing.

Pola came and sat with him for a while between infrequent customers and Brian practised a few phrases on him. Finally the barman brought him another bowl of *caponata* unasked. 'Just beer and coffee, *dottore*? You need to eat too.' Maybe the man was finally warming to him.

'Dottore' is better than 'faaarkaara' any day.

'I'm not a doctor, by the way, Pola. I was a teacher.'

'I see you are an educated man.' He waved a hand at Brian's suit. 'You are an educated professional, then you are a *dottore* here in Italy. Almost anyone can be a *dottore*. Almost you finish kindergarten, you are already a *dottore*.'

'I didn't know that. There must be a lot of doctors in Italy.'

'Too many, *dottore*. But you a teacher? Then you are a *professore*.'

'I like *dottore* better than *professore*, I think. I'm sure my mother would have preferred it anyway.'

Pola shrugged. '*Dottore* is good. You certainly dress like a *dottore*.' He picked up Brian's grammar book. 'What is this?'

'Trying to learn.'

'This is too old.'

'Ahh, that's ah, *troppo vecchio*, yes?' said Brian.

'Even in a town like this, they wouldn't use Italian this old.'

'Can I ask you a question, Pola?'

'*Sì*, of course, *dottore*.'

'What happened to the Albanians?'

'Albanians?'

'Illegal workers. Labourers or builders or something?'

'Albanians are not often seen here, *dottore*. Up north, yes. Here you maybe get Tunisians, Libyans, Africans. But Albanians? No. Not seen here.'

And that appeared to be the end of the discussion.

As darkness fell, Brian asked Pola to check the *piazza* for foreigners for him. The barman opened the door and stuck his head out. 'No *faaarkaarza* out there, *dottore*.'

He was pleased at the man's change in attitude. Maybe because he had been almost the only paying customer all day. '*Grazie*, Pola.'

'*Prego*.'

The newly crowned *dottore* slipped out of the bar and, hugging the tree line, crept back to his own place. As he fumbled with the keys, he noticed that a light had been left on over the front door of the next house. The light illuminated the steps.

Steps which had been swept.

Toasted

Brian brewed coffee in his own kitchen on Saturday morning rather than going out for it. If he could avoid the expats all day, he could avoid the drinks session. Maybe they would just forget about him entirely. Eventually. They had no reason to come up the hill from Hell town. They wouldn't be dropping in for confession at a Catholic church, that's for sure.

The house next door made him very curious. Was he getting another one-euro friend up on the hill? Maybe they could start their own group. He warily parted the velvet a couple of centimetres and looked across to the balcony next door. Nothing looked different. The light was still on over the front door. Maybe it had always been on? No, he was sure he would have noticed before.

*And the steps have been swe*pt.

He decided to risk being spotted and go and have a look.

As he opened the front door, Eric was standing there, hand poised to knock. *God no*, Brian thought. In his other hand, Eric was holding a bottle wrapped in red paper. He had a big smile on his face.

'Briannnn!'

Less enthusiastically. 'Eriiiiiiic.'

'Just wanted to come and thank you. Haven't been able to catch you. Been around a couple of times.'

'Al ... right.'

'Can I come in?'

'Ahh, sure.'

They went in and sat down at the kitchen table. Eric handed him the wrapped bottle. 'Just a token of thanks from the committee.'

'Right. Thanks, but ...'

'We didn't hold out much hope with our petition to Viviana and Franco, but we got almost an immediate result! You must be a very – how can I put it politely – *persuasive speaker*.' Was the man winking at him?

'Eric, this is very much appreciated but ...'

'Just a bottle of red from the Grampians. Victoria.'

'Yes, I know where the Grampians are, Eric. But what I don't know is what you're talking about.'

'Oh, I assumed Viviana discussed it with you first?'

'No. What?'

'Oh, dear fellow, I'm sorry. I just assumed ... She said it was all because of you. The next day after your ah, tête-à-tête, Franco and Viviana came to see myself and Salina, having spoken to all the tradespeople. They said they would provide free accommodation for some extra workers to come up here for a few months. So another plumber, tiler and painters will be arriving soon to work with the firms up here. The One Euro Club is going to chip in a little for some extras, furniture and whatnot. Not you. We thought you'd done enough. Well done, old man.'

'Oh. Yes. No problem.'

'They'll still be well behind, but it should knock a few months off all our jobs. Your work should start much, much earlier in any case,' said Eric. 'Not sure where they have found for them to stay. But they are real estate agents after all, and no shortage of vacant places around here, what?'

'No shortage at all,' Brian agreed, and thought of the light shining next door.

Hardly Working

Brian was itching to update Toby on these dramatic developments. He flipped open the laptop and clicked on the messenger program. What would it be? Early Saturday evening.

Hold on. Wait.

He hadn't been able to process things properly himself. What did it all mean? Viviana had left their meeting on what had been their usual terms: that is, he, Brian, saying something idiotic, and she, Viviana, looking at him like the idiot that he had just been. But maybe he had been a smarter idiot than he thought? This would definitely need Toby's input. But no, he would leave that until he could see Viviana again and judge the reaction in person. Maybe after the church service, if she showed.

Putting the Viviana situation aside for a moment, he thought about more practical matters. On the one hand, bringing forward the plumbing work was a very good result. But Brian couldn't help an ominous feeling rising in his stomach. That would also bring forward the time when he would have little money. And bring forward the time when he would have to do something about it. His Italian wasn't good enough to do anything practical or professional with it beyond ordering a wine or coffee. So it would need to be something in English.

Or no language at all. The fact that he hadn't completely ruled out mute lemon picking was an indication of how desperate things would become in a few months.

Brian had been using getting his bidet fixed as a yardstick for success, but it would be no good having a sparkling backside if the top half of his body was living in poverty. Despite himself, he felt a moment's sympathy for Murray and Salina. Their missing water feature was the same as his broken bidet: a symbol of failure and a constant reminder of the trap they were caught in.

Putting aside the fact that he wasn't allowed to work anyway, the only thing he knew he was good at was teaching children English. New Brian didn't want to teach children English. That was soooo Old Brian. And would it even be possible? He realised he hadn't even seen a school up on the hill. There must be something, because he had seen children, the unruly Carlo for instance. He'd ask Father Dom. Probably there were a thousand government regulations and forms to be able to teach English in schools. And although – from all reports of Sicilians so far – he assumed there were a thousand and one methods for getting around said government regulations, those would not be open to him. Could he get his visa changed? Would he even be allowed to teach with his 1965 Italian? And a non-EU citizenship? Doubtful. What about adults? Private tutoring? He tried to imagine Pola gagging to learn the use of the subjunctive. Or even trying to iron out that rolling accent. You'd need a crowbar to get an Italian to let go of that last syllable without adding half a dozen vowels. But maybe. That's all he could think of at the moment.

Would things get so desperate that he would have to try and write? He remembered his joke on the plane about penning a bloke's version of *Eat Pray Love* and *The Joy Luck Club*. He was doubtful about his prospects. English teachers automatically assumed they could write bestsellers if they could be bothered lowering themselves to try. They couldn't. Teaching English and writing English were not the same skills. He had known several teachers who had boasted about starting books. You learned not to ask about progress on their manuscripts after a few months.

He took the laptop out to the balcony. What would it take? He was always telling his Year Elevens and Twelves to try writing like Hemingway, spare, direct and without embellishment. Although Brian's unspoken, unpopular opinion was that Hemingway threw in way too many 'ands'. He looked over the *piazza* and tried typing a couple of clichéd sentences in the style of Papa H.

> The figure in the square shuffled between ovals of light and shade and proceeded – on shoes once black – with a certain dignity of movement. Bags hung from shoulders long used to the burden.

Trouble was, Piazza Spirito Santo refused to conform to any kind of bare Hemingway prose, although, to be honest, the sun *was* also rising. The leaves of the trees still looked squeezed from a tube of emerald oil paint. The gnarled roots, stubbornly, continued to resemble nothing but demon elbows emerging from the underworld. Rosa – he gave her his usual wave – rolled along like a clown on a circus bike, shoulders not troubled in the slightest by the weight of Father Dominic's shopping.

How would the old misogynist have described Viviana?

> The woman entered, put her real estate catalogue on the table and one hand on her hip.
> 'Isn't love boring?'
> 'Yes,' said the Australian. 'Shall we drink beer?'

Bleh. According to the Hemingway writers' wisdom photocopies he had distributed to his senior class, you were supposed to get more from what wasn't on the page than what was written. But how would you get from that, her eyes were dark mocking pools? Nope. He erased his novel, also in the style of Hemingway.

He put determined pressure on the backspace and erased without sentiment and without pity. The morning mist on the plain was gone and his eyes were already turned away and his chin lifted to the horizon.

Jeezus. Imagine writing seventy thousand words of that crap.

Mentally, Brian put 'write a book' below 'lemon picking' as an option. Instead of writing Hemingway, he decided to write to Toby about the Viviana situation, and his fingers flexed over the keyboard. Again he hesitated.

No. He closed the laptop, filled his trolley with shirts and underwear, so that he would have something to wear to church the next day and took off for the laundromat. He was also – surprise, surprise – actually looking forward to the expats drinks that night. Why not do a little basking in the sunlight of his possibly undeserved reputation? But no, wait.

'Of course I deserve it!'

He had taken on a Devil Woman, and a Devil Woman had seen the error of her ways. Yes, he definitely deserved to soak up some expat kudos tonight. He'd also pump them for any info about teaching or paid work.

The neighbour's door was open. Brian stuck his head inside and *buongiorno*-ed hesitantly, then gave it a 'Hello!' with feeling. His voice echoed through a smaller version of his own hallway. He could hear two people in dramatic argument, followed by music. A radio. Radio in Italy only had dramatic conversations. There was no other kind. He banged on the inside of the door, but there was no response.

A Basking Case

He had, he admitted as he lay in bed, snoozing and re-snoozing the phone alarm, over-celebrated a little with the expats the night before, this time at Lars and Susan's on Via Roma. No need to look that one up. Even Murray would know what 'Roma' was. *Hopefully.* Brian was somewhat of a temporary local hero, which was heartening considering his misgivings after taking that petition. He didn't mention he had burnt it. Very difficult to explain exactly why to them. Not sure they would understand St Matthew's influence on the whole thing.

There were many expat pats on the back. Many refills of wine. He hoped this didn't mean any more quests or tasks were going to be thrust upon him. He'd deal with that situation when it came. He'd be more than ready to parry them away next time and was determined to simply live on his enhanced reputation for as long as possible.

None of them had seen much hope in the employment situation, unfortunately. Most of the Brits were living off inadequate pensions of some kind. The Americans had investments of ever-increasing tediosity which they all wanted to tell him about, but his ears had quickly glazed over. Couldn't be that good investments if they were reduced to a one-euro home in the Sicilian sticks.

Alarmingly, Robinson and Peter were planning to get back into crypto and offered to take Brian on that journey with them. Just needed an investment of five thousand. That sounded like a very bad idea. It was the cost of fixing several toilets! Peter, he had noticed, was wearing the camouflage pants. They didn't look so bad. Well maybe they did. Now Brian was a cravat wearer, he could afford to be a little more fashion critical perhaps.

There was little hope of government work in any school unless he had been invited by a school and had the appropriate visa before coming. His visa specifically didn't allow him to work, but he had assumed he could change it. This was greeted with scepticism from all concerned. Sicilians had been expertly avoiding tax since Norman days, so there was much more chance in getting cash work, especially with the authorities so far away down the hill.

* * *

He wanted, for a change, to be at the church before the service started this Sunday. He denied himself a fourth re-snooze and got up. He was doing up his tie when the bells started ringing, so was easily at the church door before the mass kicked off.

He could have taken a seat closer to the front this time. Most of the other worshippers filed in well after him. But he didn't want to take anybody's favourite pew, if that was a thing. Probably was. He imagined the story in the English language news. 'Australian who took Sicilian's seat in church, found minus genitals.' In any case, an atheist's place was probably in the back row. He checked his phone for the time.

Five minutes to go, and no Messinas. But just as the bells stopped ringing, both Franco and Viviana walked in, finishing a whispered conversation. Viviana didn't catch Brian's eye and the pair continued almost up to the front, where a space had been left for them. Same spot as last time. Of course.

Father Dom, as usual, looked twice the normal size in his robes as he came out with a serious smile for the congregation. That was probably the intent. Like the Pope's big hat. Show who's boss. The shape, Brian thought, was a little like a giant *scarafaggio*, but he wasn't going to mention that. He wasn't following the proceedings that closely, wasting a little too much time taking in the back of Viviana's beautifully styled head and neck, and so missed a couple of the kneeling and standing cues. Still standing while the rest of the congregation was kneeling made it look like he was making an objection to a marriage.

Brian dropped just one euro in the begging box and left the church before getting the all clear to go in peace. If he hadn't given up smoking a decade before, he would have lit one now as he waited nervously outside. The rest of the congregation left slowly. Brian was plucking up courage to go to speak to Viviana, but instead she and Franco came right up to him.

'*Signore, signora*,' said Brian.

Franco, from the waist up, was as formally dressed as Brian. Sports jacket, white shirt and knitted tie. Below the belt were fancy black jeans and loafers. Viviana, her hair up again, had a shot-silk dress belted at the waist that shimmered between blue and green in the sun.

Without yet having shed his outer carapace, Father Dom emerged from the back door of the church. He saw the trio and raised his hand lightly to Franco. Franco returned the salute and left them.

'*Scusatemi ...*'

'Ahh,' said Brian to Viviana. 'I wanted to thank you for your efforts with the tradespeople ...'

She sighed. 'After I left, I was thinking about what you said. Maybe it is true. Maybe the Sicilians should be making a little more effort as well. Not that the *americani* and *inglesi* really deserve it, but you have been trying so hard, and for you—I mean, for your effort to speak Italian,' she corrected herself, 'I thought there may be a way to speed things up just a little. If a real estate agent can't find some accommodation, then who can?'

'Ahh, *molto generosi*.'

'*Grazie*. It certainly wasn't for your bread-making. Simone is still talking about it.'

'Don't be too critical. I'm using the crusts to re-tile the cellar floor.' For a fraction of a second her face was about to take on the familiar look of a person frowning at an idiot, but it stopped in mid formation.

'Yes.' She smiled. 'Very good.'

Franco returned to join them and pushed his thumbs into his belt. Brian had the impression he was not completely overjoyed that his daughter was still talking to him.

'Oh, and this free accommodation for the new painters and plumbers,' Brian continued regardless, 'Umm, *loro sono il mio vicini? My neighbours?'*

'*I miei vicini.* Not *mio*. They are your plural neighbours after all. And yes, they are next door to you. Have you seen them yet? Start work down the hill during the week.'

'Oh yes of course.' *Damn those plurals.* 'It will be good to have some new faces in the *piazza*.'

Viviana spoke to Franco. It was either too fast, or too dialect. In any case, Brian understood not a word. Franco unbuttoned his jacket with one big hand and simply said, '*Sì.*'

'*Buongiorno, signore.*'

'*Signor* Messina. *Signora.*'

They walked away down the hill. He must find out where they – she – lived. He must have walked past the place at some stage. Unless they too lived down in Nuovo. That was a thought. He hoped not. *Why don't we see what we can get out of the Lord's representative in Montegiallo? He's got to know at least something for my one-euro investment!*

The Bins of the Father

Brian found himself roped into several minor chores after following Father Dom back to his modest flat behind the church after mass. *Unpaid work. That's just what I need. It's not as if the man was ninety. Should be able to manage the bloody bins himself!* But the priest had been generous to him, and in the end, Brian was happy to do it. Plus he wanted to ask him a few questions.

Finally the coffee maker was bubbling on the small electric stove.

'Thank you for that. Rosa has had to visit her mother in Palermo today. I forget how much she does for me.'

'Happy to help.' Brian wondered how much Rosa got paid. *Maybe I could undercut her?* 'Oh, by the way, were you being my wingman earlier?' he joked.

'Wingman? It's not a term I am familiar with.'

'When you called over Franco Messina. Very subtly done.'

Dom stared at him. 'I really don't know what you mean. Franco will be generously helping out with the Festival of the Madonna again later in the year. We needed to discuss some of the details. Wing ... man? I don't ...'

Brian could hardly say, 'You know when you are out on the town chasing women, Father, and you get your friend to help, by distracting *her* friend, or to sing your praises to her while you're in the dunnies?' Besides, Brian had the feeling maybe the priest knew exactly what he was talking about. He did not elaborate further.

'Why is Viviana even allowed in the church?'

'What? What do you mean allowed?' The priest was obviously confused by this change of tack.

'Divorced, isn't she? I thought we went direct to Hell with the Protestants?'

'Oh, no. The Holy Father, in fact several Holy Fathers, have made it clear that divorce, or even living in sin as it is unfortunately termed, is not a barrier to taking the sacraments.' Brian had really been fishing more for information about Viviana rather than the ins and outs of sacrament taking. He tried another angle.

'They live up here, Father? In the old town?'

'The Messinas? The old family home is up here of course.'

But where exactly?

'Franco and his wife have a new apartment down in Nuovo. He spends his time between both locations. *Signora* Messina is not often seen up here. She prefers the mass in Nuovo. There were plans to move the office down the hill as well, but this one-euro business keeps Franco and Viviana so busy up here, those plans have been put on hold. Viviana lives up here permanently. Not far from you, actually. But everyone is in everyone else's pockets up here. Above Simone's restaurant.'

Right. Brian turned to the question of paid employment.

'I've seen a few children around up here,' he said, 'but I haven't seen a school. Have I missed it?'

'Most of the school-age children now live in Nuovo. Those left in the old town are bussed down in the morning. In fact, I volunteer to drive the minibus myself once a week on Wednesdays, when I do the religious instruction classes down there.'

Brian suddenly imagined the terrified screams of school children and frightened little faces at the windows as Father Dom performed racing gear changes down the hairpins in a school bus. Wait, they probably loved it. Highlight of their week more likely. Have to be more exciting than the religious instruction classes.

'They still do that? Teach religion in school?'

'They still do, of course!' said the priest. 'But,' he admitted, 'optional now.'

'Wow.' Brian realised his surprise sounded a little rude, so moved onto the subject of getting paid for something. He asked about the possibility of teaching English at the school. The priest frowned. Like the expats, he was doubtful that Brian could get the paperwork through the clogged government channels. 'And your Italian is…'

'*Sì.*'

'Yes.'

'But they do learn English at school in Italy?'

'Of course. Even in kindergarten sometimes. The teacher in Nuovo is *Signora* La Rosa.'

'How is her English?'

'Excellent. Better than yours!' Father Dom gave a deep laugh.

Brian produced one of his thin smiles.

'Further north they might have a choice of German or French. But English is the most popular here. Everywhere.'

Of course it was. The thought of a bronzed, rural Sicilian speaking German didn't really compute for Brian. But what would he know? Australian schools had been steadily dropping language classes from the curriculum since Mrs Calalesina's days. They'd been steadily dropping religion too, so it wasn't all bad news.

'Maybe you could get some unofficial private tutoring work for a student who was struggling. Or failing…' The priest was still doubtful.

Brian was instantly depressed at the thought of teaching the worst student in the school. Especially when the cursed child's English was probably way better than his own shitty and antiquated Italian.

Bleh.

But it might be the only option in the end.

'What about the adults, if they supposedly all learned in school? There's many who don't speak much English at all. No English, some of them.'

'Probably the same ones who were failing at school in their own day.'

'Right.' Even so, Brian would much rather teach adults than children. 'Your English is the best in town, Father. Where did you learn it?'

'Same place I learned Latin, of course. Rome.'

'*Quo vadis?*' was the only Latin phrase Brian knew, so he left it at that. He didn't know the answer to the question anyway.

The *Vicini*

The van, maybe the same one that came to his own *palazzo*, arrived next door on Monday at about an hour after *buongiorno* turned to *buonasera*. He still couldn't work out how it got up the narrow streets. Two men, possibly the same two, unloaded more plastic-wrapped furniture. He wondered if the new neighbours would have to carry their mattresses upstairs themselves. *Unless you've got a carton of beer, you may have to.*

No sign of the actual *vicini* so far though.

Brian had decided, despite the discouraging signs, to at least try to get some of the adults up the hill interested in conversational English lessons. Before the last resort of teaching child dunces. He almost wished he'd bought a printer down in Agrigento. But he remembered the tobacconist had a copier. He composed a flyer on his laptop. 'SPEAK ENGLISH LIKE A PRO!' The *Personal Italian Grammar* couldn't help much with the composition, so he tried the online translator and hoped for the best. 'PARLA INGLESE COME UN PROFESSIONISTA! CON IL DOTTOR BRIAN!'

Now. What kind of image will suggest a professional English speaker to an Italian? He had an idea. He put the Italian phrase rather than the English one into the image search. Union Jacks. Plenty of them. 'Gag. No.' Absolutely not. Graphics of women throwing around furniture and laptops were popular. *No idea what that's about.* Why would an ability to juggle furniture suggest English fluency? The dominant images that came up besides these were serious-looking men in suits and open-neck shirts holding up one finger in front of open laptops.

They look like more prosperous versions of myself, he thought.

In that case, might as well be a picture of me.

So he checked his tie in the phone camera and composed a shot with his laptop open in the background. Had to have a laptop open to teach English apparently. In the photo, his raised finger had the suggestion more of a proctologist than a teacher. He made two more attempts which were worse. He was only lacking a surgical glove. *Right.*

The result in total was, to be honest, mixed. A man in an old-fashioned suit seemed to be offering to teach English – or examine a prostate – in an ill-lit cave. Well, until Gaetano rewired the place, the lighting was going to have to remain somewhat intimate. It had a sort of appeal, he guessed. It would have to do anyway. He put the result onto a USB, walked down to the marketplace and tried to get prints out of the copier with the help of the elderly proprietor. This guy could do with a few lessons, thought Brian. He didn't seem to have a single word of English. *Class dunce, 1950?*

The image came out stretched to fit the A4 page, for some reason, which made Brian a little thinner and taller. And weirder. But he really couldn't be bothered walking all the way back up and down the hill to reformat it.

'*Venti, per favore.*' He flashed ten fingers twice to make sure the man got the message, making sure he hadn't ordered two hundred. That would be overly optimistic at this stage of proceedings. 'No. Twenty? Great.' He thought about giving the man one for himself. *Maybe that would be a little rude?*

Now. Where was he going to put them? First step maybe try them out that night at Bar Limone.

When he got back home, he went out onto the balcony, with his laptop, a glass and a bottle of the fizzy Italian mineral water he was getting addicted to. He liked the tap water in Montegiallo, but he realised he hadn't even asked anyone if you *should* drink it. Would it be racist to look that up? Come on, wait. Of course it was safe. Italy was a modern advanced country. However, he did wonder whether the ancient plumbing was doing justice to healthy mountain drinking water. He guessed he would have to wait months to find out. Maybe the taste would be *worse* from new pipes. Caligula's plumbing could be giving the water its fine character?

Something else to ponder.

So. What was it? 11 pm? Midnight in Melbourne? He wouldn't message Toby on a school night at that time. An email would do. He began, 'Devil Woman …' Maybe time to stop that. He erased it. 'Promising developments re Viviana situation. Stop. Will consult at your convenience. Stop.'

He closed the lid, took a swig of mineral water straight from the bottle and let out a small burp. His phone pinged. Text from Toby with a line of thumbs-up symbols.

Italian, subdued at first, burst onto the balcony next door, which was about a third the size of Brian's. Two Italian men, late twenties. Designer jeans torn perfectly at the knees and distressed at the thighs. Both t-shirts celebrated motor sports. Their bare feet were worn somehow as a fashion statement. If Brian had bare feet, it would just look like he was too lazy to put on shoes. *Italian sprezzatura, I guess.* Cigarettes and beers completed the look.

Brian got up. Restricting his speech to barely a single word, he tried again to be mistaken, however briefly, for a local.

'… *giorno*'.

'Hi there,' said one, in clean but accented English.

'You are Brian?' asked the other, struggling a little with a name that didn't end in a, e, i or o. Brian ended up sounding a little like Brianna.

'L'australiano?'

'Si.'

'*Signor* Messina told us ... We are Andrea, and Salvo. We are the ...' they put their heads together. 'Extra plumb and tiler.'

'It is good to see you here. Andrea, you can't weld by any chance?'

'Welt?' he asked.

'Weld.' Nope. Not in his vocab. 'Wait a second,' said Brian. He went back into his bedroom. The grammar didn't have weld either. He stepped back out and queried the phone. The results were ambiguous.

'*Saldare? Sa saldare?*'

The men put their heads together again. '*Certo*. Why?'

Hmm. Interesting, thought Brian. 'No reason.'

A raised woman's voice inside the house got their attention. The men waved their beers at him. '*Ciao*, Brianna.'

The *Dottore*

Brian took a deep breath at the dark and dusty door of Bar Limone that night. He had a fistful of flyers in hand, and the rest in his bag. Four would have been sufficient. That was the extent of the patronage. Giuseppe, who he recognised, seemed to exist solely on *caponata* and beer. A woman, possibly a wife, was across from him, and another elderly gent in a moth-eaten grey fedora sat alone at the corner table. One of either Akil or Taysir completed the crowd. How did Pola ever make any money? Whatever cash he did make was not being spent on the interior of Bar Limone, that was for sure. Or the exterior to be honest.

The man himself greeted Brian from behind the bar with a quiet '*Buonasera, dottore. Birra o vino?*'

'*Birra, grazie.* Umm, I was wondering if I could leave a few of these around, Pola?' He handed the barman one of the flyers. He took out the rest of the stack of twenty from his bag.

Pola looked at it, then at Brian. 'Is this supposed to be you, *dottore*?' Without waiting for an answer, he looked around the almost deserted room and added, 'You can try.'

'Giuseppe's wife?'

'*Sì*. Maria.'

Brian first laid out some flyers on the empty tables. He stopped in front of Giuseppe and Maria. They didn't really look like candidates for English lessons. Giuseppe had barely spoken a word, even in Italian, as far as Brian could remember. The old man in the corner looked ready to croak any moment. If he didn't speak English already, was it really worth wasting what was left of his life learning it? But Brian was determined to go through with it. They might know someone who needed the services of *Dottor* Brian, at least.

'*Buonasera*, Giuseppe, Maria.'

He put a flyer in front of Giuseppe who looked at it as if he'd been handed his own death warrant. Maria squinted at the absurd photo of Brian holding up one finger, and whispered, '*Grazie*,' into her glass of wine. The North African turned out to be Taysir, who was a Tunisian. He took a flyer with a terse nod.

Brian moved onto the old man who was nursing a very small beer. Brian gave him his most cheerful *buonasera* and handed him the piece of paper which he took with a trembling hand. He stared at it for a very long time. He then slapped it down on the table and let out a long and loud stream of dialect of which maybe the words '*inglesi*' and '*americani*' could be discerned. Brian was not expecting this. He took an involuntary step backwards. The old man screwed up the paper and threw it on the floor at Brian's feet. Giuseppe and the woman loudly replied to the man in equally incomprehensible dialect. Pola called out to him in his deep rumble as well, which calmed him down a little. Brian picked up the flyer from the dusty terracotta.

'*Mi scusi*,' he apologised to the crown of the fedora. He returned to the bar and sat in front of Pola. He smoothed out his flyer with a sigh.

'Do not be discouraged, *dottore*. Perhaps they are not your ideal students?'

'What did he say? I didn't catch any of it.'

'Well,' said Pola, slightly embarrassed, 'it is maybe too difficult to translate literally,' he lied, 'but in general he was saying that all the English and Americans are *faaarkaarza*.'

'Why such strong feelings?'

'Why? It's always the same when someone new comes. The same

everywhere, no? Probably the same where you come from, *dottore*. Been like that for a thousand years here. Two or three thousand. Greeks, Normans, Tunisians, even Germans for a short while. And these particular *faaarkaarza* the English and Americans, are not good. He says you don't even *want* to belong.'

Suddenly some of the frustrations and anger of the last months finally surfaced for Brian – the divorce, the shit settlement, the plumbing, the electrics, not winning Teacher of the Year – everything. Being lumped in as English or American was absolutely the final straw. 'I'm NOT American or English!' said Brian, loudly. 'I'm Australian. There's a huuuuuuuuge difference!'

'Still unfortunately the same as an American *faaarkaara* in his eyes, *dottore*, I'm sorry,' said Pola. He looked truly apologetic.

Brian raised his voice again. 'And, by the way, it's not *faaarkaara*. It's fucker! It's fu, fu, FUCKER! Not *faaa, faaa, faaarkaara*. The English are FUCKERS. The Americans are FUCKERS. I'm a fucker, you're a fucker, we are all fuckers! There is no *faaarkaarza*.'

The bar went silent. Which was pretty much its usual state, but this time, it was a very different kind of silence. They all stared at him.

'Ahhh, I'm sorry, Pola, I just … Everything has just been …'

The man stared down at him. A Sicilian of this size was probably not the right man to be shouting at. He could fold Brian in half and use him as a bar rag if he ever decided to start cleaning this hole.

Pola opened his mouth but then closed it. He took a deep breath and said, 'Faarka.'

'I know,' said Brian, 'it was completely unacceptable for me to take it out on you. Please accept my apologies, Pola.'

'No,' said Pola. '*Faaarkaara*: how do I say it?'

'Oh, ahh. Don't worry. You can say it how you want, I was just …'

'No,' said Pola. 'If I'm calling someone a *faaarkaara* in English, I want the *faaarkaara* to understand it.'

'Oh, alright then, umm. It's a short u. Uh, uh, uh.'

The Montegiallo School of Swearing

'Ahhhra, ahhhra, ahhhra,' said Pola.

'Uh.'

'Ahhhra.'

'Uh.'

'Ahhr.'

'Uh, uh, uh.'

'Ahr, ahr, ahr.'

'Getting closer. Wait. First, beer.' Brian drained the rest of his glass.

Pola filled it from the tap, waving away his card as he attempted to pay. 'And you,' said Brian. Pola pulled another glass from under the bar, filled it with beer, and drained it in one gulp. 'Ahhh. Farka,' he attempted it again with a slight burp.

'That's it. Getting there!'

Giuseppe and Maria came up to the bar and started yammering at Pola in dialect. This time Brian understood most of it because they were both obviously giving him advice about his pronunciation. Incorrectly. Each time worse than the last. 'No! Ahhh, ahhh, ahhh,' said Giuseppe. 'Urrra, urrrra, urrrra,' said Maria, with a flourish of one arm.

Now the old man came over wagging his finger. 'No, no, no: faaarg, faaarg, faarg,' he said. There was now a ring of people around the bar, barking at Pola. 'Furrka, forrrka, faaaaga.' His head turned from one to another. The African also weighed in. His French accent did not improve things.

'Is fargair,' he said.

'Faaargaza,' said the old man.

'No, no, furrraka,' said Maria.

'Forrrka,' insisted Giuseppe.

Pola tried to follow this advice with little success. 'Faggarza?'

Brian did not need the grammar book for this.

'*Silenzio!*' he shouted. They all stopped.

'OK, *allora. Tutti*, everyone.' Brian had an idea. Now he did need the grammar book's dictionary. 'OK, wait.' What was to cough? '*Tossire*'. Really? Didn't sound right. Guess it must be.

'Alright. Everyone cough. *Tutti, tossite!*' Nobody made a sound. Brian demonstrated with a very short cough. 'Uh. Everyone, after me. Uh.' The group coughed quietly. Brian stepped up the volume. 'Uh, uh, uh.' They all followed him. '*Bene, bene, bene.*' Brian hoped this wasn't going to kill the old man. Every cough might be his last.

'Now, like this. Fff, (cough), ka. Slowly.'

They all followed him. 'Ff, (cough), ka.'

'Fucking beautiful,' said Brian with both thumbs up. 'Now let's put it together.

'Fff, uh, ka – fucker. Fff, uh, ka – fucker,' went Brian.

'Fff, uh, ka – fucker. Fff, uh, ka – fucker,' they replied.

'Fucker, fucker, fucker!' called Brian.

'Fucker, fucker, fucker!' shouted back the patrons.

'*Birra* and *vino*, Pola. Quickly!' Brian waved his fingers at the other 'students'. The barman poured out more glasses. All off them threw back their alcohol between chants.

'You fucker!' Brian shouted, pointing at Pola.

'You fucker!' the barman pointed back.

'You fucker!' to Maria.

'You fucker!' she pointed back.

'You fucker! You fucker! You fucker!' Point, point, point.

'You fucker!' 'You fucker!' 'You fucker!' All five of them pointed back at Brian in unison.

Brian mopped his brow with a napkin from the bar and took another mouthful of beer. They were all breathing heavily. '*Molto bene*, everyone,' he panted. 'Very good.'

'Now this is the English you should be teaching, *dottore*,' said Pola. 'People are only interested in the swearwords in any new language.'

'Well, if used only as a guide to pronunciation, I guess it could be useful,' said Brian doubtfully. *What am I talking about?*

They did more rounds of drinks and more rounds of 'fuckers'. Brian felt his frustrations begin to melt away with the satisfaction of being able to call them 'Sicilian fuckers' at the top of his voice. And they in turn were revelling in calling him an 'Aussie fucker', too. Brian even threw 'Tunisian fucker' into the mix and Taysir replied with gusto.

'You Italian fuckers!'

'You Aussie fucker!'

'Tunisian fucker!'

'Aussie fucker!' Brian had switched from beer to wine, but hadn't realised that he was slurping down the *vino* at the same rate. He stood and faced them all, and the alcohol started to put a little harder edge to his profanity. 'You fucken Sicilian fuckers! All of you!'

From the look on Pola's face, Brian realised he was getting a little too enthusiastic. 'Ahh, *dottore*...' They were pretty well all exhausted anyway so the barman brought the lesson to an end.

The customers made to leave. The old man clapped Brian's shoulder with his leathery, bony fingers.

'*Buonasera*,' he said, looking into Brian's face. 'Fucker,' he added. He reached past and took the crumpled flyer Brian had smoothed out and then chuckled all the way to the exit.

Pola beat the man to the door, and Brian could see he was holding a small glass jar. He waggled it at the old man.

'*Per il dottore*,' said Pola, tilting his head to Brian. The man, still laughing, dropped in a couple of coins. '*Grazie, grazie*.' Taysir did the same.

'Umm,' said Brian, 'I'm not sure that we should be...'

'Fucker, fucker, fucker,' laughed Giuseppe, swearing powerfully at the ceiling beams.

'Fucker, fucker, fucker,' shouted Maria, spreading her arms wide to the room. They also dropped coins into the jar and were both taking away a flyer.

Right, thought Brian, and frowned.

Pola, however, was grinning like a madman and shaking the jar, which rang with the sound of one-euro coins. As Pola poured them into his hand, Brian saw that it was six times what he had paid for his house.

'With this maybe I could buy the whole fucking *piazza*,' crowed Brian.

'Maybe you need some sleep first, *dottore*.'

After Class

Brian made his way back across the dark *piazza*, his sweat-covered forehead chilled by the breeze. He closed his front door behind him and leaned back on it. What had just happened? He moved through to the kitchen and also quizzed Skeletor on top of INDES.

'What the actual fuck was that, old mate?'

He was tired, but he was way too wound up to sleep. He couldn't really process the speed of what had happened. In the space of five minutes, the crowd had turned from indifference and even hostility to enthusiastic paying customers, belting out correct English pronunciation. The fact that they were pronouncing 'fucker' correctly was *perhaps* not the point. Brian jangled the coins in his pocket. He felt he had had a real teaching workout. He hadn't had such an enthusiastic class since the Year Elevens had finally realised that the King was having a red-hot poker shoved up his arse in Marlowe's play *Edward II*. *How tedious Marlowe is, arse-pokering notwithstanding.*

He was beginning to think he really had deserved that Teacher of the Year nomination. Turning hostile students into *Good Will Fucking Hunting* – or was he thinking of *Dead Fucking Poets Society?* – was not something just anyone could do, was it? And even the Viviana situation was showing some promise, wasn't it?

Weariness suddenly dropped on Brian like a curtain.

The Morning After

Brian slept late in the soft, velvet darkness of his room. After the debacle involved in purchasing the house, he had promised himself to ease up on the drinking. 'Errk.' The enthusiasm of the night before had evaporated. He had made a total fool of himself at Bar Limone, hadn't he? He cringed at the memory of screaming at the Sicilians – oh God, and a Tunisian – and calling them all fuckers. What had possessed him? He was grateful for the darkness. He got up and went into the bathroom without turning on the light. He wasn't quite ready for green-and-red tiling. He splashed some water on his face, then, leaving it running, bent down and drank straight from the ancient tap.

He went downstairs one step at a time, keeping one palm on the wall.

They'll find my broken body at the bottom of these steps one day. Who would 'they' be though? Nobody would miss me for weeks.

He sat in front of his laptop. It was time to talk to Toby about this. As he opened the browser, there was a banner ad for travel. First a bear, advertising a North American cruise. Then a giraffe for Africa, and finally a kangaroo. He felt sick and lonely in his dark stone cave. He hovered the cursor over the kangaroo. He could still afford a flight back... 'Nope.' He resisted that urge to click. He'd already made the decision to stay. 'That's it.'

Toby, via his small square of laptop-screen real estate, was less interested in what had happened at Bar Limone than what was going on with Viviana.

'You swore at some Sicilians and they swore back. One all. Who gives a shit? *Cherches* the fucken *femme*, mate. The woman's into you. Get one of those eight bedrooms cleaned up. You're on.'

'I'm not sure.'

'Are you kidding? She hates the whole load of Poms and Yanks, but drops everything just for you?'

'It's my willingness to be part of the community, I think. I'm pretty much the only foreigner to have bothered to speak a word of Italian. Probably nothing more to it than that.'

'Jeezarse, Brian mate. What is wrong with you? Part of the community? Listen, you total fucken plonker. The goal's wide open! You just need to tap it into the back of the net without falling on your arse. God, I wish I could be over there as wingman, to stop you launching into any of that goat dying under the ledge stuff. Real romance killer.'

Brian didn't see the sense in telling Toby that a priest had recently played the wingman role. 'We'll see.'

'Try the bread again. That was a good idea.'

'Talk to you soon, Toby.'

Brian had gone back upstairs, fully intending to go back to bed, but the iron ring in the lion's mouth on the front door began pounding. He glanced at the time on his phone. Twenty past ten. He went out onto the balcony in his underwear, pausing before he stepped out, to scratch his backside.

'Good morning, *dottore*,' came a loud voice from below. There was a pause. 'You ... fucker!'

'Errr. Pola. What?' He wished the man would keep his voice down.

'I was about to throw stones at your window, *dottore*.'

'Wait.'

Without bothering to put on any more clothing, Brian walked downstairs and opened the door. The man filled the entrance space. He came in, looking around.

'You've really cleaned up this fucker,' said Pola, poking his head through the arch.

'Yes. And I see your pronunciation is still good.' Brian led him into the kitchen, handed him the packet of coffee and the coffee maker, and without another word, went up, had a shower, and got dressed.

When he came down, the coffee was bubbling and Pola was looking through a *Pussycat*.

'This filth is as old-fashioned as your Italian, *dottore*. But I'm beginning to think that old-fashioned suits you.' Pola took in Brian's shirt-and-tie combo. Brian flicked over the *Pussycat* to check the cover. 'Oh, yes. This is the moustache man and the two nurses.' He got two cups and poured the coffee. 'So, Pola. I want to apologise for last night.'

'*Dottore?*' Pola reluctantly closed the *Pussycat*. 'Apologise for what? I came here to ask you when you will do your next lesson.'

Brian goggled at him. 'What next lesson?'

'Maria came in this morning asking. She and Giuseppe want to sign up. They had the time of their lives.' Pola lowered his voice. 'And, *dottore*, she said that afterwards, Giuseppe was like a man twenty years younger, if you know what I mean?'

'I very much hope that I don't.'

'They have told their friends. Two that I know from Nuovo will come too.'

Brian checked his phone, still a little bewildered. 'Nobody has contacted me for a class.'

'Well, *dottore*, they did not feel confident enough to contact you directly, so they asked me to find out when the next one will be.'

'Giuseppe, his wife Maria and your friends want English lessons? After that nonsense last night? That's great. I wasn't expecting pupils so soon! We could start with some basic conversation. Slowly add a little grammar. It's the spelling that catches many second-language students out …'

'Oh, *dottore*, maybe you misunderstand me. They don't want English lessons exactly. Just the swearing part.'

'Ahhh. What?'

'Only the *parolacce*, the ahh what is it called? The profanity, *sì*?'

'Yes, but ... So, swearing-only lessons?'

'*Sì.*'

'No grammar, no spelling?'

'No. *Assolutamente no.*'

Brian sat in stunned silence for a moment. 'I'll have to think about it,' he stammered.

'I hope *Dottor* Brian won't disappoint them.'

'Wait, let me ... let me ... Just to get this straight, you are telling me that they are willing to pay? To be taught to swear like an Australian?'

'At Bar Limone, *sì*. As I told you, *dottore*, Giuseppe and Maria haven't had such a good night in years. And don't worry about the money. For a modest venue hire fee, Pola will take care of that fucker for you. Let me give you my personal phone number.'

'I need to keep it unofficial. I'm not really supposed to work. And what about the tax?'

'The tax?' said Pola. He stood up laughing. 'I did not realise you were a man of humour, *dottore*.'

After Pola left, Brian began to think hard about the proposal. Maybe using the novelty of swearing really could be a gateway to more traditional lessons. Could it work? He had not felt as good teaching English in *years* than he had last night. And the students had voluntarily paid. Maybe it really *could* work. Would it be better than picking lemons? Yes. Would it be better than teaching the dumbest children in town? Absolutely. Did he have any better ideas? No, he did not. He would have to prepare properly, obviously.

He picked up his phone. 'Pola. Brian. Fuck it. Let's do it. Tomorrow night, seven thirty, OK?'

Pre School

The next day was spent preparing teaching materials, as he would have done with any of his high school classes. The 'pupils' might be going to treat the lessons as fun, but he was going to make sure – as a former Teacher of the Year runner-up – that he did it properly. The ultimate aim was that serious lessons would eventuate afterwards.

Isn't it?

That's what he would focus on. If he could hook them with a couple of novelty classes, they could then move on to a more serious program. If he could make some money along the way, then that would be even better.

Maybe he *would* need a printer, since he was back and forwards several times to the tobacconist printing out and copying materials. He felt busy. He felt he had a purpose. He tapped on the window and waved jauntily at the interior of the Ideale office as he went past, not knowing if either of the Messinas was in there.

He wondered what Father Dom would make of it? Would he disapprove? Obviously. Maybe. *Probably*. But it was hard to tell with the priest. He might drop in and see him later, as long as he didn't need the bloody bins emptied. Might be good to get the old papal blessing on the enterprise.

No. Hold on. Possibly better to keep church and profanity separate. *Just for the moment.*

The Montegiallo School of Swearing

He felt like a comedian about to go onstage, standing outside the bar. Nervous as his first day at Hawthorn High. But of course, teaching a class *was* a live performance, wasn't it? He was determined to act as professionally as possible. He tightened his tie knot, polished the tops of his boots on the backs of his trouser legs, tucked the folder of teaching materials under his arm and pushed open the door.

Six pupils plus Pola. *OK, I can handle this.* Giuseppe and Maria were back, sitting at the same table, with another couple, who twisted round to look at him. No old man tonight. Brian hoped he hadn't overdone it. Pola's two friends were with him behind the bar. Women in their late twenties. One had a low-cut orange dress, the other tight jeans and expensive-looking green leather jacket. They looked like they should be smoking. Like any classroom before the teacher arrives, there had been a hum of conversation. The beep of Pola's iPad as drinks were paid for was the only sound that was out of place, but the vibe was definitely similar. Brian looked round for a spare table to set up.

'Ahh, *dottore*, no, no, no,' said Pola motioning towards him. 'I have cleared this section of the bar for you.' He shooed the two women out from behind and they went and sat at the closest table with their drinks. Pola gave Brian's teaching area a wipe with a rancid-looking rag. So he does have a cleaning cloth. As a teaching lectern, Brian thought it was as good as anything. It certainly commanded a view of the room. He opened his folder, and Pola put a beer down next to it, then introduced him to those he hadn't met.

'*Dottor* Brian is a *professore* from Australia.'

Brian employed the word *allora* again like a real Italian.

'*Allora*' was a word that starts off many Italian declarations and its definition was sometimes hard to pin down. A cross between 'OK, ready' and 'shut up and listen'.

'*Allora. Buonasera a tutti.*' Nothing. He tried again, a little more forcefully. '*BuonaSERA*, everyone.'

Pola got it. 'Ahh, ahh, ahh.' One of his hands conducted the crowd.

'*Buonasera, Dottor* Brian,' they all said together in the singsong voice of students the world over.

'Good. *Bene.* Now tonight, the lesson will be "Know Your Arsehole".' Brian straightened his stack of papers. 'For *americani* and *inglesi* or Australians ...'

'Fuckers!' called out Giuseppe standing up.

'Thank you, Giuseppe, *grazie*. I appreciate your enthusiasm, but let's please concentrate on the lesson. *Questa lezione, per favore.*'

Maria pulled him back down.

'So, as I was saying. Did you know that *americani* have different assholes to *inglesi* and *australiani* arseholes?'

Heads turned to each other. From the confused looks, it seemed they did not.

'So, *australiani* and *inglesi* are aaaaaarseholes. *Americani* are assssssholes.'

Brian held up a picture of a prominent and disgraced member of the British Royal family he had printed out. 'So, this guy would be an arsehole. He would never be an asshole. Only an arsehole. OK. After me everybody. Aaaaaaarsehole.'

'Aaaarsehole,' they said together, a little hesitantly.

'Let me hear that aaaaaaaah,' said Brian. 'Like a dying crow.'

'Aaaaaaaaaaah,' went the students.

'Aaaaaah,' demonstrated Brian again. 'Louder. Louder, *per favore*.'
Mouths opened wider. 'Aaaaaaaah …'
'And … sole.'
All. 'Sole-ah.'
'No AH!' scolded Brian. 'Solar is for the sun. Solll.' There was a slight improvement.
'Now let's shorten that first ahh. Like this. Ah.'
'Ah,' came from the students.
'Remember, like a dying crow. '*Un corvo morente*, I think. Aaaaaah. Aaaaaah.'
A much harsher 'aaaah' came from the students.
'OK, good, good,' said Brian. 'Let's put it together. 'Ah, sole.'
'Ah, sole.'
'Very good.' He held up the Royal's picture again. 'So, this guy would be?'
'Arse-hole!'
'Very, very good. Now turn to the person next to you. Pretend they are English, an *inglese*. Tell them what you think of them. You two,' he pointed at Pola's two friends. 'Let's hear your, err, arseholes.'
They looked at each other. 'OK,' encouraged Brian. Orange Dress went first. 'Eeeenglish Aaaarsehole.'
'Beautiful,' said Brian. 'Now you. Leather jacket.'
'*Inglese* ahhhhsole-ah.'
'Very good, but leave out the "ah" at the end. Try it again. Arsehole.' He chopped his hand to cut off the sound at the end of the word.
'Arsehole, aresehole, arsehole.' Chop, chop, chop went Brian's hand at the end of each word.
'Arse-hoL, arse-hoL, arse-hoL.'
'Great! Give them a clap everyone.' Enthusiastic clapping from all of them.
'Alright. Very good. Moving on.' He pulled out another photo. This was of a disgraced former American president. He held it up. 'Now this

guy. *Americano.* Would be an asssssshole, OK? Let's hear it,' said Brian, 'asssshole. All together.'

'Assssshole.'

'Perfect. Ssss. Like a snake. *Come un serpente.* Asssssssss.'

'Assshole.'

'Brilliant. *Eccellente!*' He held up the politician's photo again and pointed to individual students.

'Asshole, asshole, asshole,' they came back perfectly.

'And this guy.' The Royal again. There was a little hesitation, but they got it right. 'Arsehole.'

'Beautiful. *Molto bene.* Now the only other ahhhseholes are *australiani* and New Zealanders. You know *Nuova Zelanda*? As an Australian, I am ALWAYS an arsehole, I am NEVER an asshole.' Brian hadn't been able to think of a single Australian who a rural Sicilian would be familiar with so had printed a picture of a koala. 'Look at this little arsehole!' Then a picture of a Kiwi. 'Another arsehole.'

Brian paused. OK. One more review. *Inglese, australiani, neozelandesi.* All arseholes. *Americani* and the rest. Assholes. Alright. Everyone take a drink if you need it and let's take this home.'

A hand went up. Orange Low Cut. '*Italiani?* Which are we?'

'Very good question, ahh, *signorina*. Italians are definitely all assholes.' Heads nodded. 'Easy way to remember. Only English and Australians and New Zealanders are arseholes. All the rest you can safely call assholes. Russians, Romanians, French. All assholes.' Brian realised that he didn't really know that for sure. He had better check with other former British colonies. Maybe Nigerians and Botswanans were also arseholes, not assholes? *Another thing to ponder.*

Brian moved out from behind the bar. He held up the photographs one at a time to a rhythm. The Royal, 'arsehole', US politician, 'asshole', koala, 'arsehole', kiwi, 'arsehole'.

'Maria. Pola, Giuseppe. Orange Top again. Jacket. Friends of Maria and Giuseppe. Again. Again. Again. Asshole. Arsehole. Asshole. Arsehole. Again, again, again!'

'Now everyone together!' The flashcard photos flew up and down.

'Wait. What about this guy,' Brian held up a picture of an unpopular English football player now involved in the fashion industry. 'He is …?'

'Arsehole!'

'Yes! And he is also …? Come on, you know this, Giuseppe and Maria.'

Giuseppe and his wife stood up and announced to everyone, rapidly synchronised, 'Fucker, fucker, fucker!' The whole room applauded them.

Too right. Out came the pictures again, one, two, three, four. Everyone called out at the top of their voices.

'Asshole, arsehole! Asshole! Arsehole! Asshole, arsehole! Asshole! Arsehole!' Then suddenly everyone was silent. Brian turned to the door and five people were standing there shocked and open-mouthed. Three Brian recognised. Gianni was one. His two new neighbours, Andrea and Salvo. Plus a man and a woman in their thirties who looked like a couple. Maybe the new painters?

'Ahh,' said Pola, getting out his glass jar. '*Benvenuto nella nostra scuola.*' His dark eyes glittered. Welcome to the Montegiallo School of Swearing!

'Fuckers,' said Giuseppe in the following silence. Brian gave him a look he'd used a thousand times at recalcitrant Year Elevens, and the man's eyes dropped.

'Time for a break I think,' said Brian. To everyone, '*Cinque minuti.* Phew!'

Class Action

The new students all turned out to be enthusiastic natural swearers in English. Brian wondered about the cathartic effect of swearing in another language. Was it the illicit feeling? Throwing words around without quite knowing how much power they had, felt great for some reason. It was certainly deliciously dangerous, but paradoxically safe at the same time. How different to swearing in your own language, with all its long-term baggage and built-up meanings. In another tongue you were much freer, and apparently the process was extremely therapeutic. Amazingly, Brian could see the students' language confidence growing right in front of him. Nothing like the embarrassed mumbling you'd normally see in an English as a Second Language class. And not just language confidence. You *understood* that the words had great power, but at the same time you could be relieved of the responsibility and the consequences by not quite understanding them.

Very interesting. I wonder if there's a PhD in there somewhere.

At first, quiet Gianni the plumber had preferred to sit it out. But the others pulled him in like someone being reluctantly dragged onto a dance floor. He started warily, but soon was belting out profanity like an insecure actor taking on the mask of a powerful role. The couple, Paolo and Gerlanda, were a husband-and-wife painting team, subbed in for a few months by Franco. They had put their own painting business on hold in Agrigento. Both of them were calling each other assholes at the tops of their voices in no time. And loving it.

Wonderful!

Andrea and Salvo took to swearing like naturals too. At the same time, they took quite an interest in Pola's two friends as well. The barman's iPad pinged and pinged, and pinged. Carafes of wine were poured and emptied.

'I hope the draught beer lasts,' Pola whispered to Brian. 'We'll be down to the L'Agrume soon. I'll get another barrel of Messina before the next class.'

By the end of the lesson, they were all arseholing like there was no tomorrow, 'quiet' Gianni just as vigorously as everyone else. Brian considered his 'asshole' was almost at a professional standard by the end of class. Pola and Giuseppe stepped in as teacher's aides and gave him and the newcomers a bit of a catch-up with 'fucker' (*'come tossire*, like coughing, ugh, ugh, ugh') and they were up to the level of the rest of the students by the time they all spilled cheerfully out into the *piazza* around 11 pm.

'Don't forget to practise!' Brian told them as they left. He was in high spirits too. His face burned with exertion. 'Practise in the mirror!' he called after them. 'Unless you actually see that English footballer!'

Brian closed the door and sat back at the bar as Pola collected the glasses and empty carafes. 'That was exhausting. But great.'

'You were a *maestro* at work, *dottore*.'

'Really? *Grazie*, Pola. What is *maestro* in Italian?'

'*Maestro*.'

'Oh. Good.'

'But even better, *dottore* ...' Pola brought out the jar. After his own 'venue hire' was taken out, Brian's share was still over fifty euros! 'I'll get an online account set up, *dottore*. Most of them will want to pay by card. And I think we need a better flyer. This is the last one anyway. They've all been taken. Let's see. I think it should be ...' He thought for a moment. '*La Scuola delle Parolacce del Dottor Brian*.'

Brian could translate that relatively easily, he thought. Doctor Brian's

School of Profanity? 'I like it. But ... maybe we should just keep it a little under the radar to start with. Wait, it's not going to be illegal, is it?'

'You think the *carabinieri* are going to drive most of an hour from Agrigento – although it would be half an hour the way those fuckers drive – because somebody is swearing and not even swearing in Italian? It's ridiculous, *dottore*. These words won't even have a legal meaning here. Just sounds.' He thought for another moment. 'But you may be right. It might be better to just call them "Special English Classes" for the moment. Some people might get the wrong idea.'

'Yes, and I'm not supposed to be earning money either. Don't want to attract too much attention. Let's just go a little Fight Club for the time being. The first rule is, that you can't talk about The Montegiallo School of Swearing, but you *can* talk about "Special English".'

Church and State

'Hmmm,' said Father Dom, looking at Brian's flyer. 'Special English?'

'My thought was to get them interested in English language learning with a little fun, and then they might continue with some, you know, serious lessons.' Brian watched the priest carefully for his reaction.

'And you say *Giuseppe* is taking these classes? Giuseppe *Marina*? I can't believe that!'

'Well, I don't know his family name, but we saw him the first time we met in Bar Limone. Eating his *caponata*.'

'Yes. And his wife Maria? Are you absolutely sure?'

'Giuseppe is one of my best students, Father.'

'I still can't believe it.'

'Come down next time and see for yourself. I'll comp you.'

'Comp?'

'Free ticket. What would it be? *Un biglietto gratuito?*'

'I don't think it would be a good idea for a man of the church to be seen at such an event.'

'Think of it as entertainment, or a performance.' Brian almost added, 'Like the Pope on the balcony', but fortunately did not. 'Contentious words in a language you barely understand? It is an interesting concept don't you think? Do words have power if you don't really know the meaning? What do they actually mean in that situation?'

Definitely PhD material.

'Well, I suppose it is communication, although …'

'Yes, that's it! Expanding communication skills! What could be wrong with improving international communications?'

'As long as there is no actual blasphemy involved. And that serious academic lessons will result.'

Brian tried to think. He hadn't brought Jesus into it anywhere, had he? Christ, he hoped not! No, he didn't think he had. 'Absolutely not. And yes, of course, eventually, serious lessons will of course follow.'

'Then, I suppose I …'

'You approve? Wonderful!'

'No! Of course I don't approve, you idiot!' The priest raised his palms to lower the force of his reaction. 'I suppose I'll *turn a blind eye*, is what I was going to say. I won't condemn you from the pulpit in any case. For now.'

'I couldn't ask for more than that, Father.'

Brian was handed back his flyer. 'I'll see you at mass on Sunday.'

Local Colour

And it wasn't just the students who were growing in confidence.

'*Come sei gentile*, how kind you are!' The *dottore* flattered, as the coffee *signorina* added a tiny *biscotti* to his saucer. He then completed a full paragraph in perfectly comprehensible Italian, praising her skills with the La Cimbali coffee machine.

Sitting out in the cobbled marketplace, Brian sipped his *caffè con latte* like he owned the place. His tie – after just five minutes on YouTube, and only slightly longer in front of the mirror – was a perfectly formed, 'four in hand' knot, exactly the right size and style for his antique shirt collar. His calfskins gleamed below the cuffs of his suit trousers.

Viviana and Franco arrived to open the office and Brian raised his cup to them both. Franco nodded. Viviana gave him a wave. Brian reached into a bag of shopping and held up a packet of flour for her to see.

'I'm trying again. I think I had the wrong flour,' he called across the cobbles.

'Ha-ha, let me know how it goes.' Viviana followed Franco inside the Ideale offices.

There, thought Brian. You're perfectly capable of speaking to the woman without making a total knob of yourself.

The online bread arsehole community had, it turned out, been quite helpful in critiquing Brian's nightmare loaves. He had apparently had the wrong protein count in his flour. Or something. He had several more 'can't fail' remedies he was ready to try.

Italian Angels

There were an unbelievable *nine* students at the next lesson.

The class almost taught itself. Brian had downloaded a famous Australian rock-and-roll song by the Angels, which he transferred by USB to Pola's music system. The song was perfect for Brian's purposes. Australian teenagers at live performances in the 1970s and 80s had for some reason incorporated raucous, synchronised swearing into their interaction with the group. It had been so successful that the band had embraced the new interpretation and encouraged the crowd's response at every performance.

Originally the song had been more or less endless repetition of its title, 'Am I Ever Going to See Your Face Again'. But by some telepathic Australia-wide group agreement, crowds began answering that question by screaming, 'No way, get fucked, fuck off!'

What could be better for teaching Sicilians public profanity? Made even more effective with a few glasses of Birra Messina.

The first line of the song was essentially gibberish, regarding Renoir offering wall painting services in Santa Fe. It was not comprehensible at all – even to an Australian – so Brian didn't even try to explain. But the title was perfect for timing, pronunciation and emphasis. Brian sang it along to the music and the Italians were soon able to respond – as well as any drunk Australian teenager from the early 1980s – to Brian's repeated queries as to whether he would see their faces again.

'No way, get fucked, fuck off, *dottore!*'

Singing and repetition, Brian knew, were both excellent aids to learning. Now educators could add swearing to that list.

Another great night of instruction. Brian was still humming the Aussie rockers' greatest hit as he walked back across the *piazza*.

Maybe this thing can actually work!

Mental Fatigue

Brian really was going to need a printer. He was three times down to the tobacconist, first printing the newly designed flyer, then all the teaching materials for the next lesson. If he was going to get that many pupils every time like that last class, he would probably be able to afford one! Maybe that was being too optimistic. He could still hardly believe how well the last classes had gone.

Amazing.

While a hundred flyers were copying, he looked through the window, across the roof of the Mercedes, and into the Ideale real estate office. Should he invite Viviana to class? He had been worrying about it since the last lesson. What would she think? Maybe he should give her a flyer? Would she take offence if he gave her a free lesson? Would she take offence if he didn't? Would she look at him like he was an idiot? Well, that was probably a given. He was starting to love that look. *Is that weird?*

He looked at the new flyers. These were much better. For a start they weren't stretched and distorted. And he had jiggered around with image filters so that his picture was now in black outline, very much like the ink drawing of the teacher in the old-fashioned *Personal Italian Grammar*. As an illustration, it had lost the whiff of proctology as well, which was a bonus.

Good. He popped the flyers in his folder, and then started copying the last of his teaching handouts. How many? He texted Pola. 'How many attending tonight, you know?'

Maybe explaining the set-up at lunch to Viviana would be best. He wouldn't want her to hear about Doctor Brian's School of Swearing from someone else. Especially as she seemed to have warmed to him somewhat. It would best be a concept explained in person. Maybe when he'd baked a successful loaf of bread. No. Why not now? He'd go over and ask her if she had time for lunch at Simone's.

Through the reflections on the window, he couldn't see if she was in the office, frowning away at her laptop as usual. He was getting to love that frown. Was *that* weird?

'Maybe 10–12,' came back the text from Pola.

'10! Wow,' he texted back. 'See you 7.30 before class.'

He put back the master sheet under the lid of the copier and made another half-dozen handouts. Just as the last one was emerging from the end of the machine, he saw the Ideale office door open and Viviana walk to the car.

'Oh, shit, wait…' He grabbed his folder and the handouts and was about to rush out when he realised he hadn't paid. He scrabbled to pull out his card and rubbed it on the machine until it beeped. He impatiently waited for his receipt. For some reason, it was compulsory to take one in Italy. Something to do with the tax police. The tobacconist finally tore off the receipt, gave it to him and Brian rushed out of the door, just in time to see the brakelights of the Mercedes turn the corner out of the marketplace. The rattle of the tyres on the cobbles retreated down the hill.

OK, no worries. Plenty of time.

He put the materials in the granny shopping trolley and started dragging it back up the hill.

Hopefully this is the last time today.

* * *

Back at the shop, the tobacconist lifted the lid on the copier and saw that Brian had left the master sheet in there.

'*Signore, signore!*' The man stepped outside and looked up the hill waving the paper, but Brian was already out of sight. He turned the sheet over and looked at the other side. There were two words, printed in the largest possible typeface to fit the piece of A4, formatted for landscape. The words were marked up with pronunciation instructions. The tobacconist's English was almost non-existent, but he mouthed the syllables quietly and quite close to correctly. 'COCK SUCKER'.

He grunted in surprise. 'Eh?' Then he went back inside and stuck the page up behind the counter for the next time *il dottore* was in the shop.

* * *

Every time Brian went through his front door, he loved to take a deep breath of the cool air. The heat from the plains of Sicily never made it that far inside. '*Buongiorno, Dottor* Skeletor; g'day, *Maestro* INDES; *buongiorno, Dottoressa* Becky.'

INDES had been saving a nicely chilled Messina for him. Before taking it upstairs, Brian texted Toby a copy of his flyer. *Heh-heh.*

He put the beer down on the balcony table, where the condensation on the chilled glass with the *piazza* in the background looked like it was from an advertisement. Even the sound of the beer pouring into the glass was perfect today. 'Ahhh.'

The text from Toby came back. 'Dr Brian???? Who is this cunt now?'

Exactly. Who is this cunt now indeed? thought Brian but didn't reply to Toby.

Let him stew a bit.

He must get Pola to take a picture of him teaching the class. He would love to see the looks on the faces of the Victorian Teacher of the Year committee if they found out a former runner-up (who should have won that bastard) was teaching Sicilians the correct usage of 'fucker'. *Maybe I should tell them!* He sank into a pleasant reverie about receiving an honorary Teacher of the Year award for his specialty arsehole work.

'Ehhhh, arsehole!' The very word came at him from the next-door balcony, jolting him out of his fantasy.

'Hi, Andrea. How you doing?' Andrea was wearing his exquisitely torn jeans and an open yellow linen shirt revealing a lightly muscled torso. Fashionably barefooted again too.

'*Bene, bene.* So, *dottore, cosa deve saldare?*'

'Huh?'

'You ask me before? Welt.'

'Oh, weld, yes.' Brian realised that *saldare* was like solder.

'*Sì,* weld. What I say. What you need?'

'Ahh, don't you have dozens of jobs before mine? I don't want to get anyone in trouble.'

'Fuck those asssssholes and aaaarseholes. Let me have a look.'

In a few seconds he had gone back into the house and emerged from the front door. Brian let him in, looking furtively around the *piazza* as he did so. He first showed Andrea the stairs without rails, then took him down to the cellar where the pieces were.

Andrea inspected the broken posts at the bottom of the rails. 'You have the bottom pieces?' he asked. Brian hunted up the flanges with the bolt holes.

'*Uno, due, tre, quattro.* Another.'

There was another sitting on the rough masonry at the far end of the cellar. Andrea juggled the pieces in his hand. 'I don't know in English, *dottore. Fatica del metallo.*'

'Oh, metal fatigue?'

'*Sì, sì, sì.* Many years of using. Bending, bending, a little, a little and then one day the fucker snaps.'

'Can you fix?'

'*Sì,* of course but, *dottore,* you should throw out this asshole and get a new one.'

'But if I want the old one?'

'OK, sure. Take half an hour. I'll bring the machine up couple of days.'

'How much?' said Brian warily.

'It will be a favour, *dottore.* Maybe just a few euros for the rods.'

'*Grazie mille*, Andrea! What about Franco and, err, Viviana. Won't there be problems if I jump the queue for jobs?'

'Ehh, fuck those—ehh, *italiani*, are assssssholes not ahhhhseholes, *sì?*'

'*Sì*. Correct.'

'*Grazie*. So, fuck those assholes too.'

For just a moment, Brian had a quick and disturbing vision of Viviana frowning. And this time he didn't love it.

'See you at class, *dottore*.'

I Can't Hear You

At 7.30 that evening at Bar Limone, Salvo and Andrea were smoking outside, pre-class.

'Ahh, *dottore*, sorry.'

'No, no, plenty of time.' For a second Brian's hands twitched with the muscle memory of bumming a smoke behind the teachers' lounge, but that was two Brians ago. No, no, no.

Pola's woman friends whom he still didn't know the names of, or for that matter their relationship to Pola, were with them doing the same. The boys didn't seem worried that Pola would crush their heads, so … I guess not girlfriends? Brian realised he had never asked if Pola had a better half. Although, due to his size, it would be 'better third'.

'*Dottor* Brian.' Low-Cut Dress smiled at him, looking straight into the back of his head with lamp like eyes. Brian's own eyes flicked involuntarily down and realised she was low-cut red tonight.

'Ahh, umm, B, B—' *Don't balbettare, you idiot!* '*Buonasera, signorina.*' Leather Jacket friend buzzed a long line of soft rolling rrrrs at her in Italian or dialect and they all laughed. All of them except Brian, who missed every word. He got out of there. '*Scusi, scusi.*' Waving his folder in the air, he pushed past and stepped into Bar Limone.

Oh my God! There were thirty people inside. *Not going to be able to keep this secret for too long.* Must remind them it was Special English. It was noisy with laughter and conversation. Even the old man from the first night was back, as well as Taysir and Akil, the North Africans.

A sweating Pola was struggling in from the back of the bar with a stack of folding metal chairs.

'Ahh, *dottore*,' said Pola, 'could you …?' Brian put his folder on the bar and helped carry in the chairs. 'If you could put these out, *dottore*, I need to …' There was a line of people at the bar waiting to buy drinks. Brian forced the old chairs open one by one and found space for them where he could, while Pola's iPad card reader beeped like a flock of seagulls.

Brian was only slightly surprised to see Gianni with a spot right at the front. 'Ahh, *Signor* Chapman—*scusi*, I mean *Dottor* Brian.'

'Gianni, great to see you!' Brian looked around. 'Gaetano?'

'Ah, no. I told him I needed to do some English lessons, to improve my standard.'

Interesting, thought Brian. He didn't tell him it was to learn English profanity. Calling them Special English Classes on the flyer had been a smart move.

'It's always good to do some self-improvement, Gianni.'

'Ahh, *scusa*, Gianni.' Pola moved Brian aside with a giant arm around his shoulder and steered him back to the bar. '*Dottore*, I thought I'd let you know, we may have *una spia*.' Brian looked around.

'A spy!? What? Who?'

'Shhh. Back corner. Don't look.' Brian looked anyway. It was Rosa from church who also carried two cloth bags across the *piazza* every day, sitting next to the old man with the fedora. 'You mean Rosa? Really?'

'*Sì*, Rosa,' Pola lowered his voice as far as he could in the crowded bar. 'Father Dominic's housekeeper. I told her it was a private function, but she wouldn't leave. She says she has *un biglietto gratuito*.'

'Oh, a comp? Yes, yes, she does. That's fine.'

Pola looked doubtful. 'Maybe best to keep the church out of it.'

'Really, it's OK.'

Pola shrugged. 'Alright. So you all set then, *dottore*?'

Andrea, Salvo and the girls came inside.

'*Sì*, but there's one problem.'

'*Cosa?*'

Brian held up one of his printouts. 'I didn't do enough. People are going to have to share these cocksuckers.'

* * *

An hour later across Piazza Spirito Santo, Franco and Viviana Messina were standing outside *numero trentaquattro*, next door to Brian, with a box of household items for the newly arrived workers. How number thirty-four could be next to number five was a secret maybe Manfredi III Chiaramonte could have answered back in 1360, but the arrangement would not have surprised any Italian.

Viviana sent a text. Franco shook his head and dropped the carton outside their door. Viviana looked up at the *australiano's palazzo*. Nobody seemed home. In the dead quiet of the *piazza*, however, there did seem to be some activity on the other side, perhaps in the vicinity of Bar Limone. Was it applause? A crowd? Didn't seem likely to Viviana. The place was usually near comatose. Glancing once again at Brian's velvet-fortified upper windows, she led Franco across the square. They stepped around the benches and tree roots under the seedy yellow lights and up to the bar entrance. There was some kind of loud chanting, and then – now she was sure – another big round of applause.

On the door was a photocopied sign printed in a heavy black font, '*EVENTO PRIVATO*'. Another cheer rocked the interior.

Viviana and Franco peered through gaps in the shutters and the grime-covered windows. Viviana tried to rub a cleaner spot on the glass. The *australiano* was standing on the bar, waving his hands and shouting.

'WHO AM I?'

The crowd yelled back, 'AN AUSSIE COCKSUCKER!'

'AND WHAT DO I DO?'

'YOU SUCK COCKS! YOU SUCK COCKS!' chanted the crowd.

'I can't hear you!' called Brian, his hand behind his ear. 'WHO am I?'

'AN AUSSIE COCKSUCKER!'

'And what do I do?' Brian pointed down at someone in the crowd.

A man screamed, 'You suck cocks!' He turned to the room. 'He sucks cooooooooocks!'

This was greeted by cheers and whistles.

Gianni? Was that the quiet and shy Gianni the plumber? Viviana and Franco turned and stared at one another in complete shock then back to the window. And surely that wasn't Rosa who cleaned for Father Dominic? Viviana put her hand to the door and raised her eyebrows in a question. Franco shook his head. They hurried away down the stone stairs, but neither of them spoke on the walk back. Or even after they were inside the old family apartment above Simone's restaurant. Maybe they would *never* speak of it.

Confidence Trick

Andrea and Gianni sat at Brian's table the next morning sipping coffee. Andrea had a small welding unit on wheels next to him. Gianni had a box of metal bits and pieces with a large electric drill sitting on top of a scarred heavy-duty power cord. *God. I must put those* Pussycats *away when I have visitors. Way too big a distraction.*

The men put down the *Pussycats*. They first examined the holes in the stairwell then, down in the cellar, the broken stack of metal. They conversed, in rapid Italian, and Brian couldn't follow either the speed or the technical words.

Gianni picked up the drill. 'You haven't got much plugged in, *dottore*?'

'Mainly just the fridge.'

Gianni plugged the drill carefully into one of the old bakelite sockets, and commenced to re-drill the holes on the edge of the stairs.

'Let's bring up the pieces, *dottore*,' said Andrea. 'Will be easier to do it up here than drag the machine down the stairs.'

They struggled up with the metal pieces, the complicated curved sections tangling in with each other. Hmm, Brian thought as they navigated the stairs up from the basement, maybe Andrea is right. Maybe it isn't worth fixing. But they got it all up and got the sections roughly where they had to go. Gianni unplugged the drill, and Andrea began to plug in the welder's flex. There was another long and fast technical discussion.

'I think you better unplug the *frigorifero* as well, *dottore*. And the laptop charger. And anything else. Just for a minute. Since I know your electrics.'

Brian did so.

'OK, hold this still,' said Andrea. Brian and Gianni held the rail. Andrea slipped on a pair of dark goggles. 'Now look away, *dottore*.' He and Gianni turned their heads to the ceiling as the welder sparked and buzzed, the intense light flashing their distorted blue shadows around the room.

It took about half an hour to reattach the bases. And another twenty minutes to get the rail back in place and bolted to the stairs tightly, using some big shiny bolts from Gianni's box. They stood back with a Messina each and surveyed the work.

Messina, thought Brian. There were a couple of Messinas who he would rather did not know about this queue-jumping.

'Just need a coat of paint, *dottore*.'

Brian had a wallet stuffed with euros in small bills from the classes. He tried to offer the men some, but Andrea refused. 'Consider it a favour, *dottore*.'

'That's so generous, guys!' said, Brian, plugging his electrical appliances back in. 'But seriously.'

'And Gianni,' Andrea went on, 'what a disgrace that *Dottor* Brian's electrical system is in such a state!' They argued in Italian for a moment. For Brian's benefit, Gianni switched to English. 'We will get to you as soon as we can, *dottore*, I assure you.'

'That's OK.'

'Tell those assholes they are fuckers,' said Andrea slightly confusingly. 'Why are you letting your father and those assholes at Ideale push you around? The *dottore* has money to pay. Why not do his job next?'

'Ahh, hold on, Andrea,' said Brian. 'You don't live here permanently like Gianni.'

But Gianni acted like he hadn't heard. Almost to himself he said, 'What if I *did* tell those assholes? Could I? *Perché si chiama Gaetano Idraulico?* Why it is not called *Gianni Idraulico?*' Gianni's face became beatific and his eyes shone – even more brightly than the starry-eyed Madonna around the corner – and they were seeing something wonderful through the back wall of the *palazzo*. He took a sharp breath in and, staring into the middle distance, he whispered, 'Or why not ... *Gianni Internazionale!*'

Brian was worried. Only a couple of swearing classes, and the young man's confidence had grown so much! Maybe too much. Maybe way too much. Why wasn't it called Gianni's Plumbing instead of Gaetano's? Whoa! This was escalating a little too quickly. But, on the other hand, if he did start Gianni's Plumbing, maybe that would be a good thing for the boy? It would certainly be good for Brian. Maybe Gaetano would be supportive?

This could all get complicated.

Still, might need to keep a lid on it for as long as possible. Which didn't look like it would be long at all. Keeping it all as Special English was going to be extremely difficult. Not that he really cared if he gazumped the expat renovation jobs. He was a lot more concerned about the reaction from a certain *signora* formerly known as the Devil Woman.

Brian looked cagily out of the front door to check if the coast was clear as they left. Gianni casually wheeled the welder back next door. The *piazza* seemed as empty as it usually was, but there were always eyes in a place like this. But, no. It looked OK.

He went back inside and shook the railings. Solid as a rock. Brian patted Skeletor on the head. 'I think we got away with it, Big Guy.'

Love vs Plumbing

'So let me get this straight,' said Toby's lagging face from the other side of the world. 'You are worried that getting your reno jobs before it's your "turn" will flush away all your hopes and dreams with this Viviana creature, and your name will also be shit with every other foreigner in town?'

'Yes. Exactly, although I couldn't really care less about the other foreigners. And I want the bidet done pronto too.'

Toby's image appeared to have frozen. *The connection must have dropped out.* Brian waited, but still nothing. He waved the cursor over the screen. 'Are you still there? I can't hear you.'

'Yes, I'm still here. Just not sure what I could possibly say to that.'

'It's a tough one.'

'It's not a tough one!' yelled Toby. 'It's more like the stupidest thing I've ever heard. What are you even talking about?'

'Just need your advice, Toby. What do I do?'

'What do you do?' Toby spluttered. 'What do you do? I'm still trying to get my head around that you're *also* teaching a bunch of Sicilian hicks how to say "Fuck me with a dead dingo's donger"!'

'Oh, I forgot about dingo dongers! That would be great for a lesson.' Brian made a quick note on a piece of scrap paper. 'But that side of it is fine. Made most of a week's pay as a teacher in a couple of nights.'

'Is there someone else I can talk to?' asked Toby. 'Is there an adult in the room there by any chance? Do I need to come over? I'm not made of interventions, you know! Wait, are you high? Am I high?'

'How do I get a bidet fixed quickly and still have a chance with a woman? That's all I'm asking, Toby. It's a simple enough question, isn't it? No need to be rude about it.'

Toby sighed. 'Orright, orright. Let's break this down. You haven't really got very far with her yet anyway, apart from some longing looks and cracking her desk with a loaf of bread. Maybe you need to get her so enamoured with your charms that she will be gagging to fix your plumbing. And can I say, I never expected to say that last sentence and it not be a euphemism. Wait, better still, get her to come to one of these so-called Special English classes. When she sees that powerful runner-up Teacher of the Year technique, she'll turn to butter.'

'Wow. That's almost sensible advice, Toby. I've been meaning to go down and explain the concept.'

'OK. Can I go to bed now?'

'Thanks, Toby.'

'You will keep me informed about any developments in this fascinating bidet-based love triangle, won't you?'

'Thanks, Toby. You're a good friend. Goodnight.'

The Straits of Messina

Well, Brian now knew where Viviana got that look when she was staring at an idiot. It ran in the family. Both of them, she and Franco, were giving it to him now in the Ideale front office. There seemed to be a little bit of wariness and pity mixed in there too, if he wasn't mistaken. He wasn't sure where the vibe was coming from, but something had happened. Had they found out about his illicit visit from Andrea and Gianni? Surely they would raise it if they had. No, it was something else. He abandoned his plan of asking her for lunch again at Simone's. He placed one of his flyers on the desk and backed out with a hesitant *buongiorno* and his trolley full of dirty clothes. *Ahh, that's not good. That's really not good.*

* * *

Gianni himself was in the laundromat, talking to the woman behind the service hatch. 'Ehhh, *dottore*!' he greeted Brian enthusiastically. 'I would like you to meet Anna. We have just got engaged.'

'Oh, congratulations, Gianni! Congratulations, Anna. Yes, I've met Anna. She fixed my suit. When is the big day?' Anna's English was not as good as Gianni's, and she left it to him.

'We've only just decided,' he said. 'Sometime after the festival of the Madonna we think.' Anna nodded.

'Wonderful!'

'*E dottore*,' said Anna, searching for the words, 'Gianni is so enjoying the English lessons. He's getting very confident with his ah,' she

The Montegiallo School of Swearing

switched to Italian, '*come si chiama in inglese? Pronuncia.*'

'Yes, pronunciation.' He glanced at Gianni. Not told her exactly how the classes work either. Just then, Martina passed by the laundromat window.

'Arsehole!' barked Gianni, easily loud enough to be heard through the glass. Martina shot a puzzled look inside, but kept walking.

'Ahh, Gianni,' said Brian. 'Maybe we should tone it down a little in public, don't you think?' But Anna beamed up at her fiancé and hugged him very tightly. 'He's so confident now, *Dottor* Brian. So, so, confident. *Grazie, grazie, grazie.*'

'Err. OK. *Prego.* You're welcome.'

* * *

Giuseppe and Maria were in the *supermercato* as Brian picked up some essentials. '*Buongiorno*, fahker,' said Giuseppe. Maria waved and smiled. 'Good morning, arsehole!' she said cheerfully.

Brian glanced nervously around. Giuseppe's pronunciation had slipped a bit, but now was not the time for a remedial class.

'Umm, *buongiorno*, Giuseppe. Maria. Good shopping, umm, *buoni acquisiti?*' he asked, simply to forestall further public obscenity.

'Oh, *Dottor* Brian. Maria makes *gambero rosso 'sta notte!*'

Rosso is red, but what the hell is gambero?

In answer, Giuseppe plunged his hand into Maria's shopping bag, and brought out a huge pink-red prawn, halfway in size to a lobster. The crustacean – as brandished by Giuseppe – was unmistakably lewd, even without his satyr's leer. Red tail held upright, Giuseppe waggled it suggestively in front of Maria's lips. 'Very good eating, this fucker, *dottore*, ha-ha.' Astonishingly, Maria began giggling like a teenager.

Well, this is fucking disturbing.

'Ahh, sounds *molto delizioso*.' Brian looked for an escape route. 'You two kids have fun, OK?'

Oh my God! The old fedora man was in there as well. He raised a claw to Brian. No doubt a cocksucker was about to be declared! Yikes.

Brian hurriedly left the store before he had collected everything he needed. Outside he looked around quickly to make sure that there were no more of his pupils around, ready to swear at him. He escaped up the hill. Had he created a monster? *Maybe hold off on those C-bomb lessons for now.*

* * *

Later that day, it was a quiet and thoughtful Viviana who left Father Dominic's apartment after being let out by Rosa. She had Brian's flyer in her expensive red *buona borsa*. She walked past Brian's apartment on the way back and almost, but not quite, knocked on his door.

Teacher Evaluation

At the next class, later in the week, Brian had to put his foot down when two children came with their family. Carlo and Giulia. He hadn't seen either of them since their encounter in the *piazza*.

'Pola, I'm not going to teach children the ten ways to say motherfucker!'

'We could give them a junior discount, *dottore*, if you prefer?'

'Junior discount?! It's not the cost! Why would their parents even want them to learn this? It's offensive language'

'But it's not their language, *dottore*, so it's not offensive to them. It's just an entertaining night where you can wear *una maschera*, a mask of another culture. Like acting in a play maybe.' For some reason, Brian suddenly thought of the red-hot poker up the King's arse in Marlowe's play.

He couldn't believe he actually considered it for a second. 'No! What am I thinking? No. Absolutely not.'

'OK, OK,' said Pola, 'I'll talk to them.' Carlo and Giulia both glared at Brian as they were led out the door. The loss of the kids and their parents still left a class of well over thirty students.

Brian had been attempting to sneak in a little grammar here and there to the classes, still harbouring the illusion that the swearing was leading to 'legitimate' English lessons. He tried again this evening.

'So, the past perfect. "After he had been fucked, the motherfucker fucked off back home." '

But the class didn't seem as enthusiastic for what felt like 'actual learning'. They enjoyed the theatre of flamboyant swearing, and the Italian style of overdramatic vocal declarations with accompanying hand gestures certainly suited it. He had to admit that their pronunciation had improved beyond belief, which *was* a legitimate language-teacher goal. He still hadn't quite admitted it to himself, but his students were never going to go on to formal classes. This was it. He abandoned the grammar. 'Alright then, the ten uses of motherfucker. Number one ...'

* * *

Pola came up to him at the break. 'Good class, *dottore*. I did not know you could call someone a motherfucker in a friendly way.'

'Only if you know them, remember. Another good time to use it would be if they did something surprisingly good, and you'd say it slowly with a bit of a pause in the middle, like 'mother ... FUCKER!' As I say, you can even call yourself a motherfucker.'

'I'm worried this motherfucker will never learn all ten ways to say it, *dottore*,' said Pola, slightly crestfallen.

'You'll get there, don't worry. Start with the angry one. It's the easiest.'

'Hey, motherfuckers!' Gianni came up and put his hands on each of their shoulders. 'Great class, *dottore*. Ahh, there's a few new people. Do you want me to give them a bit of a briefing on arsehole versus asshole before we start again?'

'Oh, that's OK, Gianni, I was going to review the arseholes right after the break.'

'Cool, cool. Oh, and, *dottore*. Andrea and I have been talking. We're going to move your plumbing job up the list.'

'Really, that's great!' *Or is it?*

'*Sì, sì, sì*. And forget about that foreigner price we gave you, *dottore*. We can do better than that, of course.'

'Wonderful.'

'My father Gaetano does the electrics, so that will still have to wait, but Andrea and I should be able to start the pipes very soon. I'll bring some choices for new toilets and bidet and we'll have them sent up from Palermo. I've got a new water heater that I was going to install in some ...' he thought for a second, '... asshole's place. But they don't have to know that, do they?'

'Ahh, good.' Brian decided to worry about the consequences later and turned to the students who were chatting together. He clapped his hands. 'OK, motherfuckers. One minute more for drinks, and then we'll be back.'

Pola manned his end of the bar. Low-Cut, tonight in a ribbed turtleneck – which, if anything, was more revealing – was holding out her glass.

'*Rosso.*'

'*Sì,*' said Pola.

Brian had found out her name was Audenzia.

'*Dottor* Brian,' she smiled as the glass filled, then walked over. 'My friend Valentina and I,' she indicated Leather Jacket, 'are worried we may be falling behind. Maybe we could get some private *parolacce* lessons sometime?' Brian suppressed a gulp. He glanced at Pola, who raised his eyebrows. 'Ahh, mayyybe.' He edged aside. 'We'll talk about it another time, OK?'

'ANY time, *dottore.*'

'OK. Take your seat, please.' He imagined one of Father Dominic's long and disapproving 'hmmmmmmms'.

A Catalogue of Disaster

True to his word, Gianni came around with a catalogue of bathroom products the next day. 'These are the best quality, *dottore*. Designed in Milano by Sandra Delotta. Very simple to install too. Beautiful units. You don't need too fancy for the other five. But for the main bathroom, you should get these. With the hand basin that will match the new toilet and bidet. Much smoother lines than those old gold motherfuckers you have now.'

'Oh, I was hoping I could keep those. I love the gold!'

'You want to keep those two old assholes? Maybe OK. Those fuckers were made good back then. Still need new pipes.'

'The bidet doesn't work though. Maybe that will have to be replaced?'

'OK. I didn't look when I did quick fix on the place. Let me see now.'

They went upstairs and Gianni pressed the flush lever. The water still barely oozed out.

'Probably just the nozzle, *dottore*. I don't have my tools, but wait.' He went out onto the balcony, and called over to the next one. 'Andrea!' he shouted. 'Andrea, you cocksucking motherfucker!'

Andrea eventually came out with a cigarette in one hand, no shirt and mirror aviators.

'*Chiave inglese?*' asked Gianni.

'*Sì. Aspetti.*'

'*E pinze,*' Gianni called after him.

Andrea came back holding some tools. Hanging the cigarette from the corner of his mouth, he tossed them one at a time across the gap, and Gianni caught them deftly. A *chiave inglese*, translating as 'English key', was apparently a spanner. Brian wondered why. '*Pinze*' did make sense as pliers, however.

He received two texts from Pola, nagging him about printing more flyers. 'OK, OK!' he replied.

Back in the bathroom, Gianni turned off the taps supplying the bidet. 'Make coffee, *dottore*. Be fifteen, twenty minutes.'

Brian went downstairs and put the coffee on the stove. He looked through the catalogue again. Why were Italian toilets so much more attractive than Australian ones? Every piece looked like someone – Sandra Delotta, presumably – had made every effort for them to look effortlessly good. One was like a scallop shell, with its pink seat raised, waiting for Venus to rise from its waters. Maybe that was a step too far. *Bloody hell!* But the colours and proportions of even the cheapest lines were beautiful.

There was a knock at the door. 'Jeezus, for fuck's sake, Pola, I'll print the bloody things. Just give me five minutes!' He checked to see the *Pussycat*s were out of sight this time and went through the arch to the front door. At the precise moment he turned the knob, he knew exactly who was going to be standing on the other side.

'Ah, Brian.'

'No, Viviana. I mean yes, Viviana.' She was dressed beautifully but casually in a sky-blue silk blouse and a blue knee-length denim skirt. She held a paper bag from which a small loaf of bread poked out.

'How is your baking going? I thought I'd show you what bread is supposed to be like.'

'Oh, that's ...' Could she see the sweat that had instantly appeared on his forehead? 'That's ...'

'Can I come in?'

'Can you come in? What a question, Viviana, hah-hah.'

That frown again.

'And what's the answer?'

'Ahh, of course.' What else could he do? He led her inside like a sleepwalker. Her saw her noticing the repaired stair rail. 'Ahh, I got that back up myself. Was pretty dangerous to be honest,' said Brian. Her hand rested on one of the brand-new welds halfway up. Her eyes took in the shiny bolts. But she said nothing and they went through to the kitchen area. Brian glanced at the ceiling nervously. *Be quiet up there, motherfucker.*

'Looks like I came at the right time,' she said.

'How's that?' asked Brian, who could not have imagined a worse time for someone to have come round in the history of coming round.

She looked at the coffee pot now spluttering on the stove and the two cups and smiled.

'Oh, yes, yes.'

Viviana took a few steps and checked out the room. While her back was half turned, Brian swooped the toilet catalogues underneath his teaching folder with the other illicit documents, the *Pussycat*s. She came back to the table. 'These are nice chairs.'

'Yes.'

'Could I ...'

'No, no, please. Of course, yes, take a seat.'

She put the bread down and sat. 'Are you OK? You look a little ...'

'No, no, just working on my next class. Oh, you don't know about those.'

'At first I wasn't sure what you were doing.'

'Oh, you *do* know about them? They are going so well, but ...'

'My father and I saw a few minutes through the window. We were very confused.'

'Oh, really? That must have been ... Ahh, well to explain, it's really about improving international communication. And also like a kind of therapy. It's confidence in your expression, you know. It's wonderful for pronunciation practice.'

'I spoke to Father Dominic,' she said. 'Rosa mostly. She said she had a surprisingly good time.'

'Oh, good. Maybe you might like to come along one night. There's another class on Friday evening. You won't have to pay of course.'

'That sounds OK. I would like to see a whole class of swearing. It is a very interesting idea, but I still don't really understand.'

'Oh, OK, OK. Yeah, yeah. I'd really love to see you there. Franco too, but … mostly you.' *There, I've said it.*

If she was surprised, she didn't show it. She smiled the big smile that Brian had only seen on the website of Ideale real estate. If New Brian had been a little bolder than Old Brian, he might have reached for her hand, but instead he began, 'You know …'

Then it came. The unmistakable sound of robust spraying, coming from the nozzle of a gold bidet – that nobody would remember had been made by Ceramica Majestica, a company that had gone out of business in 1973 – followed by the sound of water draining and filling noisily.

'Ahh,' said Brian.

'Oh, I'm sorry, I didn't realise.'

'Ahh, it's not what you …' Wait, Brian thought. Maybe it would be better if it was what she thought? No, that wasn't good either. As long as Gianni didn't come down, maybe he could …

'All done, *dottore*! That fucker is working again.' Gianni stepped in, carrying the tools.

'Errk,' gargled Brian.

Viviana stood up. The stylish chair fell back. She looked at Gianni. Angry. Mouth open. This was way beyond frowning. In fact, she looked very much like a Devil Woman of legend. She turned that look at Brian, and his stomach shrivelled. She turned back again to Gianni, accusing finger pointed right at his face. '*Tu!*'

There began an argument between them in such strenuous and rapid Italian that Brian was completely lost. But that didn't really matter.

He was getting the gist of it. No doubt he, Brian, was a fucker. And Gianni too. Absolutely no doubt. Viviana also pointed furiously at the repaired stair rail.

Gianni, who would have cowered under this onslaught just a few weeks before, was not holding back, and ended up shouting over the top of her, 'NO! NO! NO! Nobody tells this motherfucker what to do! Only Gianni tells this motherfucker what to do!'

'Viviana turned on Brian and gave him a paragraph or two of scorching Sicilian dialect, not remembering or more probably not caring if he could understand it, which he didn't.

'I'm sorry, I didn't ...'

'Let that asshole go, *dottore*!' said Gianni dismissively. 'Let her fuck off.' He waved his *chiave inglese* imperiously.

'Shut up, you idiot,' Brian told him.

As he turned back to Viviana, the hand-baked artisanal loaf hit Brian right between the eyes, and even from that brief contact, he could tell that the crust was light, airy and crisp.

The door banged like the final closing of a tomb.

* * *

After Gianni left, Brian went upstairs. He went into the bathroom and sadly pressed the flush lever on the bidet. The nozzle sprayed upwards, powerfully focused, like an absolute dream, as if it were Plato's perfect form of a bidet. The spray fell back like tears into the golden bowl.

Pariah

Toby could barely breathe from laughing. 'And then she catches you with the plumber, and he comes down and calls her an asshole, and tells her to fuck off, which you, YOU, had previously taught him to say! Ahahahahahahahahaha.'

'It's not funny, Toby!'

'It's not funny he says, ahahahahahahahahah!' The resolution of the online chat window was not clear enough for Brian to see the tears running down Toby's face, but they were definitely there. 'It's not funny, he says, oh I'm going to pass out from a lack of oxygen. Oh my God.' Toby disappeared for a moment then reappeared dabbing his eyes on the hem of his t-shirt.

'Are you finished?'

Toby took some deep breaths 'I'm ... wait ... OK ... I'm fine, really.' But then he was off again. 'And then she hits you in the head with the bread! Ahhahahahaha. Oh, how I wish I could have been there to see it. Oh my God! The perfect shot!'

'What do I do now?'

Getting his breath back, 'Nothing.'

'Nothing?'

'Nothing to do. You're fucked. You wanted it all. Love and plumbing. But your ambition exceeded your abilities, mate.'

Brian remembered the fallen, broken Icarus outside the temple in

Agrigento. That all was like a lifetime ago. He had indeed flown too close to the sun.

'There must be something I can try.'

'Enjoy squatting over that gold bidet, mate. Only thing to do.' Brian terminated the chat before Toby could start laughing again.

'*No way, get fucked, fuck off!*' he said. And then yelled at the ceiling. 'Fuck, cunt, AAAAAAARSE!'

* * *

Early the next morning he crept down to the market area, hoping to get into the *supermercato* before the real estate opened. He poked his head around the corner. No Mercedes. He was in and out of the shops in a few seconds and almost ran back up the hill, dragging his trolley behind him like a broken anchor.

On with the Show

What else could Brian do but prepare for the lesson on Friday? He transferred money to Gianni to purchase the plumbing supplies in Palermo. He still had a few thousand left in deposit with Franco and Viviana, but he didn't dare ask for that now. Maybe someday, somehow, this would all blow over and they could laugh about it. Then maybe he could casually bring up the subject. He remembered that look on Viviana's face and shuddered. *Not for a while perhaps.* Maybe that overconfident fucking idiot Gianni could go in and demand it. It was the least he could do.

He sat out in the *piazza* in front of Bar Limone with his morning coffee. As usual, Rosa came past. But this time she was walking together with the old fedora man. She swung the two bags in her hands, quietly singing some kind of opera tune.

'Beautiful day, *Dottor* Brian.'

'*Buona mattina*, Rosa,' he said glumly. Must every day be hideously beautiful here?

Giuseppe and Maria passed along the far side of the *piazza*. Too far away to call Brian a fucker, fortunately. They looked more concerned with each other anyway. *Are they actually holding hands?* Pola came out of Bar Limone and sat beside him. Paolo and Gerlanda exited the house next door to Brian in their white paint-spattered overalls. They both waved at Brian, then Gerlanda gave Paolo a playful but substantial slap on the backside as they left for the lower levels of Hell. The remains of their laughter reached them even after they disappeared, echoing off the stone alleyway.

'At least all my students seem happy, Pola.'

'You are an inspiration, *dottore*.'

'Yeah. Fantastic.' The irony that his swearing tutoring seemed to be releasing a powerful therapeutic effect on his students' relationships – while he didn't have the faintest hope of one himself – was not lost on Brian. He touched the spot between his eyes where Viviana's artisanal loaf had hit him.

He wasn't in the mood to detail Viviana's disastrous visit to Pola just yet, so he finished his coffee, handed Pola the empty cup and went back to his house. He sat in front of his laptop.

'What to do for Friday, Skeletor?' he sighed. *Something a bit more advanced perhaps, and maybe a role-play or two?*

The video call alert buzzed. Brian hesitated accepting Toby's call. He wasn't sure he could handle more mockery. But he tilted his laptop camera and clicked on the green button. 'Can I help you, Toby?'

'Orright. On some reflection I realised that I may not have been as supportive as I could have been yesterday.'

'You don't say?'

'Yes. No matter how funny the situation genuinely is, and when she threw the bread ...'

'Look, I'm busy here.'

'Yeah, yeah, I'm supposed to work in wellbeing. I'm sorry. Truly. You OK?'

'Just getting on with the swearing classes. Thanks for the dingo donger suggestion.'

'See, this is the dedication that almost got you Teacher of the Year.'

'It seems these classes are helping everyone else's relationship except mine. Swearing has unblocked every sex hormone in town. Even the elderly are throwing a leg over, left, right and centre, apparently. It's crazy.'

'No, I can totally understand it. There are lots of legitimate therapies like Rage Rooms and Scream Centres. Heaps of that type of shit. You can get it paid on your health insurance here. The swearing is like a release of inhibition for them. And a release of inhibition in one area can help in another, such as the libido. No wonder everyone is getting it on. Yours is a way better concept though. They get to learn English as well. You should patent it.'

'Sounds like total bullshit, Toby. But I'm making a bit of cash, which is all I'm focusing on now. As long as the Italian government doesn't get wind of the money.'

'Well, I hope you're charging one hundred and fifty an hour.'

'Why?'

'That's therapy rates. Maybe less for Group, but face it. You're a Sicilian Sex Therapist now, start charging like one.'

'Ha-ha. Sounds like something you'd need qualifications for.'

'Mate, every second cult leader and serial killer has got an alternative-therapy side hustle. How many have appropriate qualifications do you think?'

'Err?'

'Well, actually, quite a few of them. Maybe a bad example, but I'm basically a therapist for students myself. I did one unit of psych as an elective. I might as well have gone to clown college, and look at me! *Dottor* Brian, Sicilian Sex Therapist. It's a thing.'

'Very funny.'

'So are you feeling better now? That will be one hundred and fifty bucks.'

'Thanks, Tobe. I really do feel better. Going to prepare for class.'

'I mean it. Patent that shit.'

Brian ended the call in a far better mood. He cracked his knuckles and began to type.

* * *

Somebody else was preparing for the class on Friday as well. Phone calls and texts were being made, in which the phrase '*Le cosiddette lezioni di inglese*' was used quite frequently. Which, if Viviana had been subtitled on a three-part special on a major streaming service, would have translated as 'The *so-called* English lessons'.

The subtitling would have continued: 'Anna? I wonder if you would be interested to know exactly what Gianni is getting up to in these so-called English classes?'

'Gaetano?'

'Rocco?'

'Fantino?'

'Giovi?'

* * *

Brian slipped into the market square again to get to the copier at the tobacconist. He edged inside. When the copies were underway, he peeked out at the Ideale office. He couldn't see who was behind the desk, because it was obscured by Eric and Murray. They looked like they were complaining. But then, they always looked that way. Maybe it didn't concern him? *No way, get fucked, fuck off, of course it did!* Had Gianni already told them he was pulling one of their jobs? Probably. Had he called them an arsehole and an asshole too, with the correct usage? *Almost certainly.* The proprietor handed him his lost copy of 'Cocksucker'.

'Oh. *Grazie.*'

'*Prego.*'

He grabbed it and his copies and all but ran back up the hill. On the plus side of everything, he was getting a hell of a lot fitter tackling this medieval StairMaster several times a day. But that wasn't much compensation.

* * *

When Brian got back, the first thing he noticed was a mattress propped up outside his front wall with a bag. The next thing he noticed was Andrea standing next to them. 'Oh no.'

'Eh, *dottore*.'

'Let me guess, the free accommodation is over?'

'*Sì*.'

'Ah.'

'*Sì*. But I'm taking the new mattress. Fuck those assholes.'

Brian sighed. 'Well, you better come in.'

'Gianni mention you have eight bedrooms, *dottore*, so ...'

'Sure. You are welcome. What about the others?'

'Just me. They are all still doing the jobs for the foreigners.' Brian didn't have time to appreciate the fact that he was temporarily not a foreigner for this conversation.

'OK, choose a room and we'll drag the mattress in. Some of them have got a bit of furniture. One upstairs has a cupboard, I think. You know I've only got one bathroom?'

'Not for long, *dottore*.' They pulled the mattress inside and shut the door.

'Sorry about this, *dottore*. *Grazie*.'

'No, it's not your fault. It's two hundred and twenty-five percent my own fault.'

'With the new pipes, you will probably need some re-tiling in the bathrooms. I'm sure Salvo would rather come over and do your job instead of those assholes.'

'Oh God,' said Brian. He sat down and put his head in his hands. Andrea opened his bag and pulled out some food items, including cheese, olives and a pack of beer with one missing. 'Salvage from the refrigerator next door.' Andrea tore through the cardboard packaging and handed Brian a beer. Of course it was a Messina. They removed the caps and Brian raised his bottle in an ironic toast.

Andrea scouted the house. 'I think I'll take the one up here with the desk, *dottore*,' he called down.

'Choose one with a window if you are going to be smoking.'

Andrea came to the top of the stairs and leaned over. 'Oh, *dottore*, I can go outside if you want ...' But Brian realised he was beyond caring. 'No. It really doesn't matter.' Second-hand smoke from some Italian high tars was the least of his problems.

* * *

After dragging the mattress upstairs with Andrea, Brian went around to Father Dominic's while his new roommate made himself at home. Rosa let him in.

'Ahhh, *Dottor* Brian.'

'Hi Rosa. *Il padre* in the *casa*?'

'*Sì.*'

Brian sat glumly in front of Father Dom. After the Andrea incident, he now really did need to talk.

The priest listened in silence until he had told him the whole grim story. 'Hmm, you ended up trying to serve two masters after all? Did you not remember the advice of St Luke sixteen: thirteen?'

'Luke? I thought you told me it was Matthew six: something?'

'Did I? In any case, they both say it.'

'Really? Matthew and Luke both came out with that independently? Did they know each other?'

'It was a lesson worth repeating, which I think you would agree with now,' said the priest a little testily, and apparently not wanting to get into a theological discussion about Gospel authorship.

'I don't think I am serving two masters now, am I?' Brian asked, a little confused. 'More like: Get behind me, Satan? Or like I'm some kind of dead Samaritan by the side of the road? Anyway, maybe she'll forget all about it, eventually?'

'Unfortunately, Sicilians are not the most ... "forgetting" of people,'

Father Dom replied diplomatically. 'They are still angry about the Norman invasion.'

'When was that?'

'About eleven thirty.'

'The year?'

'Yes, of course the year! Did you think I meant before lunch?'

'Lunch. That's the time just before you change from *buongiorno* to *buonasera*,' sighed Brian, remembering one of his first conversations with Viviana. 'I may need to skip church for a couple of weeks, Father. Might be a little uncomfortable, you know.'

'Hmm.'

'I don't suppose God would miss an atheist in church anyway,' Brian joked weakly.

'He would miss one of them the most of all,' said the priest. 'The most of all.'

Performance Anxiety

Brian paced Bar Limone before the class. Breathing in Andrea's second-hand smoke had, after all, made him irritable. As if he had given up just the day before.

'You are distracted, *dottore*,' said Pola, dropping the tower of folding chairs on the tiles with a crash.

Brian finally told him about the Viviana visit. Unlike Toby, Pola didn't show the slightest sign of levity.

'This is serious, *dottore*. Anyone could have told you. Don't fuck with a Sicilian's business.'

'I didn't mean to,' Brian wailed. 'It's all just got out of control. What do you think she'll do?'

'Maybe Franco will put some pressure on Gaetano to pull Gianni into line.'

'I think it's gone beyond that, Pola.' Brian had a hideous vision of Gianni calling his father a 'fucker asshole'. 'I've already got Andrea living with me now. Viviana kicked him out. I'll probably have the whole fucking lot on my doorstep by the end of the week.'

'I didn't realise that you had feelings for the *signora*, *dottore*?'

'Well, it doesn't matter now. That's all over isn't it …? Isn't it?'

Pola replied with a serious silence which indicated eloquently to Brian, 'Yes. It's over. You fucked up.'

'Well, *dottore*, if you need *company*, my cousin Audenzia is a great admirer of your teaching skills.' *His cousin? Who? Oh yeah, Low-Cut.*

'Also her friend Valentina ...'

'Lovely girls, I'm sure, Pola. But maybe a bit too young for me.'

'OK, *dottore*,' he sighed. 'I'll open the doors. Time for class.'

Brian pulled himself together and psyched himself up for the lesson. Never let the students see a weakness. He'd learned that pretty quickly from his first class of Year Eight boys.

Gianni swaggered in, and Brian wondered what he was going to do about him. Maybe just leave it alone. Things were so wrecked with Viviana now, that he might as well get his fucking waterworks done.

Good-sized class again. Brian waited until Pola had sold a few litres of beer and wine, then began.

'*Allora*. Let's have some fun tonight. A bit of novelty ...'

* * *

When the class was well and truly underway, a group of eight people approached Bar Limone. At their head was a determined-looking Viviana, followed by Franco, Gaetano, and Gianni's fiancée, Anna, plus a few confused others connected with class members. They were only missing pitchforks. Viviana strode up to the door, looked at the '*EVENTO PRIVATO*' sign, ripped it down and threw it on the ground. She flung open the door and marched in.

'Oh shit!' said Brian.

'Fuck me like a dead dingo!' cried Pola.

The whole class, some of them with drinks in hand, turned to the group. The place was silent. Viviana launched into Italian with frequent finger-pointing at Brian and Gianni, and also Andrea.

'What the fuck is she saying?' Brian asked out of the corner of his mouth. Pola translated into his ear.

'She's saying, *dottore*, that your classes are a fraud and you are nothing but a, errr, filthy, err, degenerate ... I'm not sure how to say ... Oh yes, yes! You are a pervert, and maybe your school is illegal ...'

My school? thought Brian.

Viviana strode over to the bar. Pola and Brian both shrank back. She snatched Brian's folder off the bar and marched back to her group. Brian understood the next bit. Something like 'This is what they are learning …'

She opened the folder and pulled out the first handout and waved it aloft. Bringing it back to her eye-line, she read, 'Dry as a dead dingo's donger.' This stopped her in her tracks for a moment. She stared at it like it was hieroglyphics. '*Aspettate.*' She then went over to one of the tables and snatched up another printout. 'Winston Churchill wanked off corgis,' said this one.

'*Primo Ministro Churchill e con un, ahh, tipo di cane inglese …*' She made a vaguely masturbatory action. Brian had to give her credit. She had made a solid attempt at translation.

Gaetano stared at the paper and made a similar action in a questioning manner. 'Ehh?'

'We're not here to fuck spiders' was the next handout, and although the translation seemed quite straightforward, even to Brian, it did little to lessen the confusion of the group.

The next sheet said 'No Wukkas!' This one finally and completely flummoxed Viviana. Brian thought that *balbettare*-ing was sure to follow, but finally Gianni's fiancée, Anna, put up her hand.

'*Aspettate tutti!* Everyone wait!'

She went up to where Gianni was standing at the front and said, 'I don't care about words. My Gianni would never have ask me to marry him before he start here with *Dottor* Brian's classes.'

Gianni boldly announced, 'I told her, "Let's do this fucker!"' They put their arms around each other.

Gaetano now made his way to the front of the bar. He twisted a cap in his hands. His English was too poor, so Pola had to hiss the Italian translation into Brian's ear.

'He is saying that he has no idea what is going on in this insane class, and perhaps he doesn't want to know, but he is so proud of how his son has become confident enough to take over the plumbing side of the business and, ahh, he says, *dottore*... from now on it will be called Gianni Idraulico and Gaetano Electrics.' The crowd cheered. Gianni put both hands in the air, grinning wildly and then kissed Anna again.

'It's a triumph, *dottore*!' said Pola.

Errrk, thought Brian, looking at a horrified and unbelieving Viviana, hands on hips near the door.

As the cheering went on, Gaetano came over and shook Brian's hand. Brian couldn't hear or understand what he said to him, but Gianni came over. 'We start on your electrics next week, *dottore*! Fuck those assholes!'

Oh no, thought Brian desperately. *No, no, no, no. No way, get fucked, fuck off, no!*

The rest of the class was forgotten, as it threatened to turn into a party. The other members of Viviana's vigilantes were welcomed by the other students. Even Franco looked a little like he would rather stay, but Viviana gave him the look, then turned on her heel and stormed out. Brian struggled to get through the crowd to follow her and ran out the door after the departing Messinas.

'Wait! I'm sorry. I didn't mean any of this!' But they didn't look back. He stood outside by himself, banging his fist on his thigh. 'No way, get fucked, fuck off!' he screamed into the branches, and it echoed around the Square of the Holy Spirit.

Finally, he went back inside. Pola had put on music. Carafes of wine and jugs of beer were being passed over heads. Some swearing was still going on in pockets. Rosa was standing on a chair for some reason. She was singing in a vaguely operatic style to the pop music from Pola's speakers, 'I'm not here to fuck spiders, la, la, la! Fuck spiders! Fuck spiders!'

The words 'No wukkas!' in an almost perfect imitation of an Australian accent came out of another corner of the bar from Gerlanda.

It was the event of the decade at Bar Limone. Pola ran out of wine. Some poor souls had to turn to lemon liqueur. And it was one of the worst nights of Brian's life.

Castle Greyskull

Well, why don't I just surrender to the fucken fates? Brian asked himself as he helped Salvo bring his stuff from next door. The tiler had decided to join his friend in Brian's *palazzo*. Am I the Dark Side? he thought, with a glance at Skeletor. Salvo was happy with Brian's old mattress. Just the husband-and-wife painters, Paolo and Gerlanda, were left next door now, and probably only because Brian didn't need any painting done. They might be glad to have the place to themselves.

'Only six bedrooms left to choose from, Salvo.'

'*Grazie, Dottor* Brian.'

Brian liked both men, and they certainly added some life to the place. He was willing to put up with both of them coming through his bedroom and using his bathroom for a limited time.

'Won't be for long, *dottore*,' Andrea and Salvo had assured him again.

This Saturday the boys were off to the 'fleshpots' of Nuovo. Brian declined an offer to accompany them. A tower of cardboard reels stood next to INDES with electrical wiring of white, red and blue. Next to Becky was an enormous cardboard box containing his new hot-water heater poached from some expat's job. It was a box that Brian would have killed to play in as a child. He felt like climbing in and pulling closed the flaps.

Salvo had brought up the boxes of surplus lurid tiles from the dusty cupboard in the basement. 'Probably enough,' he told Brian, hefting a box. 'At least three metres. You sure you don't want me to do the whole motherfucker bathroom? Nice shade of cream or white. Maybe very light-green glass tile?'

'No, these are an Italian classic, Salvo!' Brian held up one of the red-and-green glass rectangles that appeared to glow with radioactivity.

Salvo looked dubious, but made no objection. 'I'll be careful, *Dottor* Brian. Take just where the pipes have to come out. Put these assholes back like new.'

'*Bene, bene.*'

Brian had not set foot one step down the hill since the big class party. It was like he was on a desert island surrounded by sharks. He ate despondently at Bar Limone. On Saturday night, Gianni's van appeared from the road behind the *piazza* and the boys squeezed in for a night in Nuovo. Apparently there was some kind of nightclub. It was called, if Andrea could be believed, Hubba Hubba.

'Not like Palermo, *dottore*, but better than nothing.'

* * *

Brian was woken early on Sunday by two people giggling and trying to be quiet as they came out of his bathroom. Both wore towels. Andrea and Valentina. 'Shh, shhh, shhh. Ohh, sorry, *dottore.*'

'Aargh.' Fuck it, he'd get up. Salvo had already stripped some of the old tiles in the bathroom but showering was still possible. Afterwards Brian went downstairs to make coffee. Now Audenzia descended as well – in mauve G-string lingerie – Salvo behind her in nothing but hot-pink silk boxers.

'Oh, right. Good morning. How was the nightclub?'

'*Buongiorno, dottore.* Is terrible. After half an hour Valentina and Audi tell us they "not here to fuck spiders", so we come home.'

Could they stop grinning at me? Brian thanked God for the thick stone walls. Hadn't heard a thing that night.

And let's keep it that way.

How had they even got the girls back here? Surely not in Gianni's miniscule van? Would have got to know each other pretty well on that drive.

'That's ... good to hear.'

Bleh. Brian decided he might as well go to mass, just to get out of there. He went up and put on a tie and his boots. Right at this moment he couldn't care less if he saw Viviana or not. And, fortunately, he was an atheist, so he didn't have to go to confession for that vision of mauve lingerie that probably should have been left at the church door.

No Viviana at church. Probably avoiding it too, so he claimed his bravery in turning up as a sort of moral victory. He was too distracted during the service. He realised the priest was staring at him. Again he was still standing, long after the rest of the congregation was kneeling. He left before communion with a nod to Father Dom and the starry-eyed Madonna, and sat on the bench under the trees, watching small patches of yellow Sicily and blue sky flowing and changing with the movement of the leaves.

A Rum Rebellion

Viviana was not absent from mass because she was avoiding Brian. That morning she was facing a crowd of nearly thirty grumpy expats crammed into Eric and Martina's half-tiled living room.

'We paid for furniture for those new workers,' Martina called at her. 'Now we find out they are working on Brian Chapman's house? What happened to fairness? It's not his turn.'

'We were next!'

'We should complain to the government.'

Complain that you got a house for one euro? Good luck. 'I can assure you that they no longer have free accommodation,' she said.

'How does that help us, lady?' shouted Murray.

'We want our water feature,' yelled his wife, Salina.

'Our tiling is still not done. We were promised …'

'Our rain showers might as well be on the moon!'

'What are you going to do about it?'

'Our en suite is being treated as a second-class citizen!'

Eric stepped to the front and held his palms out. 'I'm sure Ms Messina will have a strategy for dealing with the situation.'

Viviana stared down the crowd until there was total silence. '*Signor* Chapman has *temporarily* negatively influenced *some* of the tradespeople in town. I hope they will soon see the error of their ways and order can be restored to the renovation schedule in a very short time. The arrangement we have with these businesses and operators is informal, so I can't order anyone to do anything, but again, we will do what we can, and I think it will be a temporary situation only.'

'We have heard that Mr Chapman has an especially friendly relationship with you, Ms Messina. And maybe that "friendship" might be why he is suddenly getting all his work done. Is that true?' asked Peter.

'I have no relationship with *Signor* Chapman, friendly or otherwise,' she replied icily. '*Quello scarafaggio*, bleh!' she muttered under her breath.

'But it's not just that,' English Chris cut in. 'A ninety-year-old man stopped me in the street and called me an arsehole! Has Chapman got something do with that?'

Viviana paused. 'I have no idea,' she lied.

'Oh! I'm sure that plumber called *me* an arsehole when I walked past the laundromat!' said Martina, suddenly realising what had happened that day. 'I'm sure that Australian was behind it. He was right there.'

'*I* got called an asshole too!' from the crowd.

'The guy in the tobacconist had a sign saying "Cocksucker" behind the counter. Was that aimed at us? He doesn't even have a word of English. Must be someone else behind it, and I know who,' said Lars.

'Gianni told me, "Hey, asshole, your job is delayed",' said Christopher.

'AND some old man called me a fucker three times in a row, in the middle of the supermarket,' said Chris. 'What's going on?'

Right now, Viviana couldn't really have cared less if these idiots' jobs took twenty years. It was the betrayal and humiliation. *That* was something no Sicilian could accept. So-called '*Dottor* Brian' needs to be taught a lesson, she thought. But what would be the best punishment?

She addressed the expats again.

'What do you want me to do about any of this?' she asked angrily. 'It's not my fault if everyone has taken a dislike to you. What do you expect? Why don't you just do the same back to them?'

'I don't think that old guy knows any other English and I certainly don't know any Italian curses.'

'Really?' said Viviana. She thought for a moment and then gave them a determined smile. 'Well, maybe there *is* something I can help you with after all.'

Guerilla Action

Brian and Gianni sat on the balcony taking a break. It was a still, hot day, and the heat from the plains was baking the top of the hill, which it didn't always do. If the heat reached the *piazza* by midday, it would be a hot night too, from Brian's short experience. A skip sat below them filled with crusted old ceramic, and rust-roughened metal pipes. They had indeed looked like they could have gone in during Caligula's reign. Brian had enjoyed acting as Gianni and Andrea's plumbing assistant. There was great satisfaction in ripping out the old pipes and putting in the new. The stainless steel and PVC had been installed in the main bathroom in only a couple of hours, and Salvo was right then completing the repaired tiling before Gaetano was to cut the power to start the rewiring. Salvo had refused Brian's offer to help. 'For the tiling, you need to have it in your fingers, *dottore*.'

'You and the boys might need to take a piss at the bar for the rest of the day, *dottore*,' said Gianni. 'Once the cement and grout is dry, should be OK. I'll help my father get the wiring done, and then we do the pipes for the rest of the toilets when those motherfuckers arrive coupla days. They confirmed on their way from Palermo. We already have plenty rain showers in the shop for both bathrooms. But might not have power for a day or two, OK?'

Brian didn't have much in INDES and he could charge his phone at Bar Limone. 'OK. No worries.'

'Don't you mean "No wukkas"?' said Gianni.

In reality, Brian had plenty of wukkas.

The only other thing in the fridge was a bottle of champagne Brian had bought to open when the repairs were finished. *Doesn't matter if that gets warm at the moment.*

'Paolo or Gerlanda can sneak you in next door if you really need a shower as well. Pity you're not asking for painting, *dottore*. They'd be right over.'

'They'd be right over living here, too,' said Brian.

'You don't want a water feature, *dottore*? Got one at the storage.' Brian assumed it was Murray's, and though he was slightly tempted to rub a water feature in the American's face, that might be going too far.

'*No, grazie*, Gianni.'

Completely unexpectedly from around the corner, Robinson appeared from his level of Hell and stood looking up at the balcony. Brian could see on the paving the stretched dark shadow of another person around the corner. Peter maybe?

'Umm?' said Brian.

Robinson was consulting something written on his hand or some kind of note. He cleared his throat and looked straight at Gianni. While he spoke, the shadow of the other figure gesticulated emphatically, their hands clawing and chopping.

'*Tua madre faceva le spaccate sulle pannocchie!*' said Robinson uncertainly in his strong British accent. Gianni stood up slowly, white-faced. Robinson turned and looked towards the hidden person. The shadow hands on the stone paving exhorted again. Brian leaned over the rail to see further around the corner and instantly recognised the shape of the shadow puppetmaster. *Viviana!* No mistaking it.

'What did he say?' Brian asked Gianni.

'He says …'

'What?'

'*Tua madre faceva le spaccate sulle pannocchie!*' Robinson called up at them more forcefully.

'Tell her, I mean, tell him, this.' Brian whispered urgently in Gianni's ear.

'You have an arse like a wombat!' Gianni called down, less confidently than usual.

The two men stared at each other awkwardly for a moment longer, then Robinson turned and hurried away around the corner. As the shadow turned with him, Brian ran down the stairs, leapt the rail at the bottom, and sprinted out the front door and around the corner. Nothing. Gone. He thought about pursuing them, but didn't. What would he do anyway?

When he got back up to the balcony, Gianni was still standing, looking down at the street. 'Really, Gianni, what did he say?' Brian put his hand on the young plumber's shoulder and sat him back down.

'*Dottore*, my mother was a saint!'

'Something about your mother? What? What?'

'He says,' Gianni struggled with emotion, 'that my mother used to do the splits on corn cobs.'

Brian goggled at him. 'Come on, Gianni. It's just words.'

'You are right, *dottore*,' he said. 'But Italian words are different maybe?' Some of the young man's recently gained confidence seemed to have been rubbed off.

'Maybe not mention it to Gaetano.'

Gianni nodded. 'And, *dottore*?'

'Yes, Gianni?'

'What is a wombat?'

'An Australian animal with a giant arse.'

'Ah.'

The work went on slightly more thoughtfully for the rest of the day.

* * *

The next morning, Gaetano needed to return some incorrectly sized light fittings to Agrigento and was away the whole day.

The afternoon saw another couple of attempts by expats to disrupt the young workers. While Andrea was coming out of the *supermercato* with a carton of high tars, Eric accosted him, pulled back his shoulders and told him, '*Sembri un pene!*' 'You look like a penis.'

Andrea called him an English cocksucker in reply.

One all.

Martina tried to tell Salvo '*Mangia merda e muori*', 'Eat shit and die', but her pronunciation was so terrible that he didn't realise what she was trying to say until he got back to the *palazzo*. Another draw.

Andrea and Salvo simply laughed these incidents off, but Brian was more worried about Gianni. As he had been walking up the hill from the plumbing workshop, Murray had consulted a written note, and told him he was a '*rotto nel culo traditore!*', 'a bastard traitor'.

Crossing the market square, Salina got in another body blow with, '*coglione*', 'testicle'. Gianni had fled apparently.

'Why didn't you reply to those fuckers, Gianni?' asked Brian gently. 'You're so good at your swearing.'

'I don't know, *dottore*, I don't know. I just froze. Maybe because it was in Italian?' He thought for a second. 'I'm sure all these Italian insults are coming from Viviana Messina, you know, *dottore*? She saw me getting called a testicle in the marketplace. I think she laughed!' Gianni was outraged.

I bet she did, thought Brian, suppressing a smile. But to Gianni, he lied, 'I'm sure she has nothing to do with it.'

'She can be a scary woman, *dottore*. I wonder if I made the right decision to go against her.'

Now he wonders if he should have crossed her, for fuck's sake, thought Brian. But he tried to buck up Gianni's spirits, and with Andrea and Salvo's help and a glass or two of rough reds in Bar Limone, Gianni seemed almost back to his confident self by the time he left for his own home that evening. Brian told Pola he was not going to do a class that week, until the house was done.

'No wukkas, *dottore*, I have all their numbers. I'll do a group text.'

Brian took home the remains of the bottle of wine.

The power was still off that night, so the three of them sat at Brian's table, the scene only lit by a battery torch supplied by Gaetano. They drank the wine while Brian told them true and semi-true stories about Australia, including the prime minister who disappeared while swimming. The few *scarafaggi* with constitutions that had been strong enough to survive the spraying took advantage of the darkness to totter around looking for scraps of wild boar salami.

When the bottle was empty, the men made their way upstairs by the light of phone torches. Brian lay on the bed, thoughts churning as Montegiallo threatened to dissolve into anarchy around him. He'd got his new plumbing, and even a bit of cash, but at what cost? He'd worsened things between the expats and the Sicilians, and even managed to turn *Sicilian* against Sicilian. He recalled Viviana's smile the moment before the bread and bidet incident, and his heart lurched. It had all been downhill from there. If only fucking Gianni hadn't wrecked it all! But it wasn't Gianni's doing, was it? It was all his own work.

The Cabal

As Brian finally fell asleep, Viviana was meeting with the expat leaders Eric, Martina, Murray and Salina.

'Is this Italian cursing getting us anywhere?' asked Eric. 'That plumber from Agrigento abused me straight back.'

'And that other guy just looked at me like he didn't know what I was talking about,' said Martina.

'Forget those idiots!' Viviana told them. 'It's Gianni who will crack. If he gives in, then those other two won't matter and he will start focusing on your jobs. He has to live here, the other two don't. If you want your rain showers, you will need to focus on Gianni.'

'And our water feature,' said Murray. 'But yeah, he looked kinda rattled when I called him whatever I called him yesterday.'

'A bastard traitor is what you called Gianni,' Viviana told him. 'Specifically, a broken-arse traitor. Which he is.'

'Yes,' said Salina, 'and whatever I said had him just about running out of the place.'

Brian would have known what they were saying, thought Viviana. She thought about him looking it up in that stupid old book of his. She shook her head determinedly to rid herself of the image. He would soon find out who was in charge in Montegiallo.

'Maybe we need a *group* approach,' she suggested thoughtfully. 'Strength in numbers. Everyone *must* remember the insults I gave them. You're in Italy. Learn some Italian for once! And concentrate on your pronunciation. Some of you sound like you're speaking Albanian.'

Questi cretini.

'Write them out on your hands if you have to.'

The group grudgingly agreed.

'Everyone needs to get ready for my call. *Signor* Chapman is going to get what's coming to him.' She banged her fist into her other hand. 'We just need to wait for the right moment. It will be called,' she narrowed her eyes, '*Operazione* Wombat!'

The Battle of Piazza Spirito Santo

For two days, there was a tense peace in Montegiallo. During this phony war, expats did not appear in the *piazza*, up from their lairs in Hell, and Brian and his student workers tried to avoid leaving the *palazzo* when not strictly necessary.

Without further distraction, work on the plumbing, tiling and electrics proceeded rapidly. On the first day, the renovators celebrated the power going back on. The bright, new light fittings illuminated every room including the basement. While INDES re-cooled the warm beer, they celebrated with wine from Pola and a kilo of cannelloni Salvo had brought up from Nuovo while they had been waiting for the power to be reconnected.

The next day the new hot-water system went in. Brian wasn't allowed to assist. 'Don't want the new one to explode, *dottore*! Better leave it to the professional motherfuckers.'

When completed, Brian's bathroom resembled a photograph from a 1969 architectural style magazine, gold, red and green. The rain showerhead shone, and the gold toilet set gleamed.

'How did I live my whole life without a bloody bidet before?' thought Brian, balancing the hot tap to the perfect nozzle temperature. Although he loved it, sometimes when he pressed the lever and experienced its powerful spray, it reminded him of the disastrous meeting with Viviana.

They celebrated again, after throwing the 'deathtrap' heater on top of the skip like a corpse. The only thing left to do was to fit the new toilets for the rest of the house, which were already en route from Palermo. Everyone else was in high spirits, but Brian was still apprehensive that Viviana was just biding her time.

* * *

The crucial moment for the expats and *Operazione* Wombat came the next Wednesday. Viviana was tailgating a slow truck up the hairpins from Nuovo after dropping off Franco. She took off her big green sunglasses in annoyance. Her right hand readied to press the horn. *Un momento!* She squinted at the open back of the truck. It was stacked with cardboard cartons. She put her foot down until the Mercedes' grille was centimetres from the tailgate. 'Sandra Delotta' was the bold, stylish typeface across each carton. Below that, the unmistakable universal graphic of a toilet pedestal. Looked like at least five of them.

'Ah-ha!' she growled angrily. She pressed her foot on the brake to give herself some space, transferred the toe of her expensive boot to the accelerator and stamped on it, pulling out to go round the truck. The Mercedes was very nearly demolished by a school minibus which suddenly filled her rear-view mirror out of nowhere and blasted by at high speed, the faces of cheering children in the windows. The bus horn howled past her and the truck, then up the hill in a rapid doppler effect. That had been the last spot for overtaking, and Viviana had to crawl the rest of the way, fuming and grumbling to match the fuming and grumbling of the smoky diesel in front of her.

As the truck finally turned off onto Via Fuori le Mura, just before the city gate, Viviana's face broke into a smile. There was nothing else at the end of *that* street except Gianni – formerly Gaetano – Idraulico.

She got to the Ideale offices, cleared the paperwork off her desk and sat in the back of the office watching the market square through the window. She made a group text.

'*Operazione* Wombat initiated. Everyone must be ready to get to the marketplace. Wait for my signal!'

* * *

Forty-five minutes later, the tiny old plumbing van crawled into the marketplace. It was stuffed full of cardboard boxes of toilets. Two were precariously tied to the roof with thin nylon rope. Three were crammed into the back. On the passenger seat were more boxes of plumbing accoutrement. The van stopped in front of the *supermercato*. The driver's elbow, resting on the sill of the door through the open window, was withdrawn and Gianni's head popped out cautiously. There was barely room for him inside. He got out, looking carefully around the market square. He peered at the Ideale offices. Viviana shrank back into the shadows, phone to her ear. 'If you all want to see what happened to your rain showers, en suites and plumbing jobs, get to the market now! *Operazione* Wombat is Go! Go! Go!'

* * *

Gianni skulked out of the *supermercato* with a panini and a bottle of burgundy-coloured sports drink. He went back to the van and shifted the boxes which had fallen onto the driver's seat. He balanced them carefully. 'Fuckers.' He stood back up and looked around. He was pleased to see no expats. Very pleased. He stopped for a moment, and took a bite out of the sandwich. He started to take another, but stopped, puzzled for a second. Sounded like a football match or something. Wouldn't be. Not round here. Closest pitch was at the school down in Nuovo. But some kind of crowd to be sure. Getting closer by the sounds of it. From down the hill? He was suddenly apprehensive. He threw the panini onto the dash. From … down the hill? Wait …

Viviana stepped out of the Ideale offices as the crowd of around thirty expats poured out of the covered walkway. Viviana pointed straight at Gianni.

'There go your en suites,' she cried. 'Get him! *Il traditore!* The traitor.'

'Ohhhhhh, fuck!' Gianni dropped the drink bottle, and red liquid splashed over the cobbles and down the slope towards the mob who – '*Santa Madonna!*' – were all screaming out Italian and even Sicilian curses.

'Ohhh, fuuuuuck.' He jumped into the van, and slammed the door. '*Le chiavi, le chiavi!*' He struggled to get the keys out of his pocket in the cramped cab. He contorted himself in the seat like a fish on a line, finally got them out and rammed them into the ignition. 'Start, you fucker!'

The crowd were nearly on him. He distinctly heard, '*Intro culo di mammata!*' from one of them in an American accent.

'My mother was a saint!' Gianni screamed before rolling up the window like closing curtains against a tsunami. He jammed the van into gear and, severely over-revving, jumped the vehicle into action. Its tyres pawed the cobbles, the front wheel lifted and, like a rearing donkey it shot up the stone ramp, the crowd right behind. The tied-on toilet boxes swayed dangerously.

'*Vaffanculo!*', '*Mezza sega*' and '*Pezzo di merda*' echoed off the stone passageway from voices unused to Italian.

The alleys he had to drive through to get up the hill were so narrow that the van couldn't go at more than walking pace. But at least the mob couldn't get in front of him. He felt the vehicle lurch as someone tried to pull at one of the toilet boxes. 'No way, get fucked, fuck off!'

He contorted again in his seat, the engine and the mob screaming and amplifying in the stone passageway. Someone was banging on the back of the van. He finally got his phone out from his back pocket. His thumb flashed over the screen, eyes wide as he tried to watch both the phone and the stone street in front of him.

'*Dottore, dottore!*' he screeched into the device.

* * *

Brian was chatting to Pola in the *piazza* when the call came through. 'Wha—? Ohhh fuck!' He handed the phone to Pola who listened to the distorted voice coming through the speaker.

'Ohh, fuck a dead dingo! I'll get the students here now!' Pola yelled at him. 'We're going to need them, *dottore*.'

'*Sì*, Pola!'

The barman's huge thumbs worked like lightning on the screen.

The van came around the last corner on two wheels, the raucous crowd behind it. Brian and Pola ran over as it bumped into the skip and came to a stop with a bang. 'Andrea, Salvo!'

The two of them rushed out onto the balcony, followed by Valentina and Audenzia.

Again with the underwear? thought Brian, totally forgetting that he had appeared on the balcony in underwear several times himself.

The crowd surrounded them, shouting. Brian suddenly remembered Rorke's Drift in the film *Zulu*. Viviana was right in front of him. There was so much commotion he couldn't tell if she was screaming English or Italian. The crowd of expats repeated their Italian curses at high volume, some reading off pieces of paper.

'*Vi rompiamo il culo!*'

'*Minchioni!*'

'*Stronzi!*'

'*Sucaminchia!*'

Some of Brian's students came hurrying across the *piazza* in response to Pola's call. *Thank God, reinforcements!*

Gerlanda stuck her head out from next door, phone still in hand. 'Ya dingo fucken dongers!' she added to the roaring mix of multilingual profanity, in a perfect Aussie accent.

'Wankers!'

'Arseholes!'

'Assholes! Emu fuckers! Cocksuckers!'

'Piss drinkers!' came down from the balcony.

Piss drinkers? thought Brian. *We didn't even cover some of these.* Salvo was freelancing. A sure sign of a creative student mind.

'WOMBAT ARSES!!!' shrieked Gianni, struggling out of the van.

It was good to see his confidence returning in this crisis!

'*Vai all'inferno!*'

'Motherfucker!'

'*Leccaculo!*'

'Arse-licker!'

* * *

Father Dominic could hear the commotion all the way up to the church. Puzzled, he straightened his collar and started down towards the *piazza*. Halfway there, Giuseppe and Maria passed him, almost running, 'Fucker, fucker, fucker!' Then Rosa! Her short legs pumping.

'Rosa! *Aspetta!*'

'*Mi scusi, padre!*' she said as she accelerated away from him. The priest began to move more urgently. As he entered the *piazza* just behind Rosa, everybody was shouting at the tops of their voices. It was chaos. All were swearing – the Italians in English, the Americans and Brits in Italian.

'Please, please, everyone,' the priest begged, ranging the edge of the crowd. No-one could hear him. 'Please, please! Stop. *Basta! Basta! Fermi tutti!* Stop! Stop!'

'*Testa di minchia!*'

'Turd face!'

'*Segaiolo!*'

Pandemonium ruled.

Father Dominic finally put two fingers next to his tongue, and blew a piercing whistle that sliced through the noise. It stunned the crowd into silence.

'Now,' said the priest, very angry. 'This disrespect can be heard all the way to the church and the ears of the Madonna!' He followed up with the same in Italian. Some heads dropped. 'I knew I should have condemned this from the pulpit.'

'So,' continued Father Dom. 'There are two people here, who need to work out their own differences. They have been shamefully using other people to solve problems that they need to work out themselves.'

Everyone looked at Brian and Viviana.

'What have you got to say to each other?'

Brian was panting. So was Viviana.

'Well,' said Brian. 'What *do* you have to say?'

Viviana frowned the frown. She straightened up, looked him in the eye, and said, 'Fuck you, Australian arsehole!'

Brian responded, 'Fuck you, Sicilian bitch!'

The crowd drew in its breath, and Father Dom shook his head.

Both of them had not stopped glaring at each other when the priest stepped in between them.

'Both of you will listen to me! *Signor* Chapman, would you not agree that your inappropriate and frankly preposterous swearing classes have caused animosity in Montegiallo to an extent not seen since the days of the Vendettas? Do you not understand the disruption you have caused? Perhaps an apology is required?'

'Well …' said Brian. Viviana folded her arms.

'And *Signora* Messina,' continued Father Domenic, 'could you also not agree that *Signor* Chapman has tried to become part of our community and, despite the often surreal nature of some of his activities, Montegiallo is a far more interesting place than it was before he arrived? I know that "sorry" is not part of a Sicilian's vocabulary, but an acknowledgement of his efforts might also be appropriate?'

'Hitting you with the bread may have been … a mistake,' conceded Viviana.

They stood facing each other. Pola caught Brian's eye and urged him forward with a nod of his head. But it was Viviana who closed the gap. She put out her hand and Brian shook it.

The crowd was so astonished, that after a pause, a spontaneous but polite round of applause broke out. As the handshake ended, everyone, Italian, English and American, turned to each other. There were murmured apologies, slaps on the back and hugs. Some of the same swearing was now being used in a friendly way, just as Brian had taught.

'Hey, motherfucker!'

'Ha-ha, you're the motherfucker!'

Andrea emerged with Brian's bottle he had saved for the house warming. He shook it and popped the cork, showering the pair and the rest of the crowd with champagne. A baffled Franco arrived in the *piazza* just in time to be hit by some of the spray.

Father Dom blessed the scene quickly – in English and Italian, then he looked up. 'And put some clothes on, Audenzia!' he scolded, but nobody heard him, and he didn't press the issue.

* * *

For the rest of the afternoon, and into the evening, a party raged between Brian's *palazzo* and Bar Limone. The *piazza* was filled with revellers, some even dancing to a playlist of 1980s Australian rock-and-roll, DJ'd by Gianni from the balcony. The plumber had the Angels' biggest hit almost on repeat, singing the title and asking the crowd if he would ever see their faces again, and everyone below yelling back, 'No way, get fucked, fuck off!'

As the twilight shadows grew darker, Brian and Viviana walked together side by side under the trees.

'Look,' said Brian, stopping. She turned and faced him. 'Look,' he began again.

'Are you giving up on your Italian?' she asked.

'Sometimes I think I should give up speaking in any language.'

Viviana smiled. 'Well, as Father Dominic says, Montegiallo is certainly a more interesting place than it was a few months ago.' She caught his eyes. 'A better place.'

Brian took this in, then in slightly hesitant Italian, said, 'You know, *tu mi piace*, right?'

Viviana placed her palm on the base of her throat and in feigned surprise said, 'You like me? With the correct grammar? What woman could resist that?'

'I know, but … *e tu*? Or should that be *e lei*? Not sure if I should use the polite form in this situation.'

'Now you are worried about being polite? After almost causing a full-scale riot in Montegiallo? I think we can leave the polite version behind now, don't you?'

'In any case …'

'I must admit that I was intrigued when you dropped that loaf of bread on my desk. It is not an approach many Italian men would make.' Then, as Gianni started playing one of the Angels' few slower songs, 'Be With You', Viviana put her hand on Brian's cheek and kissed him.

'Does that answer your question?' For a moment he tried to think of something else to say in Italian, but words failed him. And although her eyes, close up, were not a million miles from mocking pools, he saw in them a New Viviana.

* * *

Everyone in the *piazza* practised their swearing to laughter and even some tears. Gianni promised plumbing and electrics to everyone, whether they needed it or not. Murray declared, 'I'm the biggest asshole in all Montegiallo,' to anyone who would listen, and found nobody to disagree. Gaetano and Samantha from Seattle met for the first time and seemed to hit it off. Franco began calculating what all this meant for the real estate prices. The *scarafaggi*, hungry for food, wondered when everyone would go to bed. Which, in the general celebrations, nobody noticed Brian and Viviana had done around midnight.

Another Dawn

And that's how it came to be that on *another* Sicilian summer morning, Brian woke again into a new life, just weeks after he had started the last one. Viviana lay beside him, still sleeping. On the bed made by the two brothers in 1923. *Beautiful.*

Brian brushed hair from across her face and smiled. She stirred but didn't wake. Nobody had dared try to share the bathroom.

He got up quietly and put on just his underwear. Opening the velvet the bare minimum, he slipped out onto the balcony.

'Eeehhhh, *dottore*! Motherfuckaaaa!' There was a piercing whistle. The whole crew – Gerlanda, Paolo, Andrea, Audenzia, Gianni, Anna, Valentina and Salvo – were on the next-door balcony, drinking coffee and eating pastries. Brian put his finger to his lips and mimed sleeping and they lowered the volume ever so slightly.

'Wait, *Dottor* Brian.' Valentina came to the balcony rail and tossed across a bag of pastries, which Brian caught in one hand. He pulled one out and grinned at them, jamming the whole thing in his mouth.

Brian returned to the darkened room, where a line of light from the open curtains lay across the bed. Viviana was awake. Brian held up a pastry enquiringly, but she shook her head, smiling, holding out one hand to him.

* * *

Later, and way too late for what would be considered appropriate for breakfast, they sat out on the balcony drinking espresso and eating custard-filled treats. Across the *piazza*, if Brian could believe his eyes, Murray and Pola were laughing together at something. He couldn't hear what they were talking about, but Murray's hah-hah-hah reached all the way to the balcony. Rosa and the fedora man stood on their own balcony across the *piazza*. He waved at them. Brian's feeling of wellbeing seemed to have extended all across Montegiallo. This thought was interrupted by Gianni and Salvo emerging from next door and starting to wrangle his Sandra Delotta toilet boxes off the van, which still stood up against the skip from the day before.

'You need my help?' Brian called down.

'You two fuckers just relax. We'll have this done in no time,' said Salvo.

'No rush,' said Brian.

'We are putting in that asshole's water feature later,' said Gianni, nodding across the *piazza* in the direction of Murray and then at Viviana.

Brian noticed Peter and Robinson were sitting on one of the benches. Robinson was planting a kiss on Peter's ear.

'All that is because of you,' said Viviana, with a gesture that took in the two Englishmen, Rosa and the fedora, Murray and Pola and the whole of the hillside.

'*Dottor* Brian, Sicilian Sex Therapist,' he said under his breath.

'*Cosa?*' said Viviana.

'Oh, I was just wondering how much one hundred and fifty dollars per hour was in euros.'

A Million Views

'Me being cussed at by an old lady in Sicily LOL' was the graphic over a short shaky video online posted by Krystal_why_not. 'Check this out.' A close-up of a young traveller's face was replaced by vision of a stout middle-aged woman standing on a bench in what looked like a small *piazza*. 'I'm not here to fuck spiders, lalalalala,' sang the woman.

ElEnA	😂😂😂😂😂😂😂😂😂😂
Krystal_why_not	I know right!!!!!!!!!!!!!!!!!!!
JAXXXon	What the actual?????? 😂😂😂
Sassy_sassim	She's not cussing at you. She's cussing at the state of the world
Begay221	You shaming mental health. No cool 😂🙏 😂🙏😂🙏
Krystal_why_not	Montegiallo

This video initially got a relatively modest 4,000 views. The next one was a little different. Jermyn_roamin posted a video from Montegiallo of being addressed as 'Hey wanker' when handed his coffee by a young woman. Two Italian men cheerfully discussed 'dingo dongers' in the street.

Jermyn_roamin	Gotta check this place out. Everyone swears ALL THE TIME 😂😂😂😂😂 ENGLISH AND ITALIAN!

Santa_Jelaybee	ewwww 😭😭😭😭😭😭😭😭
Vixers_travel223	i really love the place 😇 Where is it?????????????????
Jermyn_roamin	Centre of Sicily. Montegiallo
Blakest_ace23	you need to get here dude
Sharry_19_for_life	Why? What? 🙏🙏🙏🙏🙏
Jermyn_roamin	When I say everyone, I mean everyone! It's wild
SabudoobyDOO	I'm there! 😂😂😂😂
Maru23!!	Opinion? You on?
Lillibetter23	Sicily is lovely but srsly need to avoid this 😭😭😭
Darrenty_live	I'm booking now LOL

This upload got 250,000 views. But a video of the old tobacconist wearing a cap with the words 'Aussie Cocksucker!' plus Giuseppe and Maria saying 'Fucker, fucker, fucker' in sync, received a million views in just three days.

Six Months Later

Six months later, in the studios of International News in Rome, an editor was putting together a story for distribution. He forwarded through some rough footage of a dozen tourist coaches jammed into the tiny area outside the Montegiallo town gate. Tour guides, with flags, led crowds into the town. It cut to a reporter checking her makeup on her phone camera. She sucked excess lipstick off her front teeth, before putting the phone back in her pocket. The cameraman's fingers appeared in front of the lens and counted down. The editor paused, marked the spot, and then continued viewing.

'Montegiallo, the town that never stops swearing, once just an internet sensation, is now a major *travel* sensation. Cursing in Italian and English has taken over the whole village within these gates. Some claim it will eventually rival the popularity of the Running of the Bulls as a European tourist destination.'

The reporter stopped and asked direct to the cameraman. 'We good?'

The editor rolled to just before the start of the next take. He pulled up some other footage. The reporter continued in another location outside the *supermercato*. 'We can't play you the unedited footage, but Italian and foreign locals actively take part in the swearing experience for visitors. And if you think they look happy, then they should be. The swearing sensation has made Montegiallo one of the fastest growing real estate markets in the country, with properties, some bought for only one euro, now reaching unbelievable prices.'

The footage switched to a cheerful group – Robinson, Murray, Martina and Salina – greeting tourists with a steady stream of obscenity. The editor added sounds, to mask the swearing.

'Welcome you *beep, beep beeeeeeps* to Montegiallo.'

'There are swearing-based souvenirs, drinks, clothing and even culinary dishes. There's swearing therapy and, I've even been told,' said the reporter, 'there are plans for a swearing-based cryptocurrency.'

The editor pulled up various images of merchandise and he blurred out the swearwords with clicks of his mouse. These included t-shirts, water bottles and caps with the words 'I Fucked Off to Montegiallo', and a sign in Simone's restaurant window that read '*La Casa Del Bastardo Burger* – Home of the Bastard Burger!'

The reporter made the 'cut' sign across her throat, and the editor moved to the next clip, which was set outside the church.

'We spoke earlier to Montegiallo's priest, Father Dominic Cremasco.'

'Father Dominic, what is the church's view on what the town is now famous for?'

'Well, in the end, it's all about international communication, isn't it?'

'You mean you approve of it, Father?' the reporter cut in.

'No of course I don't approve you, id—' he began to snap, then softened. 'Everyone has work, the town is thriving. *And* the church is full on Sunday. If this is the way God wants it done, then who am I to argue?'

* * *

A six-seat electric trolley, one of several smart new vehicles that serviced the town, wound through the narrow curves of Montegiallo's streets. It was full of visitors and their luggage coming up from the gates, many of them going to accommodation in the bustling and lively Piazza Spirito Santo. As usual it stopped first at the *supermercato* for its passengers to stock up on merchandise, and to experience the thrill of being sworn at by the staff. Also as usual the passengers were greeted by some friendly expat profanity as they alighted.

'Absolute fucking pleasure to meet you,' smiled a thin English woman.

'You arseholes are going to fuckin' love it here!' beamed a stylish Londoner with skin the colour of mild butter chicken. A pale man with a huge smile was standing next to him. They were both wearing t-shirts with the slogan *'Ask me about sHiTcOiN'*.

Some tourist were not sure whether they should reply in kind and just laughed in embarrassment. One man, however, was up for it already. 'No wukkas. Nice to meet youse cunts, too.'

Back on the trolley as it wound its way up to the square, one of the others asked him, 'You sound like you've been here before?'

'Nah, mate. Got a fucken job here. I'm the new Swearing Wellbeing Adviser!'

As the trolley rounded the last corner, Toby looked up from his phone and could see Brian and Viviana waving to him from the balcony of the now completely restored home and treatment centre. He jumped off, grabbing his bags.

Toby checked the brass plaque on the front door: 'The Chapman & Messina Clinic'.

The other passengers went on to their accommodation around the *piazza* in the electric vehicle. Tourists buzzed around Holy Spirit Square together, some coming in and out of the world-famous Bar Limone, which in physical appearance had not changed in the tiniest way. The interior was still as grimy as ever, apart from a shiny new set of beer taps that allowed Pola to dispense bigger amounts of Messina beer. Gift packs of L'Agrume lemon liqueur sat on the end of the bar ready for sale and to be sent all over the world. Nobody drank it of course, but as a gift it was hard to beat.

With a glass or two of Messina beer or red wine, many visitors were now confident enough to return some of the profanity directed at them.

* * *

As Toby entered the clinic, he was met by a stunning woman in a low-cut dress. 'Oh, hi!' he said in surprise.

'Hi! Welcome to Palazzo Parolacce, the Chapman and Messina Swearing Relationship Clinic,' she said. 'Excuse me for a moment. I'll just get your form.'

'Form? Wait, I'm …' As she left him, Toby took in the room. An impressively designed interior. The only original items were a curvy old fridge and a giant weird wood stove. Beanbags were scattered around whiteboards.

A curtain divided off the next space. Toby poked his head through. A solid man in an olive t-shirt and Crocs was addressing three couples on beanbags. 'My granny could give a better asshole than that, Phillipa, hah-hah. C'mon. Stand up. Let's hear it! Do you want to save your marriage or not?' From the basement, rhythmic chanting of profanity could just be heard. 'Fuck you! Fuck you! Fuck you …!'

Toby withdrew his head as the woman returned, brandishing an iPad.

'Can I have your name or booking ID?'

Brian appeared at the bottom of the stairs. 'He doesn't need a room booking, Audenzia. Toby. Friend. This arsehole is also our new Swearing Wellbeing Adviser.'

'Oh, welcome!'

'Likewise.'

'Audenzia runs our booking system.'

'Excellent.'

Brian came up and hugged Toby. Brian took him upstairs, and introduced him to Viviana. They sat on the balcony, all three of them with a Messina in their hands.

Brian pointed to a building across the *piazza*. 'That's your place, next to the bar.'

Toby stood up to look. 'Wow!'

'You are very lucky, *Signor* Young,' said Viviana.

'It's Toby, for fuck's sake, Viviana.'

'Toby. Yours was the last one-euro house in town. The scheme has been ended now prices have started to rise so much. Already worth a lot of money. An expert team from Gianni & Gaetano Internazionale has almost finished the plumbing, wiring and installing your satellite entertainment system.'

'You're staying with us until it's ready,' said Brian. 'Bedroom down the corridor.'

'Fucken awesome,' said Toby.

'And don't worry!' said Brian. 'Your new place—definitely getting a bidet.'

* * *

Shortly after the Festival of La Madonna della Vita, Gianni and Anna's wedding took place, Brian and Viviana as best man and head bridesmaid, with Toby and Audenzia as members of the bridal party. The ceremony proceeded as with tradition, until the final vows, when Father Dominic retrieved a set of noise-cancelling headphones from beneath his robes and placed them securely over his ears so he could bless, but not hear the personal vows of the couple. A similar set could be seen over the ears of the starry-eyed Madonna.

* * *

In Montegiallo from that year, yellow sacs still chased *scarafaggi* through the cracks in the stone walls, both of them keeping at least one eye out for Sicilian tarantulas. Cats lazed on the hot stone as they had always done. Birds still hopped from one branch to another, then back to the original branch, just like before. They all still followed tradition,
   but somehow now,
        they did it,
               in an entirely modern way.

FINE

Acknowledgements

The news that your novel has been accepted for publication is an experience a first-time author will never forget. And for that phone call I will always be grateful to Fremantle Press and my wonderful editor, Georgia Richter. The book was written in Boorloo (Perth) on the lands of the Whadjuk people of the Noongar nation, and in the town of Fairlie, New Zealand. I also thank the many angels who took time to read my drafts, for their unbelievably generous and insightful comments. And finally, Dr Agnese Bresin for reviewing my Italian, which is every bit as inadequate as Brian's.